Slap
SHOT

SLAP SHOT

A BLADES HOCKEY NOVEL

MARIA LUIS

ALKMINI BOOKS, LLC

He'll do anything for his best friend . . . *even marry her.*

I live by two universal truths:
1. When I step onto the ice, I'm a god.
2. Daisy Hall is the other half of my soul.

My teammates joke that I'm too co-dependent with the **coach's daughter**, and maybe that's true. We've been thick as thieves since college, and even when I got drafted to the Boston Blades, Daisy followed me across state lines. Which suited me just fine.

If a person can be a home, then Daisy Hall is mine.
Only, I never anticipated that my best friend might be keeping a secret from me, one big enough to rain down Hell from every team in the league. **Now they're all out for blood and I'm Daisy's only shield.**

The home we built together suddenly feels like it's made of glass.

One wrong move, and it all might shatter.

The smart thing to do would be to focus on my game. We're coming off a Cup win, and if I want another, I can't afford any distractions. But there isn't anything I won't do to protect my girl…

Even make her my wife.

Slap Shot (Blades Hockey, Book 5)
Maria Luis
Copyright © 2024 by Alkmini Books, LLC
Thank you for reading and reviewing this book. It is illegal to distribute or
resale this copy in any form.
All rights reserved.
No part of this book may be reproduced in any form or by any electronic
or mechanical means, including information storage and retrieval systems,
without written permission from the author, except for the use of brief
quotations in a book review.

ISBN: 978-1-959069-16-4

Cover Design & Artwork: Najla Qamber, Qamber Designs

Editing: Tina Snider, @3BeansBooks

❀ Created with Vellum

To those who ask, "Is it okay to not be okay?"
The answer is yes.

Good job, honey.

CONTENT INFORMATION

Please take note that Slap Shot includes discussions on mental health, grooming (referenced only and not on page), as well as manipulation within romantic relationships (not on page). Your own mental wellbeing always matters.

PROLOGUE

WESTON

Hartford, Connecticut

"**B**ottom's up, bitch."

My teammate and roommate, Jasper Connelly, clinks his glass tumbler with mine before pounding the drink back in one go. I wait until he comes up for air, spluttering like a total newb, to say, "You're an idiot."

"And *you're* a boring sack of shit." He fishes out a tiny bottle of vodka from the front pocket of his slacks, cracks the caps open with his teeth, and dumps the liquor into his empty glass. Then he peers over at me. "You gonna drink that?"

Since I'm not into playing babysitter, I hand over my soda. Maybe it'll knock some sense into him. "Just so you know, when Coach ends up handing you your ass for drinking, I fully plan on laughing in your face."

"Like a bad friend."

"A bad friend who's gonna be takin' names on the ice while you warm the bench."

"Asshole," Connie mutters, but there's a grin lurking at

the corner of his mouth when he tosses the incriminating evidence into the trash can beside him. "Come on, though. Coach Hall should have known better. Get the whole team to show up to a gala on New Year's Eve and then tell us not to drink? Yeah-fucking-right."

"You have something against kids, Connelly?"

He eyes me over the rim of his glass. "What?"

"Kids. Tonight's for charity."

"Oh."

"Did you even read the email?"

He shrugs lazily. "I generally prefer to save any reading material for bed."

"Not talking about your sexting habits, you fucker."

"I'm not either." His brown eyes practically gleam with humor. "Do sexting right, it's more like a naughty game of Pictionary. You'd know this if you weren't—"

"Don't say it."

"—A *virgin*."

If we were thirteen, not nineteen, I'd slap a hand over his mouth just to shut him up. As it is, the dick has the audacity to grin at me, like he knows exactly what's running through my head, and I have a split-second fantasy of grabbing him by his fancy suit jacket and stuffing him in the closest trash bin where he belongs.

"You're blushing, Cain."

"You need a muzzle, Connie."

He barks out a laugh, and even though I crack a small smile at our usual banter, I find myself shifting uncomfortably while the nape of my neck warms like the heat of a thousand suns is beating down on me.

Everyone's busy talking and dancing, so it's not like anyone's paying us any bit of attention, but I still feel like squirming. When I'm on the ice, playing for UConn like I always dreamed, I live and die for the spotlight. Hand me a stick, drop the puck down at my skates, and I'll run you in circles until you're begging for mercy. Off the ice, though . . . Well, I like to think that I do a decent job of at least pretending I'm the sort of hotshot hockey player who's got his shit together.

Even if that's the furthest thing from the truth.

Wetting my dry lips, I dart my gaze away, seeking an immediate exit from the conversation. Just as I'm about to make my escape, a heavy arm slings across my shoulders and pins me in place.

"Cain. Connie. I'm bored as fuck. Entertain me."

"Entertainment is underway," Jasper says to our goalie, Felix Daniels. "It's time."

Swear to God, Felix actually squeals with excitement. "Operation Get West Laid?"

Fuck. No.

Not this again.

I duck out from under Felix's arm, putting some distance between me and the two knuckleheads that I've had the misfortune to call my best friends since we met at the start of freshman year. "I'm heading out," I tell them.

Six-foot-four Felix pouts at me like I've just stolen his favorite toy. "You need this."

"I really, really don't."

Connie leans into our friend's side, putting up a united front of dumbassery. "Your *dick* needs this."

"He doesn't." I slam my eyes shut and belatedly amend, "*I* don't, I mean. I don't need anything."

"Not everything's about hockey." Connie elbows Felix in the gut. "Tell him."

Rubbing his side, Felix shrugs his shoulders in a *you-heard-him* gesture. "I mean, we've only got two more years of playing, right? One minute the game's our whole life, the next it's just a blip of a memory while we're cryin' in a cubicle. Don't know 'bout you, but I plan to spend the rest of college living it up, and that includes getting my dick wet every chance—"

"I'm going to the Show."

"What?"

"The Show," I repeat, feeling a core of iron straighten my spine. I might know shit off the ice but there's never been any doubt in my mind about where I'm ending up one day. "Maybe you're cool with crying in a cubicle but that's never gonna be me. I'm getting drafted."

They exchange a wordless glance.

Something about it feels like a punch to the gut. "You think I can't?"

"More like *won't*." Connie grimaces. "West, we both know that your dad's not just gonna let you walk away and do what you want, even if you are . . ."

"Even if I'm *what*?"

He waves a hand at me. "Even if you are halfway decent." In Jasper Connelly speak, it's the equivalent of him calling me a hockey god.

Not that the compliment does much; my mood turns dark. And the hot sensation burning up my nape? It's gone ice cold.

Logic says that I should take my ass home before I say something stupid, but if there's anything I hate more than being told that I can't do something, I haven't encountered it yet.

As a kid, it was a tactic that my dad, a real estate mogul here in the Northeast, used to fire me up.

I bet you can't make that goal, West.

I bet you'll never make it to a D-1 college, West.

I bet you can't—

I bet you can't—

Flexing my hands down at my sides, I lift my chin and give voice to the words I've ached to tell my father for years but are coming out now instead: "I can do whatever I want."

Connie opens his mouth but it's too late; I'm steamrolling right over him.

"If I want to make it to the NHL, I'm gonna hustle so hard, no one's ever gonna tell me to warm the bench. Not my dad, not the fans, not you. And if I sleep with someone, it's gonna be because that's what I want, when I want it, *how* I fuckin' want it. You get that?"

He gapes up at me, his jaw going slack.

It's probably the first time in the year and a half that we've known each other that he's heard me give a damn about anything besides hockey. Technically, this is *still* about hockey. But also, it kind of isn't. I don't care that I'm still a virgin. For years, I've prioritized the game over everything else. What makes me uncomfortable is that everyone seems to think it's a joke—that *I'm* a joke—for caring more about a sport than hooking up with girls.

I take a deep, steadying breath.

I'm so done with tonight.

"I'll see you back at the dorm," I mutter before flicking my gaze over to Felix, who's standing with his hands knotted together in front of him. The look on his face says he's about five seconds away from running away with his tail tucked between his legs. "Don't let Connie get so wasted that he wakes me up puking again."

As I turn away, I try to rein myself in. Try to—I don't know—remind myself, I guess, that it's fine if I'm not like everyone else. Guys like Connie and Felix, they're pros at multitasking, as if it takes them zero mental bandwidth to handle juggling girls along with practice and games and schoolwork.

I can't do that.

Maybe it's that I've got tunnel vision. Maybe it's that I'm just wired differently. Either way, I'm so deep in my own head that I barely notice the girl in my way until I'm tripping over her.

She lets out a gasp—not a squeak like Felix earlier, but this breathy little hitch as if she wasn't prepared for me in any sort of way—before she shoves her forearm between us to create a barrier. It's a good thing that I've spent a lifetime learning how to be quick on my feet because I right my equilibrium a moment later, saving us both from what would have been an embarrassing tumble to the ground with me in a tux and her in a floor-length gown.

"Shit, sorry." Raking a hand through my hair, I step back to give her space. "Wasn't looking where I was going—"

"Don't listen to them."

At the unexpected comment, I jerk my head up and find myself staring into a pair of warm amber eyes. "What?"

"Your teammates." She nods her head toward where Connie and Felix were just standing. "Them giving you grief about you still being a virgin? Don't listen to them."

My knee-jerk reaction is to play dumb, to tell her that I don't know what the hell she's talking about. Virgin? Not this guy.

But nothing in her expression indicates that she's judging me, and besides, she looks kinda familiar. Not like we've been in class together but rather like at some point, somewhere, she lingered in my periphery. A silent constant with pale blonde hair, delicate features, and bold, berry-painted lips that practically scream *don't fuck with me.*

Same goes for her posture; she's way shorter than I am but holds herself like she's seven feet tall. I've been around enough athletes to recognize one at first glance, and she's giving off ballerina or gymnast vibes. Elegant. Self-contained. Except, there's something about the direct way she's staring me down . . . Yeah, something about that brisk forthrightness spells all kinds of trouble.

I hear myself say, "Eavesdropping isn't polite, you know."

"Neither is hogging the only access to the restrooms." She gestures to her burgundy dress, which is soaked from her mid-section to just below her breasts. Immediately, I lift my gaze back up to her face, warmth staining my cheeks.

"Did you dive into a water pitcher?"

"One of the servers didn't see me." She winces. "It wasn't his fault. I was playing wallflower." I have no idea what that means, and she must sense my confusion, because she clarifies with a dignified sort of sniff as if she's reading aloud from a dictionary, "When a person decides to keep company with a wall, oftentimes in a secret, obscure part of a very crowded room, in an effort to avoid small talk."

"Isn't *this* small talk?"

"No way." Her berry-colored lips curve in a delighted grin. "This is me telling you that your friends are total douchebags."

I huff out a low laugh. "Tell me something I don't know."

"You shouldn't let them make you feel embarrassed about the virginity thing."

"It's not a *thing*. I mean, it's not that I care what they—" Fuck it, lying seems pointless when this girl is already reading me like an open book. "I'm a hockey player," I tell her instead, as if that should explain everything, and it must, at least in some capacity, because she rolls her eyes.

"Ah, yes. The almighty *hockey player*, winner of trophies and savior of pussies—"

Savior of . . .

My eyes go wide.

"—However shall us mere mortal women survive without your illustrious penises to keep us alive?"

For a second, neither one of us says anything. I'm too

7

busy trying to wrap my head around, well, all of that, and she's clearly trying to maintain a straight face, but then I sort of grunt out, "Illustrious penis?" because *what the fuck*, and then we're both reduced to the sort of laughter that's totally not acceptable at a charity event like this one.

"Who says that?" I gasp out, to which she shakes her head frantically as if she's one second away from crumpling to the floor in a heap of mirth. "No, really. *Who says that?*"

"I'm sorry."

"You aren't."

Her smile is all mischief. "Okay, I'm not. Your expression was *priceless*."

Something about her compels me to stick out my hand. "Weston Cain."

"I know."

I figure she did. But still. "This is when you tell me that your name is . . ."

"Right. Yeah." She straightens her shoulders, apparently content to ignore the fact that she still looks like she got into a fight with a water pitcher and lost, and then slides her hand into mine. It's warm and small and I feel the most ridiculous urge to hold her tight and keep her safe. "I'm Daisy Hall."

Oh.

Oh, *shit*.

Yanking my hand back, I manage to stop myself from looking over my shoulder to make sure that a five-foot-eight grumpy monster isn't coming this way to lop off my head for talking to—

"Coach Hall's daughter," she goes on, as if I really need the clarification.

Which I don't.

Coach is a good guy. At least, we all assume so. At practice, the only time he smiles is when he's making us cry. Then again, I guess his methods work because last year we won the Frozen Four. Still, it seems impossible to me that him and Daisy are in any way related. Although the connection at least explains why she seemed so familiar at first. While we've never officially met, Daisy's attended a few of the same functions that I have in the last year as Coach's plus one. From what I understand, she's in her freshman year of college.

"Aren't you supposed to be at Dartmouth?" I ask.

The light in her gaze dims a little. "I transferred."

"For a specific reason or . . ."

"I don't tell strangers my deepest, darkest secrets, Weston."

"Meanwhile, you know that I'm a virgin."

"Something tells me you don't really care that I know you haven't put your illustrious—"

"No." I hold up a hand, cutting her off. "No, you are never allowed to say that again. Or we can't be friends."

I don't know what does it exactly—the banter, the mention of friendship—but Daisy's entire countenance shifts, blossoming into something that radiates pure joy. It's hard to look at her when she's shining this bright. Can't quite bring myself to look away, either. I'm fascinated by the play of light and shadow lurking in her gaze.

"Can we be friends?" she asks eagerly.

"Kinda feels like we already are. You know that I'm a virgin and I know you're . . ."

"Not," she supplies like I was fishing for info, which I wasn't. "I have a condition, though."

I lean my shoulder against the wall beside us. "Which is?"

"Friends, that's it. I'm not interested in anything more."

Any of my teammates would be willing to face Coach's wrath just to have a chance with this girl. I'm not blind. She's beautiful. Ethereal, almost, with amber eyes shot through with threads of gold, and cinnamon freckles spilling across the bridge of her nose. Her long hair is piled into a loose knot atop her head, exposing the graceful lines of her throat and shoulders.

But I just . . . there's this innate sense of relief lifting from my shoulders. And my chest feels warm and happy, like maybe she could—like maybe *we* could—

Keep this light. Keep this fun. Don't be awkward.

So, I tease, "Should I feel offended?"

"Only if you think with just your dick."

"What if I don't?" Because that's pretty much the crux of it. I rarely, if ever, think with just my dick. "What should the rest of me think?"

"Your head's probably thinking that I don't have much of a filter. You can blame Dad—Coach Hall, I mean—for that. He's the one who raised me."

Fair enough.

I try not to let my grimace show.

Seeing right through me, Daisy points at my face. "Yeah, that."

We both laugh.

Wishing my voice wasn't so hoarse, I force myself to ask, "And what if my heart's got a say in this?"

"Then you should know that I'm loyal to a fault."

"Like Bonnie and Clyde?" I cross my arms over my chest, feeling grateful that I haven't managed to make this conversation weird, the way that I usually do with anything that isn't related to hockey. "You gonna get arrested with me, Daisy?"

"Absolutely not."

"A fair-weather friend, then. Should have known."

"I'll bail you out," she sniffs. "Stage a whole rescue and everything."

"What if it's just typical college debauchery? What if I'm hungover and dying?"

"I'll hold your hair back, princess, while you pray to the

porcelain gods. Tell you that everything's going to be all right."

"What if it isn't?" I make a point to hold her gaze, noting the way that she's matched my pose, arms folded casually over her chest. "What if everything is falling apart and there's no getting out?"

Her throat works with a delicate, inaudible swallow. "I'll probably hold your hand just so we both know that we're not alone."

I suck in a sharp breath.

This whole conversation should feel ridiculous. I don't know this girl and she sure as hell doesn't know me. Truth is, I have a lot of friends but only a few people that I'd die for. My identical twin brother, Tory, is at the top of the list, followed shortly by Connie and Felix, even though they sometimes annoy the fuck outta me.

I'm too laser-focused on the future to really get invested in people.

Everyone seems to want something from me that I'm not capable of giving. Girls want a boyfriend, or at least a hookup, and guys want a bro they can party with. Somehow, even when I try my hardest to meet their expectations, I'm often left feeling like the only part of me they want doesn't actually exist.

The way Daisy's looking up at me, though, feels . . .

Safe.

It feels like safety and understanding, as if we've both been swimming upstream for years in search of a raft—until now.

"You push a hard bargain," I tell her, my voice low.

"Desperation." When I lift a brow in response, she shrugs self-deprecatingly. "I don't have many friends."

"Where's their sense of loyalty?"

She looks down. "Sometimes loyalty isn't enough."

I want to hug her. And I never hug anyone.

I settle for tapping her foot with mine. "Hey, Daisy."

"Yeah, Weston?"

"Never been friends with a girl before."

She laughs, the sound as shiny and bright as it was before. "Just don't, like, fart in front of me and we'll be fine."

"That's it for prerequisites?" I keep my foot next to hers. She doesn't move away and neither do I. "Like, am I allowed to breathe or . . ."

"I'll take it up with management."

"You do that."

Her good humor fades. It's not completely obvious but after thirty-some minutes of talking with her, seems like I've gotten a good enough read on her to at least recognize the signs that she's ruminating on something else.

"Say it," I prompt softly.

"One more thing."

"What's that?"

"Please don't fall in love with me."

"Dating a hockey player is a bit like swimming with sharks.
They hunt. They feast. By the time they're done using your
bones to sharpen their teeth, you'll realize it was a lie when
they said that you were lucky to be the Chosen One.
Here's to hoping the mediocre orgasms were worth it."
—*Confessions of a Puck Bunny*

CHAPTER 1
DAISY

"This is a shit show."

Never let it be said that Sam Hall, head coach for the Boston Blades, isn't a drama king.

His players know it. His ex-wife knows it. As his only kid, I know it, too. Which is why I don't even bat an eye at his red-faced bluster. "It's not ideal, obviously, but hey"—I offer him a strained smile—"at least I wasn't caught having sex on camera like Andre Beaumont, right? It could definitely be worse."

"An absolute, goddamn *shit show*, Daisy."

I wince. "Dad, it's not like I—"

"*Confessions of a Puck Bunny*?" He shakes his head, his white mustache twitching furiously. "What the hell were you thinking?"

About a lot, actually. Not that he seems particularly keen on hearing any of it.

It's pretty much been the two of us against the world for the last fifteen years. He's the one I called when I first got my period and the boys at the rink made fun of me for bleeding through my leggings. At twelve years old, it hadn't even occurred to me to feel embarrassed about running to my dad for help. When life sours, Sam Hall makes lemonade. That's the way it's always been. Same goes for when he held my hand while the doctors told me that my figure skating career was over. He never left my side, not even once. Through thick and thin, we've always been a dynamic duo.

Until an hour ago, that is.

Turns out that running an anonymous social media account, ironically titled *Confessions of a Puck Bunny*, has the ability to make him look at me like I'm public enemy number one. Better yet, like I've personally betrayed him.

"Well." He closes his laptop with a decisive *click*. "What do you have to say for yourself?"

Out of sight, I dig my fingernails into my thighs. Logically, I get that he has every right to be upset. He coaches a pro hockey team—a team that won the Cup last season—while I've been secretly airing out hockey's dirty laundry for the better part of the last five years online. So, yeah, I don't blame him. But also, logic can kiss my ass. I'm just as angry at being outed as he is that this whole thing has blown up in our faces, especially when I have no idea who even pulled the plug on my alter ego.

Finally, I tell him, "I don't have anything to say that you'll want to hear."

"*Daisy.*"

"Fine. What do you want me to say?"

"That you messed up." He riffles impatiently through his desk, probably in search of a toothpick. "That you're sorry. That you never planned to get hacked."

"Who plans to get hacked, Dad? Literally no one."

"And that you're feeling a shit ton of guilt over all the careers that you've had a hand in ruining."

Well. I shift a little. "*Ruining* is a bit of an exaggeration, don't you think? I was just—"

"Jesus-fucking-Christ, where the hell are my goddamn toothpicks?"

"Second drawer, in the back."

Grumbling under his breath, he yanks open the appropriate drawer with more force than necessary, rips open the plastic casing around a new pack, and then clamps a toothpick between his teeth as if it's the only thing keeping him sane. His blue eyes are sharp and unwavering as they return to my face. "Well?"

Appearance-wise, Sam Hall isn't exactly intimidating. What's left of his hair went white years ago, and much to his chagrin, no amount of yoga ever stretched out his wiry frame past five-foot-eight. Appearances aren't everything, though, and there's a reason why he's one of the most respected coaches in the league.

For one, he's got a deep, imposing voice that could shrivel a thousand dicks.

Secondly, my dad is *intense*.

Unfortunately for him, he single-handedly raised me, which means that I have absolutely no qualms about standing up to him. "I didn't mess up and I'm not sorry. If some players spent half as much time keeping their dicks in their pants as they did worrying about the game, maybe their reputations wouldn't be—"

"That's it, I'm calling your mother."

"You've got to be kidding me. Like I'm *five*?"

"Like you're our daughter."

"I'm *your* daughter," I say before I can bite my tongue. Instead of acknowledging the bitter truth, Dad puts the call on speakerphone. And okay, I should probably keep opinions on Alice Hall to myself, but Dad and me, we've never had that sort of relationship. We say what we mean, the good, the bad, and the downright ugly. "I don't even know why you bother."

When the endless dial tone solidifies my point, Dad's jaw clenches. "She's your mother."

"If you're wanting backup, you'd be better off calling the Blades' PR team."

His brows arch toward his hairline. "Oh, I'm heading there in thirty. And you're coming with me."

"Fuck."

"Language, kid."

"You're the one who taught me to curse."

"Yeah, and I also taught you to keep your head down and not start drama like your mother, but clearly that lesson went out the window, too."

It's a direct hit. One that I feel like a knife to the chest.

I was ten when my mom took off for California. Eleven when I accepted the fact that Alice Hall had really, truly left us for a chance at making it in Hollywood. Dad has always maintained that she planned on coming back; personally, I think that my father's honest to a fault but has a hard time being honest with himself. Because Mom didn't return to Connecticut. Even worse, as the years wore on, she seemed to forget that we existed at all.

She's as flaky as Dad is dependable, like a baby bird caught in a cross-breeze, willing to take flight at a moment's notice, consequences be damned.

I'm nothing like her.

I mean, I'm an *accountant*. Boring would be my middle name if it weren't for *Confessions of a Puck Bunny*, and being Bunny has never been about being dramatic—it's always been about taking a stand for what's right, and I thought . . . Well, stupidly, I always thought that if my dad ever found out, he'd at least see that the only reason I have the courage to call hockey players out on their bad behavior is because *he* taught me to always know my own worth.

"Dad." I wrap my arms around my middle as he stabs

at his screen, presumably to try calling Mom again. "Dad, please listen. I just—"

This time, she sends him straight to voicemail.

Hollow-eyed, he stares at his phone while hurt ripples across his weathered features. I know him well enough to recognize that he wants to rage at his ex-wife—for ignoring him, for leaving him, for abandoning me, their only kid—but despite keeping Dad's surname, the woman who birthed me dumped us years ago. A fact that I'm assuming he remembers right about the time he bites down on the toothpick hard enough to break it in half.

"Fuck, this is going to be a headache."

You're going to be a headache is what he doesn't say out loud. I haven't been a headache to anyone since shit went sideways at Worlds and twelve years of hard work circled down the drain. Just like then, when I watched from a hospital bed as the medalists took to the podium, I'm at a total loss for words. There's so much that I want to say—

Ask me why I started posting as Bunny.

Don't you care that I'm actually doing a good thing here?

Please ask if I'm okay.

—but he's already gone into Coach Hall mode. And sure, I might be a full-grown adult with a decent salary and a now not-so-secret platform with almost a million followers, but as I listen to my dad panic over the Blades possibly firing him, I feel smaller, and more invisible, than I have in years.

CHAPTER 2
WESTON

I fucking love hockey.

The swish of skates. The crisp scent of the ice. Making grown men cry when I steal the puck from their clutches and leave them stamping their feet like ornery toddlers.

"You are supposed to be *old*," Bjorn Anders grunts as he hustles after me during practice. "Don't you have a bad leg?"

"Weren't you a second-round draft pick?" I chirp back at my rookie teammate. "How do you say *overrated* in Swedish?"

"Kyss mig i arslet."

"Nah, don't think that's it." I flash him a wide grin. Then I dangle the puck right in front of the poor bastard before passing it to his stepbrother, who's waiting near center ice. "Hey, Alarik! Bjorn said you're overrated."

Our other rookie smiles broadly. "He is still mad the Blades picked me first."

Bjorn drops his shoulders and actually growls. Suddenly, any display of the kid's earlier hangover disappears in favor of trouncing his brother.

Yup. My job here is done.

"You're a sadist," Andre Beaumont says as he skates up beside me. The C on his practice jersey still gives me a little jolt of surprise every time I see it. Not because he doesn't deserve to be captain but because for as long as I've been with the Blades, it's been Jackson Carter at the helm of this team. Now Carter spends most of his time behind the Plexiglas as one of our assistant coaches. Rumor has it that he might be a lot more than that soon enough.

"A little reverse psychology never hurt anyone," I tell Beaumont.

"Says the guy with more pre-game rituals than the rest of the team combined."

"Hey, now. You can pry my rituals out of my cold, dead hands."

Beaumont's dark eyes crinkle warmly. "Don't worry, I'm not about to mess with greatness." After clapping me on the shoulder, he skates backward. "Speaking of, try not to give Bjorn a complex, eh? We need him focused for tomorrow night."

"Kid's a little too focused on going out, if you ask me."

"He'll learn all about priorities when he's puking up his guts after bag skates later."

I hiss through my teeth. "And you said that *I'm* a sadist."

Beaumont taps his nose with his glove. "Just here to do Coach's bidding."

"Yeah," I say, rolling my eyes. "You're a real lackey, Andre."

Captaincy or not, Andre Beaumont is far from being an obedient lap dog. For years, the guy had a reputation for being an antisocial prick. Then he fell in love with his publicist, married her, and recently knocked her up—they just announced they're having a little girl last week. Those of us who have been with the Blades long enough know that he's a total teddy bear these days, but he keeps up with the bad boy persona to scare the rookies into falling in line. Seems to work well enough because when he barks out Bjorn's name, the kid comes running. Literally.

I turn away before either Anders brother can hear me laugh.

THE REST of practice goes by in a flash.

We're nearing the end of preseason, which means that we're taking a wrench to our lines and fine-tuning last minute details. Last year, we won the Stanley Cup. This year, we're dealing with the fall out of losing a lot of our top line to retirement. Guys like Jackson Carter and Duke Harrison, our goalie, who were fundamental to the team. Suddenly, rookies are looking my way for guidance—Bjorn notwithstanding—and I'm starting to feel every day of my twenty-eight years.

I've just shoved my right leg into a fresh pair of sweatpants when our star forward, Marshall Hunt, drops his duffel bag beside mine on the bench. He straddles the narrow plank of wood and takes a seat, resting his hands on his jean-clad thighs.

"A little birdie told me that shit is about to hit the fan."

I finish pulling on my sweats. "Is that code for *my wife told me something she shouldn't have?*" His wife, Gwen, works for Golden Lights Media, the PR agency that represents most of the guys on the team, myself included.

Hunt shakes his head. "It's code for *there are rumblings on the inter-webs—*"

"Please tell me that you're not stalking Reddit again."

"Listen, I've said this before, and I'll say it again: nothing tops Reddit. I want to grab dinner with my girl in a new city? Some subreddit out there will have the answer. Maybe I'm feeling feisty one day, in the mood to read about horrific first dates, you know?"

"Can't say that I do, bud."

"Whatever. My point is: there's a subreddit for everything."

"And?"

Instead of humoring me with some totally bonkers story that he found on the internet, Hunt's pretty-boy face twists in a grimace as he fishes his phone out of his jeans. After letting Face ID do its thing, he hands over his cell with all the enthusiasm of a man being told to walk the plank.

I stare at the damn thing like it's radioactive.

"Maybe you should sit down," he says, which is the wrong thing to say to a guy who routinely comes up with more pre-game rituals to stem off a constant flow of anxiety. Most days, I've got it covered. Other days, a teammate tells you to *sit down* like he's about to break news of the apocalypse.

In the end, I don't sit, mainly because our bags, and Hunt himself, are in the way. Though when I get a look at the headline at the top of the screen, I start thinking that maybe Hunt had the right of it.

Confessions of a Puck Bunny
Outed as Daughter of Boston Blades' Head Coach

"Maybe it's a spoof piece." Hunt's expression creases with sympathy. "You've known Daisy for how long now?"

Almost ten years.

There was some time after I got drafted and she was still at UConn where we drifted apart. Daily phone calls turned into weekly check-ins turned into sporadic texts that left me feeling strangely off-balance. I've never felt so relieved as I did the day that she sent me a U-Haul receipt for a one-way drop off in Boston. Since then, Daisy Hall has been by my side. The girl couldn't hide a dead body from me, even if she tried.

Or maybe she could.

The longer I skim the article, the warier I grow.

"Gwen said I should stay out of it. That you might know already." But I didn't know. When Hunt grimaces again, I curse my lack of poker face. "Yeah," he sighs, running a hand through his messy black hair, "I didn't think so."

He doesn't say anything else while I finish reading.

Confessions of a Puck Bunny is legendary in the world of hockey. And by legendary, I mean that most people regard the anonymously run social media account as being a perpetual thorn in the league's side.

Bunny's branding is bubble-gum pink with charming white font.

The subject matter might as well be stained blood-red.

It's safe to say that Bunny's got a real mean slap shot. It's been a long-running joke—the morbid kind, anyway— that if you find yourself on Bunny's radar, you might as well kiss what's left of your reputation goodbye. Infidelity. Gambling debts. Drug scandals. It's the sort of quality investigative journalism that has no business being relegated to a social media post. Players are lucky if they only lose endorsement deals or get benched. One guy ended up facing jail time after a slew of women came forward with sexual harassment charges.

With a casual sign off name like *Puck Bunny*, I always figured the mastermind behind the account had to be some sort of genius. I just never thought that genius might be my *best friend.*

"Fuck." This honestly has me feeling all kinds of twisted up inside. Pride because if it's true, it's just like Daisy-fucking-Hall to grab life by the throat and make it her bitch.

Disappointment, and the slightest bit of unease, because I've always been an open book with her and she's . . . Shit, I don't even know what to think right now.

"What are you guys talking about?"

I pass Hunt's phone back over to him before Joshua Kammer can get his pesky hands on it. Kid has one season under his belt, and he's been strutting around the locker room like he's God's gift to hockey since training camp. "It's nothing."

"Doesn't look like nothing."

Hunt shoves his phone into the deepest, darkest recesses of his duffel bag. "You're wicked nosey for a rookie."

Kammer straightens his spine, the look on his young face screaming *try me*. "Excuse you. Not a rookie anymore."

"You can't even grow a beard yet."

"Fuck you, West. No one in my family can. It's a curse."

Hunt shoulders his bag. Since he's so beloved that he could probably get away with murder, he flicks Kammer in the forehead before smiling the same smile that's stopped hearts all over North America. "Go away, kid. The adults are talking."

"So, you *are* talking about something!"

"We aren't," I say at the same time that Hunt replies, "It's above your pay grade."

Jesus.

"You're not helping," I tell Marshall.

Then Kammer looks me dead in the eye and says, "Does this have anything to do with Daisy crying in the parking lot before practice?" and I decide right then and there that Joshua Kammer isn't so bad after all. He's just a cocky little shit who thinks he owns the world. We've all been there.

I kiss the top of his head and then playfully push him out of my way. "Gotta go, boys."

My girl needs me.

CHAPTER 3

WESTON

It takes three tries before Daisy picks up her phone. The second she does, I know that everything I read in that article is true. There hasn't been a single day since we met that Daisy hasn't answered one of my calls with a breezy, "Stop stalking me, Cain. We've already talked about this."

Today, she doesn't say anything at all.

The silence is punctured by her shallow breathing, like she's on the verge of breaking down, followed by the distinct sound of a locker door slamming shut. Since there's no one around to watch me jam my key into the ignition, I peel out of the practice arena's parking lot like my car is on fire. By the time I'm hauling ass onto the Pike, I'm done waiting for Daisy to break the silence.

"I'm on my way."

I can hear her painstaking swallow even over the line. "I'm not at home."

"I know you're not."

"You can't come here."

"You think I won't?"

She tries to laugh but it comes out sounding ragged.

"Last time you showed up, you caused so much pandemonium, the rink banned me for a month straight."

"It's not my fault some kid posted a picture of me online and tagged the place."

"It's not your fault that people are obsessed with you, is that what you're trying to say?"

"If the skate fits . . ."

"I hate you."

"I know you do." Any other day, I'd be smiling at our usual fast-paced banter. I'm too worried to smile right now. Too worried and still too stunned, honestly, by the fact that the girl I thought I knew better than anyone, I might not know at all. "I'll be there in ten. Don't do anything stupid."

"You say the sweetest things, West. Really. I just swooned."

"Without me," I correct smoothly. "Don't do anything stupid without me."

"Ten minutes?"

Blinker on, I change lanes. "Ten minutes."

"Right. Well, I can probably hold off until then," she says in a paltry attempt to be flippant. I don't need to see her to know that she's holding back tears.

I MAKE it to Daisy in seven minutes flat.

Shouldering my duffel bag, I head for the rink's entrance, sending up a silent prayer that the local kids are still at school and there won't be anyone but staff around. Any other day, I'd love the chance to meet some fans. Some guys in the league think that they're above signing an autograph or two but that's never been how I operate.

Sure, I've made it this far in the league on my own merit, but I'd be an idiot not to account for all the love

Boston has shown me over the years, especially when I was scraping the bottom of the barrel after my hip surgery. Yeah, sometimes the notoriety gets to me, but I figure that's the price to pay for living the dream.

I signed away my privacy the second that I finalized my contract with the Blades.

So, when the guy at the front desk tries to let me through without paying the entrance fee, I not only hand over my card but pay another grand on top of it, asking politely if he wouldn't mind letting me and Daisy have the place to ourselves for the next hour. He stumbles over himself, eyes gone glassy with the sort of hero worship that has me shifting uncomfortably under all that unspoken praise, before waving me through with an effusive, "Sure, man, whatever you want. I mean, you got it, Mr. Cain. No problem!"

I find Daisy already on the ice.

She's dressed in a pair of black leggings and a cream-colored sweatshirt that hangs loosely off one shoulder. I've seen her in that UConn sweatshirt more times than I can possibly count. The fabric's faded from numerous washes, and she's worn thumbholes through the sleeves. Her wavy blond hair is pulled back in a messy ponytail that swings across her face as she completes a double toe loop with the sort of mindless ease that comes from years of repetition.

She hasn't noticed me yet.

As she goes through a series of jumps, I study her closely as I lace up my skates. To anyone else watching, they'd be hard-pressed to look past all that effortless perfection. Even her expression gives nothing away. She could just as easily be putting on a performance for thousands as she could be skating for just herself. But I know Daisy Hall. Swear to God, most days I know her better than I know myself.

The girl who supported me making it to the NHL even when my parents tried to talk me out of it.

The girl who suffered a hamstring avulsion fracture on live TV, and then desperately tried to keep going, all so she could have a chance to still medal.

The girl who puts on a brave face every day of her life when people reduce her to "that skater who could have been something great one day."

I can't help but take note of the slight hunch in her shoulders as well as the strain bracketing her mouth that's got nothing to do with old injuries. She may be skating like she was born to dominate the sport, but her head is a million miles away. I wait until she's slowed down, hands propped on her hips, to step onto the ice.

"You're a badass, you know that?"

The sound of my voice has her turning to look back at me over one shoulder. While there aren't any noticeable tear tracks staining her cheeks, her amber eyes are somber when she faces me head-on with her arms hugged tight around her middle. "You don't need to butter me up."

"I know I don't."

"I'm in deep shit."

"Not gonna lie to you, Hall. It's looking that way."

She visibly winces. "I already heard it all from Dad. And the board. And every other PR team they brought in today to tell me all the ways that I've screwed up big time. So as much as I probably need to tell you everything, too, I'm not sure that I have it in me right now to hear you say that I'm the reason why hockey players all over the league are pissed off and wanting—"

The rest of her panicky rant ends in a gasp as I wrap my arms around her.

"Weston." My name is a breathy whisper on her lips.

"Daisy." Hers is a soft exhale on mine.

"You're hugging me."

"Sounds about right."

"*Why* are you hugging me?"

"Because you need it."

"Shit," she expels raggedly, and then her small hands press flat along my spine. Even through my T-shirt and flannel, I can feel her nails digging in, like now that she knows I'm not gonna hang her out to dry, she can't bear the thought of letting go. For a second, we stay like that, me holding her, her burrowing into me, before she releases a small sigh and lets her head fall forward onto my chest. "They're right. I fucked up."

"You regret it?"

I feel her hesitation, the way she's weighing the pros and cons of being honest, before finally she shakes her head. "No. I don't."

"Then you can't really say that you fucked up, can you?"

At that, she lightly bangs her forehead against my sternum with a grim laugh. "Dammit, West. Why do you have to be so logical?"

"Part of the friendship pact, I guess. We can't both be a hot mess at the same time."

She pushes away from me gently. Immediately, the chill from the rink settles in all the warm places where her body just touched mine.

I watch her closely as she scrubs a palm over her red-rimmed eyes, trying my best to reconcile the girl in front of me with the best friend who's been with me through thick and thin since college.

My Daisy is sunshine personified.

This Daisy looks like she's been shoved under a rain-cloud and told to weather the storm.

Defeat slopes off her shoulders and anxiety has her chewing nervously on her bottom lip. Everything about her is dull and sad, and *fuck*, I hate that I can't erase the last twenty-four hours from everyone's memory for her.

She lets her arms fall limply to her sides. "You probably have questions."

Anyone would, I think, but I'm not about to kick her when she's already down. So, I go with one that feels important but won't—I don't know—crush her spirit any more than it's already been crushed. "Did you ever wish that you could tell me?"

"Oh." Surprise flashes in her gaze. "That's . . . You know, of everything you could have asked, that's not the question I thought you'd go with."

"What, not predictable enough for you?"

Her wane smile feels like it costs her every bit of effort. "I thought you'd ask why I started the account in the first place."

"I'm sure you have your reasons."

"You don't want to know them?"

"I know that you'll tell me when you're ready."

"And you aren't going to yell at me?" Her beaten-down posture tells me that she's probably spent the entire afternoon being berated by the Higher Powers That Be. After all, Kammer said that he saw her crying in the parking lot. And my Daisy, she's not exactly one for breaking down in public places—too many years, I think, spent shielding her emotions while being picked apart by coaches and judges.

Looking at her now, I clock the way she's back to chewing on her bottom lip, and my chest gets real tight at the thought of Daisy being reamed out by Coach, the GM, and whoever else sat in on the meeting with her.

I lower my head a little, our height difference so vast that I want to make sure she hears me loud and clear when I say, "You didn't murder anyone, Hall. And even if you did, I'd grab a shovel and ask you when and where to start digging."

That earns me a laugh. It's watery, sure, and a little high-pitched, but still, I cling to it like a lifeline. She'll be okay. Maybe not right now but soon.

"Weston Cain, accomplice for murder?" She playfully swats me in the gut with her knuckles. "Not a chance."

"When and where, Daisy. All I'm saying."

"Hockey's Golden Boy doesn't get his hands dirty for anyone."

"And yet, I'd get them dirty for you."

"Kiss ass," she mutters, but she's smiling—a real, soulful kind of smile—and I find myself smiling right back. It's instinct at this point, a habit embedded in my DNA. There's not much I won't do to put a smile on Daisy Hall's face. Doesn't matter that I still don't know what prompted her to start *Confessions of a Puck Bunny*. Curiosity aside, I'm not gonna push her to tell me more when she's already looking so emotionally drained. It can wait for another day.

I'm a patient guy. Ambitious, yeah, but patient. It's what I'm known for on the ice. Other D-men play with the kind of rough physicality that keeps players on their toes because they don't want to end up getting personal with the boards. Me on the other hand? I'm in it for the long haul, the shadow you can't outrun. I learn your habits, decode your ticks, then unravel that shit in front of twenty-thousand fans.

So, yeah, patience. I've got it in spades.

Which is why Daisy catches me totally by surprise when she clarifies, "It's not that I didn't want to tell you." She rolls the pink flesh of her bottom lip between her teeth. Just when I think that she's about to laugh this whole thing off, her gaze flicks away nervously. Softly, almost apologetically, she adds, "You're my best friend, West."

It occurs to me that we're slowly circling each other; that as close as were just seconds ago—physically, emotionally—there seems to be an invisible wall sprouting into existence between us, leaving me on one side with her on the other. Fuck if I know what to do with all the awkward glances she keeps sending my way. Me and Daisy, we don't do awkward. Since we met almost ten years ago, we've been glued together at the hip—to the point where the guys on the team like to joke that I'm too close with the coach's daughter.

Closeness isn't a problem right now.

Not when Daisy's watching me with an expression akin to dread. Then blunt understanding dawns a second later, and I almost rock back on my skates from the force of it. "You didn't trust me with this."

As if warding off a chill, she folds her arms around her middle again. "Me not telling you about Bunny has nothing do with trust."

"The look on your face says otherwise, Hall."

"I trust you, West. There's no one I trust more."

Five minutes ago, I would have believed her.

But there's something in her gaze that has the hair on my nape standing on end.

"Maybe, yeah." I want to be respectful when she's clearly hurting. Not gonna lie, though, it feels like all the air's left my lungs. As if I'm standing in the middle of land-mine, not knowing where the explosives are beneath my feet. One wrong move and we're both fucked. With my heart thudding loudly in my ears, I hear myself say, "Tell me whatever's runnin' through your head."

"You're a hockey player."

That's it—*you're a hockey player*—as if I haven't always *been* a hockey player. As if we haven't built a raw kind of vulnerability between us over nearly a decade of late nights and early mornings and every fucking second in between.

"When has playing hockey ever stopped me from having your back?"

She squeezes her arms around herself even tighter. "It hasn't."

"Then why would it be any different now? What, because I lack the empathy to understand that some of my peers are shit human beings?"

"Weston, it's not like that. I'm not—" She drags in a sharp breath. "I'm not explaining this well."

"You're not explaining it at all." Somewhere in the back of my head, alarm bells are going off that we can't be having this conversation here. I might have paid for some private rink time but that doesn't mean the staff can just take a hike during their shift. There are eyes and ears everywhere; though it might feel like it, we aren't alone. I know all that, I do, but my chest is aching like I've just been delivered the killing blow from the one person who's always been my safe place. Because that's who Daisy is to me.

Home.

"I didn't come here to berate you. I didn't—*fuck.*" I spear my fingers through my hair, tugging restlessly on the strands. "I didn't come here to tell you that you're wrong for calling players out on their shit because I don't think you *are* wrong. Honest to God, Daisy, you've got balls of steel to keep this under wraps for as long as you have, knowing that you've been doing a good thing when fans would rather turn a blind eye. And maybe . . . maybe I should have seen it sooner—that you're Bunny—because that kind of courage is rare, practically nonexistent. Except that every day for the last nine years, you've never failed to show me how brave *you* are."

She isn't skating now.

Neither am I.

The air has never felt so heavy between us. Heavy like there's something starting to rot at the core of our foundation. Or maybe it's always been rotten. Maybe I just never noticed that we've been building a lifetime together atop shaky ground.

"You've always wanted honesty from me." Roughened by the hurt still licking at my heart, my voice is low, raspy. "You've told me that a thousand times—that I could be the hotshot hockey player with the boys, and the dutiful son with my parents, but with you . . . With you, I can just be *me*."

She takes one hasty lunge toward me, but I skate back, maintaining careful distance. I think it might be the first time since we met that I haven't willingly dropped everything to run to her side. A fact that seems to register to her, too, because her expression suddenly crumples.

"That's what I want," she says fervently. "That's all I've *ever* wanted."

"I wanted the same from you. Thought I had it, too. Except for the fact that you clearly won't let me see all of you after you've spent years asking for all of *me*."

At that, she rocks backward, her weight shifting quickly to stay upright on her blades. I watch her press a hand to her heart as if she's having trouble breathing, and I almost cave then and there. Almost drop to my knees right there in front of her on the ice to beg for forgiveness.

Somehow, I hold my ground.

"I didn't ask if you regretted not telling me," I say quietly. "Some things are personal. Some roads you've got to walk alone. I get that, I do. I asked if you ever *wished* that you could have shared this with me, to let me stand by your side. Clearly, the answer to that is no." Because I'm a hockey player. Because she closed the door on a corner of her life while expecting full access to mine.

This isn't how I planned for this conversation to go. Emotions are running high. We're both feeling hurt. If I dig deep, I know that her posting anonymously has nothing to do with me. We can be best friends without being codependent. It's called having healthy boundaries, something she's clearly set in place for herself. Still doesn't lessen the sting of knowing that I've always poured my heart out to her while she's been keeping hers locked up tight, though.

Fuck, I gotta get out of here.

I say as much, barely waiting for a reply before I'm hightailing it over the boards. She calls out after me.

No. No, she's *begging* for me not to go.

And maybe I have even less boundaries than I thought because I can't bring myself to ignore her. She's got me wrapped around her finger, a star perpetually caught in her orbit. I turn to find her just a few feet away, panic flooding her expression. Then I drop my gaze from her face to see the way she's reaching for me, as though she can keep me from running away.

Heart thudding, I rasp out her name.

"I couldn't tell you." Throat working, she pins her hands to her sides. "I promised myself that I never would."

"Daisy—"

"Be angry with me. Yell at me, if you want." Her chin lifts as a single tear slips down her cheek. "I never wanted to risk your career, West. You've worked too hard. Overcome too much." She scrubs that tear away with a quick pass of her palm. "I told myself that I'd never, ever let you get stuck in the mess with me if I ever got found out."

Years ago, we said that we'd hold each other's hand when shit got tough. Maybe I took it too seriously, that silly promise between two naïve kids who barely knew each other. Maybe I should be down on my knees and kissing her feet for damning herself to Hell alone rather than bringing me down with her.

Maybe, maybe, maybe.

So why do I feel so short of breath? That panicky, too-quick rhythm of my pulse that I haven't felt in years, not since I was new to the Boston Blades and always feeling about ten steps behind my teammates. Then again, the only time I really ever feel like I'm on even playing field is when I'm on the ice—or when I'm with Daisy.

Gruffly, I say, "I didn't ask you to protect me."

"I know."

"I didn't—I wouldn't—" Frustrated, I inhale through my nose and let it out just as slowly. "I don't want you making decisions for me, Hall. That's not how this friendship is supposed to work."

Looking miserable, her voice is small when she replies, "I'm so sorry, West."

I know she is. Shame is written all over her—I can see that now.

So, I try to smile for her. Try my fucking best, honestly, because I shouldn't be upset when she was just trying to look out for me. Only thing is, the smile I'm offering feels wooden. It doesn't sink deep into my bones and warm me from the inside out, the way being with Daisy always does. "You're gonna be fine," I tell her. "Coach will figure it out."

"That's not—" She shakes her head, her blonde ponytail swishing across the tops of her narrow shoulders. "I don't care about that. I mean, obviously I do, but it doesn't matter . . . None of it matters if you don't—if *we* don't . . ." Trailing off with a curse, her fingers flex as if she's doing everything she can not to reach out and touch me. "Are *we* going to be fine?"

Yes.

I hope.

I don't like the way it feels, knowing that you shut me out.

But instead of admitting any of that, I just force the wooden smile on my face into something that I'm hoping doesn't reflect any of the turmoil in my heart. I don't hug her this time, and she doesn't jump into my arms, the way she's done for years.

"Yeah, Daisy-belle. We're gonna be just fine."

CHAPTER 4
DAISY

Nothing is fine.

In fact, as the firm's frat bro administrative assistant appears in my office doorway with a look on his face that says *buckle-up-sweetheart-shit's-about-to-get-rough*, I consider the idea of booking a one-way ticket to Antarctica and figuring out a way to live there for the rest of forever.

I could do it. I mean, I'll miss watching screaming husky videos and eating my weight in vermicelli bowls, but for the sake of my sanity, I'll happily move to—

"Arthur wants to see you, Daisy."

Shit.

I turn away from Trevor to set my desktop computer to sleep mode. "Sure, yeah. No problem." There is no amount of joy in my soul as I stuff my feet into an incredibly uncomfortable pair of black heels. "Whatever Arthur wants."

Trevor doesn't comment on my sarcasm.

Like a good little soldier, he marches me from my office, down a long, never-ending hallway featuring an assortment of arachnid portraiture—I see them in my nightmares sometimes—and straight into the lair of Arthur Phister. It's an unfortunate surname but not nearly as unfortunate as the man himself.

He doesn't even look up from his computer when he barks out, "Is that Daisy, Trevor?"

"In the flesh, Mr. Phister," I say.

Trevor narrows his eyes at me like he's finally catching onto the fact that my tongue can be razor sharp even when my expression is as placid as a lake. His chin dips so he can peer down at me from his eight-inch height advantage. "Arthur," he begins, as if I really care that I'm not a first-name basis with our boss, "would you like me to stay and take minutes for you?"

"Thank you, but no."

Instead of feeling the sting of rejection, Trevor's green eyes shimmer with glee. "Whatever you want, Arthur."

Gross.

"Take a seat, Daisy." Arthur waves me in, his gaze still trained on his computer, fingers flying a million miles a minute over his ancient keyboard. The *clack-clack-clack* of the keys imitates the sound of my heels clicking across the marble floor before I lower myself into the chair across from him.

If I'd known this meeting was happening, I would have prepared for it. As it is, I sit, and wait, and stare at a life-size figurine of a tarantula perched near a jar of ballpoint pens. I don't think the spider was there last quarter. Something tells me that it was a gift from Trevor. After six years of working here, it's safe to say that I've never met anyone who can kiss ass like he can. The only person who waxes poetic about Arthur even more is Trevor's wife.

I clear my throat. "If this is about the Verret account, I've already—"

"It's about Bunny."

From head to toe, it feels like I've been dunked in a pool of ice.

Arthur finally spins away from his monitor. He's in his early seventies and should already be dipping his toes into retirement. Instead, he gets his rocks off on tormenting his employees and faults all of us for not clocking in before sunrise. I've always figured that he's more likely to croak at his desk than he is to kick back on a beach somewhere with his feet in the sand. As he watches me now, from his throne of cracked leather and weathered plastic, I have the sinking feeling that he'd rather I croak first.

I clear my throat again. "Apologies, Mr. Phister. I'm not sure what—"

"Trevor filled me in, Daisy."

Of course he did.

"And I have to tell you," he goes on, "while I'd normally be in favor of letting my employees handle their private lives *privately*, I've decided that it behooves me, in this particular case, to suggest that you take a temporary leave of absence."

My mouth actually falls open in surprise.

"A vacation, perhaps."

A *vacation?* I sit up tall, trying desperately to take up more space when my petite frame often makes it so that everyone treats me like I'm something to be managed. As if I'm a doll or a child instead of a twenty-seven-old adult. "Mr. Phister, I appreciate the suggestion. Really, I do. But I have so much to get done that even if I *wanted* to take you up on this, it wouldn't benefit the firm."

He speaks over me as if I haven't voiced a perfectly valid concern. "Or you could use your sick days."

"But I'm not sick."

"Daisy." His tone is haughty and dismissive and, dammit, I really, really want to take that stupid tarantula and smash it over his head. "I'm trying to keep this simple, yes? You're clearly going through a lot—"

"I'm more than capable of doing my job, sir."

"—So, I'll let this little display of attitude slide for the time being."

He did not just say that.

I almost turn to look over my shoulder, as if I'll find someone waiting there so I can blurt out, *Do you hear this bullshit?* but aside from Trevor, who probably has his ear pressed to the closed door, there's no one around to commiserate with.

After being forced to retire early from figure skating, I was totally lost. Skating was all I knew, and it was ripped away from me in the blink of an eye. My dad, my peers, they all assumed that I'd go into coaching, and if not that, then at least a career in sports medicine or sports psychology or sports *something*.

I went into accounting instead.

Not because I particularly like it—even though I'm surprisingly good with numbers—but because of its stability. In a job like this one, no one is going to walk into my office and be all, "Oops, you broke a bone! Time to pick a new career."

Except this feels exactly like that, as if I'm on the verge of being shoved out the door.

I'm not proud of the way desperation makes me curl into myself in a last-ditch effort to make myself appear even smaller, a non-threat. Anything so that when I walk out of this office, I won't be doing so without a job.

"I'm sorry, Mr. Phister." I force the words past the knot of frustration lodged in my throat. And by "force," I mean that I choke on every syllable. It feels wrong on so many levels to apologize for taking a stand against the jerk-bags of humanity. Bunny would never, and yet here I am, swallowing my pride long enough to pathetically add, "If there's something I can do to fix the situation that doesn't include me stepping away from the office . . ."

"Many of our accounts are with athletes, Daisy. And not just athletes as individuals but Boston-based sports teams. They trust us to be professional at all times, which includes how we conduct ourselves in the office as well as away from it. You seem incapable of upholding either standard."

Before I can get a word in, he angles his desktop monitor so that I can see the screen. Immediately, my heart careens into freefall.

In bold, black letters, the headline from a tabloid site stares back at me:

Lover's Spat?
Boston Blades' Weston Cain Faces Off Against Puck
Bunny Daisy Hall

Below the headline is a picture of us from the rink in Watertown. Just looking at it makes me want to throw up. Someone captured the moment right as West twisted away from me, his slightly blurry features darkened by hurt while I bear the full brunt of the camera's focus; my cheeks are flushed, my desperation for him blatantly obvious in the shape of my outstretched arms. It's abundantly clear that we've been arguing.

I don't know the last time West and I have disagreed on anything besides what to order for dinner, and now it's been forever memorialized online.

It suddenly feels hard to breathe.

"Not a single one of our clients signed up to be exposed by someone named *Bunny*," Arthur continues stiffly. When I try to interject to defend myself, he shuts me up with a clipped, "I could fire you, Miss Hall."

"Mr. Phister. Sir. I don't think—"

"If I was really so inclined, I could even seek legal

counsel and take you to court—but I won't. Unfortunately for you, this sort of grace comes with certain . . . Shall we say, *expectations.*"

Expectations like being told to take a vacation or get sued.

Expectations like being told to shut up—permanently.

My talk with management for the Blades the other day was a mixed bag. A few people sent me sympathetic glances but on the whole, it was mandated that all of Bunny's accounts be immediately deactivated. Some of the hard hitters even demanded that the team launch a formal investigation into how much of what I've revealed online was repeated before me in confidence. There was discussion of violated NDAs, whether or not I could potentially face legal action, and if the Blades would be expected to stand by my side while I mucked about through the trenches.

By the end of the three-hour long meeting, it was wholly apparent that no one wanted to touch me with a ten-foot pole—my father included. If there's a silver lining to all this mess, it's that the decision I made years ago to keep West out of the loop will save him in the end.

He can hate me all he wants but at least his career isn't in jeopardy.

The fallout will come down on only me.

But while I felt, and still feel, pressure to keep quiet when it comes to the Blades—if only to avoid bringing any more trouble to my dad or West—I feel none of that while sitting here in this sterile office.

Arthur is still yammering on about *expectations* and *consequences.* A quick glance at the clock on his desk tells me that he's been talking at me for almost twenty minutes. Not once has he stopped to breathe. And maybe it's just that— the sensation of being perpetually talked down to, of constantly being told to lower myself and make myself smaller in order to prop up the old boys' club—but something inside me snaps.

"Excuse me, Mr. Phister."

He blinks at me slowly. I have the feeling that even though he's been laying into me, he somehow managed to forget that I've actually been present for his entire tirade. He bites off, "What, Daisy," as if I'm somehow more inconvenient than a shit stain on the bottom of his shoe.

Yeah. I'm about done here.

I say, "No need to worry about the accounts."

When I rise to my feet, he does the same, almost knocking the tarantula figurine clear off his desk in his haste to stand. "What are you talking about? Of course we're going to worry. They're our clients. Some of them have been with us for over a decade. Which you should have considered before you decided to completely disregard the reputation of this firm—"

"Mr. Phister, you don't need to worry about them because I *quit*."

CHAPTER 5
WESTON

A few days after my blow up with Daisy, the boys are giving me a wide berth while we get ready for our game against New York.

Everyone's at their stalls, shedding their game-day suits and donning their gear. Usually, the dressing room is a hub of activity and chatter, some guys kicking around a hacky sack to get the blood flowing while others choose stillness, taping and re-taping their sticks with meditative precision. Tonight, the room is as silent as a morgue.

It feels like a bad omen.

Seated on the bench in front of my stall, I try to block out the eerie silence by hunching my big frame over to pull on my left skate and then my right one. As my fingers tangle in the laces, someone across the room from me sneezes and gets shushed by one of the rookies.

Shushed.

Like he's a toddler screaming in a library.

Before I can change my mind, I'm peeling off my skates and striding across the room in my hockey socks. A few of my teammates turn to warily glance my way. Kammer, on the other hand, looks like he's about two seconds away from trotting over to me, golden retriever smile firmly in place, only for Hunt to swat the back of the rookie's head, wordlessly telling him to leave me alone.

I don't need to be left alone.

It's not one of my pre-game rituals.

What I need is music blasting over the speakers. I need the guys to not treat me like I'm a ticking time bomb they're worried about setting off. I need to pull on my gear, from left to right, and then I need to tape my stick, make the same stupid joke with Beaumont that I did last season before we won game seven in the final round of playoffs, and when all that's said and done, I need to head out onto the ice, stick held in my left hand even though I'm a righty.

The second that Journey's "Don't Stop Believin'" comes on, it's like I can finally breathe again. Although as far as music goes, I'm not exactly a fan of—

"Aw, you *love* me, don't you, Cain."

I flash our new starting goalie, Tommy Kase, the middle finger. "This song is trash, Kasey, and you know it."

The banter is enough to break the tension, thank fuck. Half the team starts blundering their way through the lyrics, singing at the top of their lungs, while the rest groan good-naturedly and hurl balled-up socks at me as I head back to my stall with my arms raised up by my head to ward off the attack. The too-tight feeling in my chest loosens.

There we go. A little bite of chaos to keep things moving along. Exactly how I like it.

After I sit back down, I start from the top again.

Left skate. Right skate.

Left laces. Right laces.

Then the door to the dressing room swings open and Sam Hall storms inside with Jackson Carter and the other assistant coaches trailing a few steps behind them. Coach signals for someone to turn off the music. Just like that, we're back to being a morgue again.

"Fuck," I mutter under my breath, slumping back on the bench.

"Gather around, boys," Coach booms loudly. I've known him since my UConn days and not much has changed in the last ten years—less hair, maybe, and he's grown a little rounder in the middle, but otherwise he's the same Sam Hall known for making grown men cry with just a single, laser-eyed glare. He pulls a toothpick from his shirt pocket and sticks it into his mouth, talking nimbly around the thin strip of wood. "I'm sure you've all heard the news."

No one asks him to elaborate.

I fold one hand over my opposite wrist, pressing my thumb against my rabbiting pulse. And I keep my gaze fixed on Coach, who drops his hands to his belted waist. His suit jacket is missing, which is how I know he's more flustered than he's letting on. Sam Hall is always pulled together; I used to think that he slept in his game day suits.

"Seems we've got a journalist in our midst, and for once, I'm not talking about Charlie Denton." At the mention of Duke Harrison's new bride, there are a few awkward chuckles as if no one's really sure whether the comment was meant to be a joke. Coach clears his throat. "There'll be a team meeting later this week to discuss *Confessions of a Puck Bunny.* You got concerns, bring them up then. I'm only mentioning it now because Morley's spent his entire afternoon making a fuss online. He's going to be a fucking menace on the ice tonight, and I want all of you prepared if he tries to start anything."

Joe Morley plays on New York's second line.

There were rumblings a few years ago that he was cheating on his wife; rumblings that cracked wide open when Bunny—fuck, correction, when *Daisy*—exposed his infidelity on social media. Turns out that Mrs. Morley spilled the beans to Daisy, but I'm guessing Joe doesn't really care to dwell on the specifics. Mrs. Morley is now the *former* Mrs. Morley, and Joe never bothered to sign a prenup. On top of losing half of everything in the divorce, he's been playing like shit the last few seasons, so I'm not surprised that he's out for blood. He's a desperate man clinging to what's left of a dying career.

Can't relate.

"This is how it's going to go," Coach says as he meets the gaze of every player. When he skips right over me, I press harder on my quickened pulse point until I can feel the reverberation of my measured breathing all the way down to my toes. "You're going to play clean. You're going to ignore any and all trash talk—"

"Oh, c'mon, Coach. That's the best part of hockey!"

Rolling his eyes at Kammer, Coach continues, "And you're going to go out there and remind New York who won the Cup less than six months ago. You hear me?"

The dressing room erupts with raucous cheering.

"Great. Now finish up—you've got twenty minutes." Coach shifts the toothpick to the opposite corner of his mouth before finding my gaze amidst a sea of hockey players. "Cain? A quick word."

Fuck.

Thankfully, he makes his way toward me instead of the other way around. Despite my friendship with Daisy, I wouldn't go so far as to say that I think of Sam Hall as a father figure. We get along just fine. I've spent holidays camped out at his dining table and more nights than I can count washing his dinner plate in the sink. We're close, friendly, even, but careful about not crossing boundaries. At the end of the day, I don't owe him my life—I would have gotten here with or without his help—but I still owe him a lot, and that includes showing professional deference as one of his veteran players.

Shifting to the side, I offer him room on the bench.

His bones audibly creak as he lowers down beside me, his shiny black dress shoes catching the florescent lighting as he plants them hip-width apart on the floor. Without preamble, he announces, "I'm considering keeping you off the ice tonight."

My stomach pitches uneasily. "All right."

Lacing his fingers together, Coach rests his elbows on his spread knees and lowers his head. To be honest, he looks like shit—like whatever comes after even the fumes he's been running on have gone dust-dry. With a rough sigh, he shoves a hand through his thinning white hair. "Look here, kid, this isn't about punishing you."

He's been calling me "kid" since my freshman year at UConn.

It's a nickname that he's reserved for Daisy, too.

I remind myself that me and Sam Hall, we've got iron-clad boundaries. Coach. Player. At the end of the day, it doesn't matter that his daughter is my favorite person in the world. In this building—on the ice, especially—all that matters is hockey. Plus, I've never been one to kiss ass to net me more playing time, and I'm not about to start now. I've more than earned my place on this team.

"Didn't think it was about punishing me." I nod toward the others with a small lift of my chin. "If you're wanting to give the rookies more ice-time, I get it. Honestly, Bjorn could use—"

"It's not about the rookies."

Tension binds my muscles into stiff knots. "Then I don't understand."

Because if it's not about the rookies, then it's about *me*, and I've never given anyone in management a reason to put me on the bench. Unlike Beaumont, who wears hockey player tears on his knuckles like diamond rings, I rarely end up in the sin bin after getting physical. That's not my style. I can do more for my team on the ice than I can from behind a sheet of Plexiglas.

My confusion must be apparent because Coach tilts his head just enough to swing his gaze up to meet mine. "You're my girl's best friend, aren't you?"

"You already know the answer to that."

"Maybe I want to hear you say it out loud."

Because he's doubting it all of a sudden?

Ignoring the lingering tension in my shoulders, I lean back and grab my stick from my stall, lowering its familiar weight across my thighs. From what he said, he's *thinking* about keeping me off the ice, which isn't the same as *you're benched*. If there's any hope in me having a good game, then I need to finish getting ready. I pluck a roll of cloth tape from my duffel bag.

"There isn't anything I wouldn't do for your daughter, Coach." I keep my focus centered on the well-practiced, fluid motion of my hands. "Told her yesterday that I'd bury a body for her, if that's what she needed."

"Would you fight a player over her?"

"Generally speaking, I leave the fighting to Beaumont."

"Generally speaking, my daughter hasn't personally lit a fuse under Joe Morley's ass."

"I'm not gonna lose my temper just because the guy can't keep his mouth shut." Over the years, I've learned to mentally disengage from what's said in the heat of the game. Most of the time, I'm so focused on the puck that trash talk just skates right past me—no pun intended. "I'm not worried about it."

From the corner of my eye, I watch Coach closely, taking stock of his perfectly neutral expression. But a quick tick of movement in my periphery snaps my gaze downward, to where Coach's knee is bouncing anxiously. The moment he realizes that I've noticed, he jumps to his feet and busies himself with plucking another toothpick from his shirt pocket. "Any other day, I'd be happy to watch you defend my daughter's honor, but not when I need your head in the game. I'll let you play, but don't—don't make me regret this, Cain."

"You won't," I start to say, but he's already turned away.

Fuck Joe Morley.

No, really, fuck that fucking cunt-face piece of—

Beaumont shoves me against the boards, panting hard as his dark brown eyes glitter with frustration behind his visor. He jabs a gloved hand at my face. "Pull your head out of your ass, Cain. He's not worth the energy."

"You heard what he said." About her. What he said about *Daisy*.

"Yeah, I did. And he'll say worse if he knows that it's getting to you."

Beyond my captain's shoulder, I spy Morley's red-and-white away game jersey as he skates off with the puck. When I make a sudden move to follow, Beaumont gives me another rough shake. "Head out of your ass," he growls in warning, "or I'll do it for you."

Then he's gone, and I'm hot on his heels.

Our exchange lasts ten seconds, if that, but ten seconds in hockey is the equivalent of a lifetime. In the time that it took for Beaumont to put me in my place, Hunt's managed to sweep up the puck in a turnover that he sends over the blue line with a clean wrist shot to his linemate, veteran winger Henri Bordeaux. From there, they jostle the biscuit back and forth like two kids playing a high stakes game of keep-away, but the shot Bordeaux finally takes on the net rebounds off the pipes and gets picked up by New York again.

I keep my cool.

Head down, reflexes sharp, I stay locked in for the rest of the second period and well into the third. It's not until there's four minutes left on the clock, and we're up 2-1, that Joe Morley's line change matches up with mine again. And even then, I do what Coach ordered, what Beaumont told me—

I dutifully ignore the fucker.

Well, as much as the game allows, at any rate. I battle it out with him against the boards, stalk him from one end of the defensive zone to the other, and keep him far away from the net every time that he so much as breathes in Kasey's direction. Beaumont sends the puck sailing past center ice, but it feels like not even thirty seconds later that we're back on the prowl, sabotaging every attempt New York makes to score.

It's only when I'm tussling for the three-inch slab of rubber with Morley's linemate, Douglas North, that shit hits the fan.

Thing is, I've spent all night enduring vitriol from Morley—gritting my teeth, biting my tongue—that when North opens his mouth, I honestly don't think twice about whatever he's said, just let it wash over me like everything else. But then he says it again, with his helmet striking mine as he tries to shoulder me out of the way, and this time, I hear him loud and crystal fucking clear:

"You into ice-cold cunts, Cain?"

My heart thuds viciously against my rib cage. "The fuck did you just say?"

"Ice-cold cunts," he sneers while slashing his stick at the elusive puck. His elbow catches me in the side. "Frigid pussies. You gotta be into freezing your dick off with the way you're always chasing Hall's daughter around. But maybe that's why she's such a two-faced bitch—must be exhausting letting her father's team run train on her all—"

Later, I'll tell Coach that I don't remember grabbing North by the jersey. No one who reviews the footage will believe me, of course, but for the first time in my career, I don't give a fuck. Because the last thing that I really *do* remember is shoving Douglas North down onto his back and straddling his waist. I remember ripping off his helmet and sending it skidding across the ice before slamming my fist down into his ugly fucking mug. And I remember doing it again, and again.

So, yeah.

Generally speaking, I leave the fighting to Andre Beaumont.

But generally speaking, if you fuck with Daisy Hall that means you fuck with *me*.

CHAPTER 6
DAISY

"So, what you're saying is that you got fired today."

"Excuse you," I mutter while playing a game of hot potato with the steaming plate of leftover pasta that I pull from the microwave. Quickly, I set it down on the counter and shake out my tingling fingers. "I quit today, there's a big difference."

On the other end of the line, Weston's twin brother, Tory, doesn't miss a beat: "Mr. Phister was totally about to can you, admit it."

I groan. "Can we not call him that? Please?"

"But it's his name."

"Yeah, but it's . . . ."

"Suggestive?" Tory's laugh echoes in my kitchen as I go through the motions of setting the table, which is tucked cozily against my bay window. "Do you think it's an inside joke between him and Mrs. Phister? Because there are about a million-and-one puns they could be dishing out daily, and hopefully they haven't let down all of humanity by having a bad sense of humor."

I gag a little at the thought of Mr. and Mrs. Phister sharing *anything* between them.

"Why did I call you again?" With a glass of white wine already waiting for me, I slide halfway down the cushioned bench and place my phone beside my dinner plate. "I have regrets."

"You called because my brother is currently playing knight-in-shining armor on ice, and I don't have a life."

"Sounds like the *Frozen* edition of Medieval Times."

"Sounds like you're avoiding the topic," Tory replies breezily, and I have the distinct impression of him sitting in his living room with his feet up on the coffee table and reruns of *Game of Thrones* playing on TV. "When were you going to tell me that Mom and Dad are fighting, and I'm about to become the child of a divided home?"

Rolling my eyes, I reach for the wine. "West should have smothered you in the womb."

"He tried, you know. Obviously, it didn't work out."

"Regrettable," I utter with mock solemnity.

"Brat."

"Nerd." Giving up the goose—ghost? I never remember how the saying goes—I slouch back against the wall, wine glass still clasped loosely in my left hand. In so many ways, Tory and West couldn't be more different, but they're both relentlessly stubborn, so I don't bother trying to change the subject again. "You saw the tabloid article, I'm guessing?"

"One of the girls at the office was passing it around."

Which means that West's dad definitely saw it, then, since Tory works for his family's real estate brokerage. And since David Cain has never had an opinion that he couldn't keep to himself, it's only a matter of time before he calls West directly to express his everlasting disappointment. "Ugh. Love that for us."

Tory makes a sound of sympathy. "It could be worse. You and West could have been caught fucking on camera, à la Andre Beaumont."

"You know, I said that exact same thing to my dad and he didn't even crack a smile."

"You sure the no-fun Phisters aren't rubbing off on him?"

I laugh so hard that I need to put my wine down. That— that right there is why I called Tory Cain.

Weston might be the other half of my soul, but his twin is right up there, too. After the Blades drafted West, Tory and I spent another two years together at UConn, him while he finished undergrad and started on his master's in computer engineering, and me while I wrapped up my degree in accounting. There were a lot of late nights spent with too many textbooks sprawled out before us, one too many beers, and a horrible habit of always saying the wrong thing at exactly the right time.

"All jokes aside—you doing okay?"

Tory's voice is soft and concerned. In this moment, in that particular tone, he sounds so much like West that I feel tears prick the backs of my eyes. Before they can fall, I drain the rest of my wine and then stare at my plate of pasta as if it has the answer to all of my prayers—it doesn't, by the way. I'm garbage in the kitchen but get by the best that I can.

Despite the wine, my throat feels like sandpaper when I whisper, "I hurt him."

"Didn't ask about West, brat. I asked if *you're* okay."

Not really, no. The last few days have been a whirlwind, and not the good kind. Self-awareness has always been a blessing and a curse for me, which means that I'm acutely aware of the fact that my decision to spawn Bunny into a living, breathing entity now has dire consequences for everyone I love. I always planned to keep her a secret. Not because I'm embarrassed, but because there's safety in the anonymity—not only for myself but for all the people who have sought Bunny out.

I've been a safe place to land for so many people. And now the community that I built from the ground up—that sense of belonging which has given me so much purpose—is gone, just obliterated with nothing more than the tap of a button.

While I feel guilty for lying to West and my dad and Tory, too, I also feel . . . at loose ends, in a way that I haven't since that hospital bed when everything went to shit.

"Daisy?"

Before I can answer, there's a heavy knock on my front door. "Hold on," I tell Tory, scooting out from the bench to walk barefoot into the tiny living room that doubles as my office. I take him off speakerphone and press the device to my ear. "It's probably Anita."

"The old lady who makes you water her plants whenever she's away?"

"She doesn't *make* me, I offered."

"You can barely keep yourself alive. Tell me exactly how many of her plants you've murdered."

"Ye of little faith." Since I live in an apartment building that includes a concierge service, I think nothing of opening my front door without checking the peephole first. "I'll have you know that her plants are *thriving* under my—"

Oh.

"Hang up the phone, Hall."

I'm only a little ashamed of the way my heart stutters into overdrive at finding my best friend standing unexpectedly on my "Oh Shit, Not You Again" welcome mat.

He's clearly just come from taking a post-game shower: his still-wet blond hair is darker than usual, the wavy strands chaotically mussed like he barely stopped to towel off before driving here, to my building in the Back Bay, rather than heading home to his place in Winthrop. I know he came here first because he's still in his game day suit—a suit that I custom-ordered for him because West has absolutely zero interest in fashion. The expensive material hugs his powerful frame, showcasing the broad expanse of his shoulders as well as his muscular hockey thighs. He's left the top three buttons of his matching black dress shirt undone, which only accentuates the column of his throat and the stubble shading his jaw.

He'd look like a model if not for the fact that he's way too rough around the edges to be strutting down a fancy Parisian runway. Instead, every rugged inch of Weston Cain seems to have been stitched together to wreak havoc on hearts everywhere.

With my gaze locked on his mossy green eyes, I speak into the phone, "It's your brother."

I hear Tory's TV shutting off. "Yeah?"

West glowers, which is definitely a sight to behold because glowering isn't exactly in his genetic makeup—unless he's chasing down his opponents on the ice, of course. My heart, traitorous organ that it is, only thuds faster. "He seems . . . angry?"

Tory hums a little. "What does that even look like?"

"Honestly, sort of like that time we found him clinging to that trash can at Margaritaville on your twenty-first birthday."

"His poor little athlete's body couldn't handle all the booze."

"He tried, though," I murmur sympathetically.

"And failed," Tory says, laughing.

"Daisy."

I raise my brows at my best friend. "Yes, Weston?"

"Hang up the phone, please."

"But I'm—"

"The phone, Hall. Now."

"Looks like I have to go, Tory. Your lesser half needs me."

"Aw, I always knew that you loved me the most—"

West plucks the device out of my hand and shoves it into the front pocket of his slacks. "Inside, Daisy. Now."

A shiver works its way down my spine.

Yes, West. Anything you say, West.

Great, now I sound just like Frat Bro Trevor.

Gross.

Still, I take my butt back inside my apartment, all the while asking over my shoulder, "Where's your key?" I don't remember the last time he's knocked on the door, if he ever has.

When I got the keys from the landlord two years ago, West carried me over the threshold like a bride, and then we laughed ourselves silly before proceeding to drink too much celebratory wine—he'd just gotten the news that he was finally being taken off Injured Reserve after months of intense physical therapy.

When West doesn't answer right away, I turn to find him standing in my entryway with his suit jacket clutched in one hand. On the rare occasions that he comes over after a hard-fought game, he's usually camped out on the couch by this point and already nodding off from the adrenaline crash. Tonight, he looks utterly drained, which is par for the course, but something . . . doesn't feel right.

I tilt my head. "What's wrong?"

"Did you watch the game?"

"What?"

"The game, Hall. Did you watch it?"

His voice is pitched low, the charmingly boyish dimple in his right cheek nowhere to be found. I'm not naïve—I know that a few days isn't enough time to miraculously erase the fact that I hurt him, no matter how well-intentioned my reasons—but my gut, which is always attuned to West, is screaming that the worry in his gaze has nothing to do with our argument.

"You know that I haven't." Not yet, anyway.

Because unless I'm physically present at TD Garden, I prefer to watch the Blades play after the game has officially ended. It's a weird, anxiety-driven habit. Between my own career-ending injury and watching West get pulverized a few years back, I like to be prepared, that's all. I keep an eye on my notifications, take note of anything that might send me into a spiral, and then watch accordingly.

At my answer, West jerks his head in a small, satisfied nod. "Good."

"Yeah?"

"Yeah," he echoes.

I find myself staring at his suit jacket, which he hasn't put away, and then at his fancy dress shoes that he's yet to take off. "Are you going to tell me what's going on?"

His gaze darts to mine before slipping away.

Right. Okay, then.

With a nod of my own, I head for the loveseat where I always leave the remote control for the TV. I've just picked it up when West growls from behind me, *"Don't."*

"You know I don't like that word."

"Yeah, well, you know that I don't like it either, but I'm telling you"—suddenly, he's right there in front of me, his towering frame blotting out the rest of the room as he tosses his jacket over the back of the sofa—*"don't."*

I blink up at him. "Did you seriously come over just to tell me not to watch tonight's game?"

Rough edges aside, a flush creeps up West's throat. "So what if I did?"

"I can just wait until you leave, you know."

"Then it looks like I'll be sleeping on your couch." His calloused fingers circle my wrist. Gently, he tugs the remote out of my grasp. "And for the record, I'll be confiscating your laptop, too."

What the fuck.

The moment that he turns away to presumably hunt

down my computer, I'm like a dog at his heels, not panting, thank you very much, but stalking every move he makes through my six-hundred square foot apartment. He comes up empty at my desk and in the kitchen. When he enters my bedroom, I finally lose my patience.

"West."

"Daisy."

I grab him by the elbow and drag him to a halt. He didn't bother with hitting the switch on his way in, so the room is full of elongated shadows thanks to the light filtering in from the hallway. Though maybe I should, I don't let him go, not even when I have his full attention. Cast in shadow, his green irises appear nearly black.

"You're freaking me out. Did something happen tonight?" I run my gaze over him, quickly assessing the familiar lines of his body for any sign of physical damage. "Are you okay?"

"I'm all good."

"You're lying to me."

He slips out of my hold. "Maybe I'm doing it to protect you."

"Yesterday, you told me that I shouldn't be trying to protect you when you didn't ask for it. And for what it's worth, I understand why you were annoyed because I'm not asking you to protect me now." Maybe it's too soon to bring up Bunny, but I don't see the point in tiptoeing around my alter ego, not when the rabbit's already out of the bag. Or the cat. Whatever. "I rate you an eight out of ten on the hypocrisy scale," I tack on with a smile, hoping to ease whatever tension seems to be scaling the walls of the room.

He doesn't look convinced. "Hall . . ."

"I'm going to find out, you know that, right? Maybe I'll live in oblivion tonight, but by tomorrow, there won't be any escaping whatever happened."

The sharp contrast in our height makes it so that I have to tip my head back to meet his gaze and he needs to hunch his shoulders so that we stay in the same stratosphere. But for all the inches that separate us—and there are many—I sense the moment that he surrenders. A harsh breath rattles across his lips, and then, slowly, he reaches into his pocket to offer me my phone in what feels a lot like a truce.

When my fingers graze his, he doesn't immediately let go of the device, though.

"This will hurt you," he utters quietly.

"More than I hurt you?" I don't know what possesses me to say it, but it feels important to get it out there between us. "Because I hurt you, West. And it kills me to know that I did."

"Yes."

That's all he says—*yes*.

I have no idea what to make of that answer, so I do what's always best in high-stress situations like this one and park my butt on the edge of the bed. A moment later, the mattress dips with Weston's added weight as he sits down beside me.

Years ago, when we first met, I was so deprived of sunlight, buried as I was beneath layers of mortification and grief, that standing beside *the* Weston Cain barely registered as anything noteworthy—until he offered me friendship. I jumped on the offer embarrassingly fast, so grateful to not feel so incredibly alone that it took me years to realize that the sun always shines brighter around him.

It took me even longer than that to understand that the anticipation I felt in seeing him was outside the scope of mere platonic friendship. I blamed being an elite athlete for giving me tunnel vision. I blamed my limited experience with dating for not recognizing the obvious signs of infatu-ation sooner. And I blamed me, most of all, because I literally friend-zoned myself within minutes of meeting him, and there was no turning back the clock.

I'm Weston Cain's best friend, and he's mine.

But I'm also so painfully in love with him, most days I think that I might shatter under the crushing weight of knowing that he'll never love me back.

So, when West sit downs next to me, I scoot away, not enough to draw attention, but a few generous inches to give myself some much-needed breathing room. Not that it helps any. I can still smell the woodsy scent of his body wash, and I've barely managed to orient myself to his proximity when his thick thighs are spreading wide and invading my space, leaving me no choice but to feel the imprint of his warm body alongside mine.

Then his whiskey-smooth voice is rumbling, "Do you remember what you said to me when we first met?" and in my mind's eye, I'm stumbling through that first meeting all over again, the vivid memory of a much younger West looking uncomfortable as his teammates teased him. They'd failed to read the visual cues pouring from him in waves—cues that I'd picked up on immediately even though we'd never officially met.

"I said that your friends were douchebags. Which, for the record, I still stand by that statement. And no, you can't change my mind."

Despite the almost suffocating tension in the room, he laughs. It's low and husky, the sound rushing through my veins like a feverish current. "Not that part," he says, sobering a little. "I meant when I asked what you'd do if things got hard and everything was falling apart. Do you remember what you said to me?"

My skin prickles with awareness. "I said that I'd hold your hand just so we both knew that we weren't alone."

West angles his big body toward me.

And then, with his shadowed gaze fixed unwaveringly

on my face, he lifts one hand to rest atop his left thigh, his palm tipped up toward the ceiling. "C'mon, Daisy-belle," he murmurs softly, "hold my hand, won't you?"

I hate him.

Or maybe it's just that I hate how much I love him.

But only because there's currently a tidal wave of emotions spinning through me, all of them so overwhelming that I'm not even surprised when damp heat resurfaces, once again threatening to spill over. Reaching up, I immediately use the heel of my palm to scrub away any tears, the motion ingrained in me after years spent working myself to the bone—my coaches never liked a crier. Then again, those days are long gone now, stuffed inside a memory box along with dashed dreams and career-ending injuries.

Through the blur of tears, I see West wriggle his fingers. "It's just a handhold, Hall. No need to cry on me now."

I mean to give him a friendly, bro-punch in the shoulder, but find myself leaning into his arm instead. On a deep sigh, I let my eyes flutter closed, absorbing the heat from his body. Existing in Weston's orbit is like a shot of serotonin to the system, and I always find myself desperate for another hit.

When I've been quiet for too long, I mutter, "I don't cry."

"Of course, you don't," West returns kindly.

"You don't believe me."

"I'll always believe you."

Fondness for him thickens in my throat. Sometimes, I wish that he wasn't so vocal with his affection, but if he wasn't, then he wouldn't be him, and I wouldn't change West for anything. With my eyes still closed, I reach blindly for his hand, linking our fingers together like it's the most natural thing in the world.

"I'm sorry that I lied to you."

West squeezes my hand. "You wanted to protect me."

"Always."

"And I want to protect you," he utters like a vow.

"Always," I whisper back. "Maybe it's enough to know that even though we can't protect each other from everything, at least we won't let go." I clutch his hand tighter, so he knows exactly what I mean.

"That's what Rose said to Jack in *Titanic* right before she shoved him into the ocean. *Don't let go, Jack*, and then just, like, goodbye, Jack. See you never."

I lose it.

It's been some of the worst days of my life, but suddenly I'm laughing so hard, I'm actually wheezing. Between near-silent giggles, I choke out, "Goodbye, Jack, say hi to the fish for me."

"Goodbye, Jack, don't let the door hit you on the way out."

"No," I howl into West's shoulder, "not the door. You went there."

He sounds so fucking proud of himself when he drawls, "Sure did."

Lifting my head, I seek out his glittering green gaze amidst the shadows. Eye contact with West is always hit or miss—there are days when he seems to crave the intimacy and others when I can tell the prolonged connection is over-stimulating for him. It's never bothered me one way or the other, but I can't deny how hard my cheeks flush when he not only looks me in the eye but presses our clasped hands to his heart.

"We're going to be old and gray one day, and I'm still gonna be holding your hand, Daisy-belle. Nothing will ever change that."

I wonder if he might act differently if he knew how I feel.

If he knew that I love him.

This time, I'm the first to look away, lowering my gaze to my phone. It looks so harmless resting on my thigh but has the power to destroy what's left of my already crumbling world. Nervously, I fiddle with the case. "Remember that time in college when we played truth or dare, and I dared you to do goat yoga in the quad wearing nothing but a jock strap?"

West's shoulders tremble with an exaggerated shiver. "I remember it being very, very cold."

"I'm sure the goats felt the same way."

"The goats weren't wearing next to nothing."

"You're right, Cain—the goats *were* wearing nothing."

He bumps my shoulder with his. "Jerk."

I flash him a blinding smile, then swallow down my nerves. "Ask me truth or dare?"

"Yeah. Okay." He doesn't pull away, just lets our shoulders stay flush together. "Truth or dare, Hall. What's it gonna be?"

"Truth." I turn my phone over with my free hand. "What happened at the game tonight?"

CHAPTER 7
WESTON

What happened at the game tonight?

Someone talked shit about you.

Someone talked shit about you, and I lost my cool.

Someone talked shit about you, and I lost my cool, and I'd do it again, no questions asked, because you mean more to me than hockey, Daisy Hall.

"Joe Morley happened," is what I end up saying.

Still pressed against me, I feel Daisy stiffen at the name. "Oh."

"And because he happened, Douglas North happened."

Her hand turns clammy in mine. "And I'm guessing that means *you* happened?"

"Might have. Yeah." Letting out a careful breath, I confess, "Did my best impersonation of Andre Beaumont and spent a little time in the sin bin. You know, just your average Tuesday night."

"Not for you, though," she says.

"Nah, not for me."

With a frustrated groan, Daisy leaps from the bed to pace the length of her bedroom. She's wearing an old pair of sweatpants that she's double-rolled at the hips so that her feet don't get caught in the hem as well as a *Hocus Pocus* T-shirt that's seen better days. This should be Daisy at her most relaxed—messy bun, oversized clothes, a pair of glasses perched on the bridge of her nose—but she's a hurricane of emotions as she roughly pulls her hair down before retying the long strands in another loose bun.

"This is why I didn't want you to know." She's barely lowered her arms before she's yanking out the hair tie again. Wavy blond strands fall down around her shoulders. "I didn't want to get in the way of your job because that's what hockey is—it's your *job*."

"Daisy—"

"If you piss off the wrong people, it's all going to come crashing down. And if it's because of me?" Up those strands go again, slipping like silk through her fingertips as she winds them into another messy knot. "To know that the choices I've made might ruin hockey for you?"

"It's one bad night. That's it. Not the end of the world."

"But it might be more than one bad night. It could be the whole season. I couldn't . . . West, I can't . . ." Her amber eyes burn with anguish. "What if I've destroyed your dream? What if—what if the Blades say that you can't—"

"Stop."

Daisy doesn't, though. She can't because she's clearly swept up in worries that have nothing to do with reality.

The Blades aren't going to trade me. For one, my contract is ironclad for another two years, and second, it's not as if fighting is against the rules. Yeah, the league cracks down on it more these days than they did when guys like Joey Kocur and Bob Probert were playing back in the eighties and nineties, but shit still gets physical on the ice, and every player knows the risk in dropping their gloves.

Even me.

Smoothly, I move from the bed and intercept Daisy with

my hands on her shoulders. I don't pull her into a hug—I don't think that's what she needs right now—but I make sure that my hold on her carries enough pressure to stop her in her tracks and catch her attention.

"Breathe, Hall," I murmur gently. "Slow down."

"West—"

"That's not breathing."

"I'm trying, but—"

"Look at me, Daisy-belle. Please."

Her glasses slip down her nose and she quickly pushes them back into place. This time, though, she does exactly what I tell her, tipping her head back so she can lift her panicked gaze up to mine. At first, her breaths are quick and shallow. So, I don't let her go. I stay right there where she needs me, measuring out my own breathing to the count of *one—two—three* until, finally, the tension in her shoulders takes a hike and she goes soft and pliant under my touch.

"I'm not angry." I might not have appreciated her making decisions for me, but clearly, I'm guilty of the same sin. "Me and you? We're good."

"But you *should* be angry, don't you get that? The world knowing about Bunny puts you at risk."

"It doesn't."

"You punched someone. Or you at least got physical with them. I'm pretty sure that's the very definition of fucking things up for you."

"If anyone fucked up, it's me." I sweep my thumbs upward so I can cradle her face, make her really *see* me when I add, "I knew better than to react, but it is what it is —I lashed out."

"Because of me."

"Because no one is ever gonna say shit about you, Daisy, and then walk away thinking that they can say it again."

With a curse, Daisy ducks under my arm to renew her

anxious pacing. She wrings out her hands in front of her and then wraps her arms around her middle before finally coming to an abrupt standstill about three feet away. Jerking her chin up, she announces, "I quit my job today."

Despite the heaviness of the conversation, I feel my lips quirk in a grin. "The job you love so much?"

"Oh, fuck off," she fires back but it lacks heat. Her expression turns sheepish. "Guess that means I'm not letting anyone think that they can say shit to my face, either."

I offer her a round of slow, dramatic applause. "Congratulations. You have standards."

"Yeah, well, having standards means that I don't have an income, and I don't think my landlord will care that I was standing up for myself when I say that I can't afford to pay rent in a few months. Obviously, adulting is overrated. Ten out of ten do not recommend."

Wanting to mess with her, I say, "We could get married."

Her face does something funny. Not disgust, exactly, but *something*. Before I can pull that expression apart and dissect what it means, she jabs a finger in my direction like a schoolteacher reprimanding a wayward student. "We are *not* getting married."

"Why not? Because you could do better?"

I'm teasing, and she knows it, but her smile still takes a second to shift into place. "I could, actually."

"Doubtful." I flutter my lashes just to make her laugh. "I am the best, after all."

"Your ego needs some work."

"Some might argue that it doesn't need any work at all."

Rolling her eyes, Daisy flounces off to her closet to rummage inside for—

Oh.

A burst of happiness fizzles in my chest when I realize that she's grabbed a sweatshirt of mine from my first season with the Blades. The hem hangs low enough to graze her knees, and the sleeves are just as ridiculously long on her, but none of that stops her from pulling the material down over her head. After a quick fix of her glasses, she bypasses me to head for the hallway. "We aren't getting married, West. This isn't Hallmark."

Curious, I follow her into the kitchen. "Is that a thing that happens? In Hallmark movies, I mean? Some poor, unsuspecting woman blows her life to smithereens and then her very kind, very respectable best friend offers to marry her, so she doesn't have to sell everything and live out of a shoebox?"

"Who said that you were respectable?"

"Out of everything I said, *that's* the only part that warrants a response?"

"Fine." She spears me with a feisty glance over her shoulder. "You aren't my best friend."

I bark out a husky laugh. "Nobody likes a liar, Hall."

"Who said that I'm lying?"

"The same person who said that you're being a brat—*me.*" When she snags her car keys from a bowl by the front door, I find myself grinning. A long time ago, I joked that we might become a lot like Bonnie and Clyde one day, and you know, aside from not leaving behind a string of dead bodies, I wasn't that off the mark. Every day with Daisy Hall is an adventure. "Where are we going?"

"The corner store. I want chips."

"Comfort food, huh? The consequence of having standards."

"I will stab you with these car keys, Weston, don't think that I won't."

"I wouldn't dare doubt you." Easing my body in front of hers, I open the door and then wave her forward with a dramatic flourish of my arm. "After you, Mrs. Cain."

She visibly freezes—

And then ever-so-slowly lifts those warm amber eyes up to my face. Somehow, she manages to keep her expression neutral long enough to threaten, "Keep that up, and I suggest sleeping with one eye open."

"Thanks for the feedback. I'll take it into consideration."

All that neutrality quivers as her mouth twists into a deep frown that I know—fuck, I *know*—is the only thing keeping her from collapsing with laughter. Instead, she plants her palm against my chest and gives me a playful shove. "I hate you."

"I know you do, Mrs. Cain. Don't worry—the feeling is mutual."

CHAPTER 8
WESTON

"Take a deep breath, man," Jackson Carter murmurs from beside me, his Southern drawl thick with reassurance. "It's going to be fine, you'll see."

Going to be fine doesn't really cut it when it's my girl's head that's on the metaphorical chopping block.

After Coach's announcement earlier this week about holding a team meeting to discuss Daisy's alter ego, I thought there'd be a stampede of angry hockey players all trying to squeeze through the door, but the meeting was scheduled to start five minutes ago, and the conference room is still relatively empty.

Only the usual suspects have shown up.

Marshall Hunt is seated beside his wife, Gwen, who I'm pretty sure is only here because she represents more than half of the team with Golden Lights Media. Two seats down from the happy couple is Kammer, though he's so focused on whatever he's reading on his phone that I doubt he even remembers why he showed up here today. The Canadians, Henri Bordeaux and Andre Beaumont, are shacked up next to each other at the far end of the table—every so often, I catch the low, rumbling notes of their conversation. Pretty sure they're discussing the beagle Bordeaux wants to adopt.

Coach isn't here yet.

As nerves gnaw away at my stomach, I reach up and readjust my ball cap. "You think he forgot?"

"Not a chance." Leaning back in his chair, Carter casually folds his arms across his big chest. Retirement hasn't done anything to shrink him down in size. Dude was known as the Beast of the Northeast for a reason. "Gotta admit, it's a weird position for him to be in. Can't imagine he ever thought that he'd find Daisy swimmin' in hot water—never mind hot water that could easily drown every single one of his players, too."

"Has he mentioned anything to you?"

It's a ballsy move, pumping the new assistant coach for information, but Carter was my captain first. We've bled together. Played together. Take hockey out of the equation—I was one of the few people he welcomed into his inner circle after his divorce with Holly, and I was right there with him last year when they figured out all their shit and realized how much they still love each other. The way I see it, history doesn't just come to an end because the timeline continues.

And look at that, Lady Luck must be shining down on me because Carter doesn't tell me to fuck off. Instead, he adopts the same intense expression that he used to before one of his game day pep talks.

"To be honest, it's been radio silence, but . . ." He gives an almost imperceptible shake of his head. "He'll be here. End of the day, he's not gonna let this sink the team when the season's barely gotten started. Not to mention that he has twenty-three players banking on him to figure it out."

"Twenty-two." Under the table, I knock his knee with mine because yeah, I really appreciate him talking this out with me. He could have easily told me to mind my own business. "Obviously, I have Daisy's back."

"Make it nineteen, then." Carter grins at me. "Every guy at this table has her back, too. Actually, might as well drop the count to eighteen."

"For Kasey?" I ask, referring our goalie who couldn't make it today.

"For me, asshole," Carter fires back with a laugh.

"Wow, name-calling from a coach? Lemme go talk to HR real fast."

In retribution, he kicks me in the shin, and no one bats an eye when I let out a yelp of surprise. To be fair, I wouldn't have it any other way.

Carter, Hunt, the others—they're my closest friends outside of Daisy and Tory. Over the years, I've heard some wild stories about shitty team dynamics come out of the hockey rumor mill. You've got players who have been traded so many times that it must feel pointless to put in effort with your new teammates when you're always living out of a hotel room, and then there are other guys who are so determined to climb their way to the top of the food chain that they seem to forget that hockey isn't a one-man show.

I've gotten really lucky with the Blades.

Even when I was on IR, no one ever let me forget that I was one of them—I had teammates FaceTiming me whenever they went on the road and others showing up to my physical therapy sessions just to keep me motivated. Can't lie, playing with Connie and Felix back at UConn doesn't even come close to the level of joy I feel every time I step out onto the ice for the Boston Blades. This is where I was always meant to end up . . . Even if living my dream comes at a cost with my family.

Guilt churns in my stomach.

Yeah, not gonna think about that right now.

Luckily, that's when the door to the conference room swings open, but instead of Coach appearing, in walks—

"Pizza order for Joshua Kammer?"

Swear to God, we all stop to stare at the rookie as he stuffs his phone into his pocket and rises to greet the entry-level staffer. With the exchange of a twenty-dollar tip, Kammer accepts four boxes of pizza and then turns back to us with a triumphant grin. "Pizza's here."

Beaumont is the first to break the silence. "What the *fuck*, Kammer."

"What?" Utterly unfazed, the rookie sets the boxes down on the table only to shoot a wide-eyed glance at the empty doorway. "Shit, I didn't think about plates. I guess we could use paper towels from the bathroom?"

Carter narrows his gaze. "You do realize that tomorrow's Opening Night, don't you?"

"I haven't been able to think about anything else, honestly." Kammer pops the lid on the top box. When he peers inside, revulsion flits across his face. "Hawaiian just for you, Cain. By the way, you're welcome, you freak. Pineapple does not belong on pizza. It's in the Constitution or something." With a flick of his wrist, the cardboard box skates across the table in my direction, stopping maybe a foot away.

I blink at the company logo printed across the box.

Blink at Kammer, too, who's tending to the next pie with the same treatment that he did the Hawaiian, sending it toward Beaumont and Bordeaux with a laser-eyed precision that he's honed after years of stick handling.

"Rookie," I say slowly, "you ever hear of a diet?"

"Don't believe in 'em." Without lifting his head, he tears a slice of pepperoni pizza away from its brethren and then drops into the closest chair, kicks his feet up on the table, and takes a bite. "I'm young. My refractory period is, like, nonexistent."

"Pretty sure that a refractory period generally refers to sex," Hunt chimes in. "And I can't believe that I need to tell a grown-ass adult this but get your feet off the table."

"Oh. Sorry." A flush creeps across Kammer's cheeks as he drops his fancy sneakers to the floor. "Back to the refractory thing for a sec—I don't need much time for that, either. Like, gimme four or five minutes, maybe, and I'm good to go."

"My wife doesn't need to hear about your recovery stats, rookie."

Dutifully, Kammer turns a repentant gaze on Gwen, who I swear is fighting a grin. "Sorry, Mrs. Hunt. Didn't mean to make you regret the fact that your husband is aging every single day and can't get it up for back-to-back sessions anymore."

Hunt's jaw falls open. "You fucking *dick*."

Beside me, Carter lets out a low, *you're-in-for-it-now* whistle.

Not to be outdone, Bordeaux says, in his Québécois accent, "*Tabarnak,* you are an idiot."

Suddenly, Kammer is laughing too hard to swallow correctly—or at all, I guess—and he ends up choking on what I'm pretty sure is a piece of doughy crust, which sets the rest of us off, too. By the time Coach walks in ten minutes later, it's to the crime scene of untouched pizza boxes littering the conference table and one unhinged rookie munching happily on his third slice of pie, not a single plate or paper napkin in sight.

Coach's mustache twitches. "Is that pizza?"

With the slice paused criminally halfway to his mouth, Kammer has the common sense to squeak out, "No?"

"Good answer. You've got three seconds to get rid of it before I get the nutritionist up here to give you a lecture on treating your body like a temple."

Almost pitifully, the rookie sends a longing glance

toward his half-eaten slice. "But, Coach, this temple really likes cheese."

Coach stares at him.

Kammer's throat clicks with an audible swallow.

"You know what," Coach mutters, "I'm not even going to dignify that with a response." He shuts the door behind him with the heel of his shoe and then takes a moment to skim over the rest of us with a critical glance. "This it?"

Beaumont tilts his chin. "Were you expecting the whole team?"

"Don't know what I was expecting." Claiming the chair nearest to the door, Coach lowers himself into it—but not before pulling a fresh pack of toothpicks from the back pocket of his slacks and tossing them onto the table in front of him. "All right, let's hear it. Who here has an issue with Daisy?"

Silence.

Or rather, silence except for the fact that Kammer is currently making a racket while trying to stuff one of the pizza boxes into the garbage can.

Coach presses his thumb to the furrow between his brows. "Rookie," he utters on a tired sigh.

"Yeah, Coach?"

"Just—" He waves a hand. "Just fucking put them to the side and sit down."

"Oh." Sheepishly, Kammer sets the boxes down by the door and returns to his seat. "Sorry, yeah. I'm here. I mean, I'm ready—what did you ask again?"

Coach's pale cheeks burn such a bright red that I'm surprised his head doesn't automatically explode.

Maybe I should be annoyed by the rookie's ability to turn every situation into a bonafide circus, but I find myself feeling endlessly grateful to him instead. Sure, the kid is a ball of chaotic energy but since we've all been asked here today to either defend or condemn Daisy like some modern-day witch hunt, Joshua Kammer's antics are single-handedly keeping shit from getting too tense.

Even Coach cracks a smile after thirty seconds of stewing.

"Moving on." He leaves one hand resting on the table while the other fiddles restlessly with his pack of toothpicks. "Management suggested that we hold this meeting today to give all of you the chance to voice any grievances. With that said, if you don't feel comfortable sharing your opinions in a public space, you're more than welcome to come to me directly. End of the day, we want to keep lines of communication open, and if I'm not the guy you want to talk to—on account of Daisy being my daughter—it's why we've asked Gwen to sit in on the conversation as well."

Gwen waves hello.

"All right, then," Coach says, "where are we at?"

Beaumont immediately lifts his hand. "I'd like to know what the team is doing to protect Daisy."

"Same here," Hunt jumps in after briefly meeting my gaze. "Off the record, Gwen and I have been talking—we're worried about how the public backlash might be impacting her."

Sam Hall looks visibly shaken.

It's not often that he's caught off guard—I can probably count on one hand the number of times that I've witnessed him stunned silent—but anyone can see that he's scrambling. He clears his throat. Somehow manages to look at us without truly making eye contact. For a man who prides himself on always being prepared, I'm surprised that instead of breaking out a concrete, step-by-step plan on how to get his daughter through this, he's fumbling the puck, so to speak, and stammering his way through a series of excuses.

"It's been a long week. For everyone, not just me. That

is, Daisy and I haven't had the chance to sit down to have that conversation. I've been . . ."

Busy.

The word is clearly on the tip of his tongue, desperate to escape, but he clamps a wooden toothpick between his back molars instead, effectively ending whatever other B.S. he was about to dish out.

Part of me doesn't blame him for trying to duck the question.

Like Carter said, it's Coach Hall's responsibility to handle any potential damage control with his players. If he doesn't, then the GM might start looking at him like he's incapable of doing his job—and that's never been the case. Since my days with him at UConn, Sam Hall has always been the one-percent of the one-percent of hockey coaches. We're lucky to play for him. Hell, we're even luckier when you think about how often he sticks his own neck out on the line to make sure that we're all good. And here he is, doing it again.

Still, it's impossible to miss the heavy bags under his eyes or the way he keeps surreptitiously checking his watch as if he's expecting someone to come along and rescue him from the conversation.

As one of his veteran players, I appreciate the work he's doing to put us first, but what about Daisy? Who's putting *her* first?

Before I can think better of it, I admit, "She's freaking out."

Coach visibly flinches.

"She's worried about what this means for us"—for *me*, I almost add—"and what it might mean for the rest of the season."

"We want another shot at the Cup," Beaumont says plainly. "I don't know about the rest of you, but I'm not about to let what happened the other night with Morley get in my head."

"Told her that, too." Kicking my chair back a little, I lower my elbows to my knees and clasp my fingers together. Keep my stare locked on my teammates, though, because they need to hear what I have to say. "I lost my cool, and it won't happen again. But Daisy . . . she's letting the worry eat away at her. Just because she puts on a brave face doesn't mean that she's okay."

I'm watching Coach closely, so I notice the second that he drops his gaze.

In shame?

Frustration?

"Her personal social media accounts are a dumpster fire." When I direct my attention to Gwen, she offers me a strained smile before continuing: "The board gave her explicit instructions to deactivate any accounts linked to Bunny—which she did—but no one said anything about the ones listed under her real name. I took a look at them this morning, and they're . . ." Biting her lip, Gwen winces. "They're not great."

Hunt reaches for his wife's hand. "Gwen's sugarcoating things. It's fucking awful."

As one, the rest of us all reach for our phones.

There's an uncomfortable feeling crawling under my skin as I pull up Daisy's Instagram profile. Something worse than dread. It clings to my lungs. Turns my palms clammy. I run my hand along the thigh of my jeans and get on with it, not even surprised to discover that Daisy hasn't bothered switching her account from public to private— she's never been one to hide, not even when under fire, apparently. I want to wring her fucking neck for giving the trolls of the internet free access to her. In the same breath, I want nothing more than to drag her into my arms, turn my back against the fire, and weather the flames in her stead.

Beneath the weight of my hand, my knee starts jumping nervously.

Bypassing her bio, I click on her latest photo, scroll down to the comments, and—

"Jesus," Carter breathes.

Across the table, Bordeaux makes a small sound of distress.

"It's a fucking bloodbath." The words slip out before I can snatch them back. "Bloodbath" is a devastating understatement. It's not just random strangers on the internet flinging nasty words at Daisy, but comment after comment telling her to do unspeakable things. Things that I . . . I can't even—

Lurching to my feet, I make it to the trash can just in time.

My periphery goes dark. Beneath my hands, the trash bag crinkles as I tighten my grip on the bin, squeezing hard enough that I'm almost surprised when I don't break the damn thing in two. There's movement behind me. The muffled sound of a chair being scraped back over thin carpet. The gruff demand for someone to grab me some water from the bubbler down the hall.

Letting my head hang low, I drag in jagged breath after jagged breath, trying to pick my way through the landmine of emotions pummeling me from all sides.

Disgust. Anger.

Most of all, I've been sidelined by the horrifying realization that the same people—the same *fans*—who come out to support us at every game could be so cruel to the person I love most in this world. And all because she made the decision to help those who probably felt as though they couldn't help themselves.

A hand settles between my shoulder blades.

Every muscle in my body turns to stone for—

One heartbeat.

Two.

—And then the tension in my body simply fades away.

I know that touch. Know the shape of those delicate fingers and the weight of that small hand. Turning at the waist, I peer down to find Daisy standing so close that I can smell the floral-scented perfume she only wears when she's worried about the world taking her seriously. Cozy Daisy prefers vanilla. I personally don't have a preference—I'll take Daisy however she wants to present herself to the world.

"Hi," she whispers.

"Hey," I whisper back.

Though her eyes are more tired than I've ever seen them, she offers me a crooked grin. "What did the garbage do to you to deserve such treatment?"

"It was trash talking."

Her nose wrinkles. "Gross."

"I know."

"No, I mean that Dad joke. Be ashamed, West. Be very, very ashamed."

I'm not ashamed, or embarrassed, about the way I loop both arms around her waist and pull her into a hug that lifts her onto the balls of her feet. I'm not ashamed, or embarrassed, in how I immediately tuck my chin into the crook of her neck, where I inhale the sweet scent of jasmine straight from her skin. I'm not ashamed. Or embarrassed. Because fuck me, but just holding Daisy in my arms feels like a balm to the anxiety ravaging my soul.

Someone clears their throat.

Lifting my head, I catch sight of Coach studiously looking at his phone. With one last squeeze, I set Daisy down and step away. Reach up and lift my hat from my head, raking my fingers through my hair before pulling my cap back on and situating the brim just how I like it. A quick glance over at my best friend reveals that she's watching me closely, so I offer her what I hope is a reassuring grin.

Her cheeks are pink as she gives me a tiny smile in return.

"Sorry," I mouth to her, but before I can do more to apologize for the PDA, Coach draws my attention back to the meeting.

"It was Gwen's idea for Daisy to come in today. We thought we'd start the meeting without her and then bring her in to hopefully find some common ground." Beneath his bushy mustache, his lips tilt upward in a humorless smile. "Clearly, we overestimated how many on the team might have an issue that they'd like to see addressed."

Gwen tucks a strand of red hair behind one ear. "If I may?"

Coach waves a hand. "Floor is all yours."

"I don't think anyone on the Blades roster has an issue with Daisy. They all know her. I mean, some of them—the guys in this room especially—have known her for years, which means that they know Daisy isn't out to get them. Right, Daisy?"

Everyone turns to stare at my best friend.

"I wouldn't," she blurts out, her already flushed cheeks deepening to a ruddy red. "That's not how I . . . What I'm trying to say is, I've worked really, really hard to make *Confessions of a Puck Bunny* a last resort. Like with Amber Morley—she spent over a year trying to get Joe to do the right thing. He was hooking up with girls all over the country, even telling them that him and Amber were in an open relationship."

"Guess they weren't?" Beaumont asks dryly.

"Amber was so upset with him, she wouldn't have agreed to it, anyway. But no, he never even mentioned it to her."

"What a fucking douchebag," Hunt mutters.

Daisy jerks her head in agreement. "It was really bad. He was stringing these poor girls along and putting them all at risk because he wasn't being careful . . . Anyway, Amber had had enough but Joe wouldn't sign the divorce papers. That's when she DMed me." Daisy pulls in a slow breath. "I don't sit around like some internet sleuth hunting down a conspiracy trail. And maybe it's wrong. Maybe I should send these people away and tell them that none of it is my problem, but I can't, you know? I'm like—like—"

"You're like Robin Hood."

Clearly flustered, Daisy swings her gaze over to the rookie. "I mean, not really like Robin Hood, but I guess the comparison kinda works? Sort of. Not really." She wraps her fingers around the strap of her purse, clinging tight to the leather. "I've helped a lot of people. I know that it might not seem that way—that it might seem like I'm stirring up drama—but I've tried to be a shoulder to lean on when no one else is listening. I-I've given so many people closure they might not have had otherwise. And for what it's worth, I've never used my connections with the Blades, or my dad, or West, to get information just so I can make content. I have too much integrity for that."

"And you've never monetized the account," Gwen murmurs.

"No, never." Daisy's quick to shake her head. "That feels icky, you know? To make money off people who are hurting."

"A lot of people wouldn't care so long as they're collecting a paycheck," Gwen points out.

"I'm not most people."

She's not. She never has been, not for as long as I've known her. And while I know that she can stand on her own two feet, I find myself closing the gap between us, anyway, until I'm standing behind her like some ancient warrior guarding his queen. Not doing it because she needs the backup—Daisy is uniquely qualified to stand up for herself—but because I want her to know that however hopeless the situation might feel, she isn't alone.

Her loose blond hair slips over one shoulder as she flashes me a grateful smile. It's quick, barely anything worth mentioning, but still, warmth floods my chest.

Gwen taps her pen on the table. "Here's the thing. As much as I'd like to see you do an exposé and educate people that not every player deserves to be put on a pedestal, I don't think bringing more attention to *Confessions of a Puck Bunny* is the way to go, not right now while it's still fresh. We need to bury the lead. Give fans something else to talk about. Maybe—"

"I offered to marry her."

"You did *what?*" Dad growls.

"I offered to marry her," West says for a second time.

And for a second time, he manages to completely obliterate my every train of thought because what the *heck*, Weston. If I didn't know any better, I'd swear that there's a blinking ERROR sign plastered to my forehead.

As it is, I don't have the chance to get my brain back online before he's stepping forward to stand directly beside me. Without a word, he puts us shoulder to shoulder, our hands so close together that if I stretch out my fingertips by an inch, maybe two, we'll be holding hands as if it's us against the world. Like partners—soulmates—husband and wife.

No. Stop that. Not at all like husband and wife.

Fully intending to shut this whole thing down, I open my mouth only for West to speak up first: "According to Daisy, that's what happens in Hallmark movies when one of the leads is down on their luck."

"Oh, yeah," Hunt says, "the marriage of convenience trope."

You could hear a pin drop, the room goes so quiet.

When Gwen lifts a brow at her husband, Marshall shrugs a bulky shoulder. "What? Reddit told me all about it."

"Jesus," Andre groans, "not Reddit again."

Kammer perks up. "Was there a listicle? I always save those. Like, I have a million tabs open because I never want to forget that I wanted to watch—"

"Stop. Talking," my dad grits out from between clenched teeth, prompting Kammer to snap his mouth shut and mime throwing away the key. With that sorted, Dad turns the full force of his incredulity on my best friend. "Explain yourself. Now."

To his credit, West doesn't even flinch under the weight of my dad's infamous, dick-shriveling stare—although that might have more to do with the fact that West has been putting up with it for over a decade. I'm sure that it's lost some of its effectiveness by now.

"Not sure what else there is to say, Coach." He rolls one shoulder in a loose shrug. "I said that I'd marry her, and Daisy refused."

"Because it was a *joke*." I can't believe we're even having this conversation right now. Then again, maybe it's a dream. Maybe if I blink hard enough, one of these times I'll open my eyes to discover that I've landed in an alternate reality where my best friend is doing the craziest thing ever by telling my *father* that he's open to marrying me.

Unfortunately, the universe must have it out for me because I blink, and I blink, and I blink again, and the scene before me remains tragically unchanged. The audacity, honestly.

Firmly, I say, "I'm not marrying West."

Kammer shoots me a bright, strangely encouraging smile. "You could do better."

Hunt heaves a sigh. "You really need to stop talking, rookie."

"What did I say?" The kid purses his mouth, and I swear, you can practically see his brain whirring along at top speed. "All I said was . . ." His eyes widen. "Oops, sorry. Meant to say that you *can't* do better than Cain because he is obviously the best of the best. Quality husband material right there. A slab of grade-A man meat, if you will. He brings all the fans to the yard—hey! I was just saying that Daisy—"

"*Aweille*, rookie." Without breaking his stride, Henri hauls Kammer toward the door by the back of his sweat-shirt. He waves his free hand over his head. "Carry on, friends."

Just like that, the rest of us are abandoned to the tension bleeding out from one particular source—Sam Hall.

Somehow, this moment feels worse than any other that I've had to deal with in the last week. And sure, I could pin the blame on bone-deep exhaustion—who has the mental bandwidth to consider *marriage* after the week that I've had —but the truth, I think, strays a little closer to home.

I can't marry West out of convenience.

I can't marry West at all.

No way can I survive living in such close quarters with him twenty-four-seven. I don't want to know if he walks around in low-slung sweatpants or if he prefers to only wear a pair of briefs. Or the shower. I have absolutely zero interest in learning how long he takes to wash himself— actually, scratch that. I don't even want to think about him *in* the shower. Down that road lies only madness and I'm not keen on driving myself to the brink of insanity, thank you very much.

Marrying West is a bad idea. Horrible.

I mean, there's no playbook for when your best friend proposes marriage but obviously the only way to survive it is to pretend that said proposal never happened at all. Which would be a whole lot easier if he didn't just casually announce it to all of his closest friends and my *dad*.

Honestly, fuck my life.

"We aren't getting married," I reiterate again because this is me standing my ground. No, sir, I am not about to buckle, my knees are made of steel. "It was a joke—an *inside* joke, at that." I narrow my eyes at West, who doesn't even have the decency to look embarrassed. Fighting back a growl, I turn to Gwen. "If you want to help with getting the heat off my back, I'd really appreciate it, but marriage is off the table."

She returns my gaze steadily. "It could work, though."

Wait, what—

No.

Has everyone's common sense just walked out the door? Is this a boomerang situation—like, can I get an ETA on when their brains are due to come back around or are they officially gone forever, lost somewhere in the ether?

I want to cry. I want to stomp my foot like a child.

In the end, I utter only one word: "No."

No, I am not marrying West.

No, I am not signing myself up for inevitable heartbreak.

No, no, no.

"How would it help?"

The way my neck nearly *snaps in half* from how hard I swing my head to look at my dad.

He did not just ask that. But clearly, he did. And clearly, he's expecting an answer because instead of throwing his hands up and shouting, "Just kidding!" he actually presses Gwen for more information. "You said that it would help—how?"

"Misogyny, mostly," she answers bluntly. "Put it this

way. Fans love West. Our stats put him directly behind Marshall in terms of merch sales."

"Clearly, they don't have taste," Andre drawls.

"And when it comes to social media followers, he's only fifty-thousand or so behind Jackson—but Jackson's numbers skyrocketed last year after he and Holly got back together." Gwen uses her pen to twist her red hair into a loose knot. "None of this is news, exactly, but I think if marriage *was* on the table, we wouldn't need to worry about fans claiming that Daisy is somehow corrupting him."

"Excuse you, I don't have the *plague*."

"Even if you did," West points out wryly, "you'd already have given it to me by this point."

"My best guess," Gwen continues, ignoring us completely, "is that the select group of people who are seriously upset about this Bunny business would see marriage as a way for West to assert control over Daisy, which would mean that she's less likely to cause trouble down the line for their favorite players."

"I'm not a *dog*." My God, I have never been so close to raising my voice in my entire life. "And West doesn't tell me what to do—"

"Because I don't have a death wish," West mutters.

"—So please explain to me how *anyone* would think that I'm just . . . rolling over and obeying whatever he says."

"Because the people who actually have a problem with *Confessions of a Puck Bunny* will never believe that their favorite player is anything less than infallible," Gwen says. She doesn't sound condescending in the slightest, and the heaviness in her gaze tells me that she's taking this seriously. "In their eyes, hockey players are gods. And like gods, who cares if they're good people so long as they have superhuman talents? Look at it this way. Say Marshall, for example—"

"Shots fired," Andre murmurs, only for Hunt to flash him the middle finger.

"—Is winning games for the Blades, who cares about what he does behind closed doors? To them, it's a non-issue. Some people have no problem separating the artist from the art." Gwen's gaze turns empathetic. "You won't change their minds, Daisy. I'm not saying that you *can't*, but it's highly unlikely. They aren't your audience."

"But marrying West . . ."

"Isn't a cure. You'd have to do a lot of legwork—letting the Blades issue a statement, for one, and maybe even outreach to some of the players that you've . . . wronged," she tacks on belatedly as if the word tastes funny in her mouth. "I'd put that one on the backburner for now, see what else we can do instead. But if you really want to sell it, you'll have to at least pretend that you're in love with West."

But I already am.

I'm shaking, I think. Trembling so hard that I wrap my arms tight across my middle in an attempt to stifle the nerves eating away at me.

There's no way that this is my life.

For the first time all week, I regret creating Bunny. I regret being a shoulder for others, and I regret seeking justice for those who struggle to find it on their own. I regret *everything*. In the grand scheme of things, marrying West wouldn't be the worst thing to ever happen to me— although it would definitely be masochistic—but this entire plan is the very antithesis to what I've spent the last ten years trying to overcome.

Being the silly, naïve girl who fell victim to the lies of a married man.

Working my butt off every day, every night, and every second in between, to believe in my own self-worth again after being so horribly led astray.

Seeking out a platform that allowed me the space, emotionally and mentally, to be to others what I had to survive on my own.

Bunny saved me.

I saved me.

And now, to save the team, and my dad, and West, I have to claw at all my old scars, rip them back open, and allow myself to be flayed alive—because I'm in the wrong, *again*, I'm dirty, *again*, I'm seeking forgiveness, *again*.

There are tears pricking at the backs of my eyes.

I blink them away, as I always do, and look to my dad, who's had my back through thick and thin since Mom left and never came back. I'm not sure what I'm searching for, exactly, but it's definitely not the bleak hope staring back.

He wants me to say yes.

Despite everything I just said about Amber Morley, he wants me to say *yes*.

Dimly, I feel my heart shatter.

Dimly, I feel myself reach for Weston's hand. His fingers curl around mine, holding tight. If I refuse, I know that he'll put a stop to all of this in a heartbeat, no questions asked. But my dad . . . I squeeze my eyes shut just so I don't have to look at him again.

He hasn't made the announcement yet, but this is his last year with the Blades. He wants to retire from coaching and take a job doing commentary for one of the big networks like Sports 24/7. Only, that dream might not become a reality if the league thinks that I'm a stain on his career. As it is, he's clearly been losing sleep over the thought that the Blades might decide to pay out the rest of his contracted salary and kick him to the curb. The money might pad his bank account but the damage to his reputation would be irreparable.

If I say no, will he get that same troubled look on his

face that he does whenever he thinks about Mom? If I say no, will he resent me the same way that he resents *her*?

If this is what unconditional love is—ruining myself to protect those who matter most to me—it feels funny under my breastbone.

It feels *wrong*.

I push all of it down, twisting the lock on the box where I keep the rest of my insecurities and regrets and fears. None of it serves me any good, not when it feels like I have the weight of the world resting on my shoulders.

With a single word torn from my throat, I seal my fate for good: "Okay."

CHAPTER 10
WESTON

In unspoken agreement, I follow Daisy back to her place after the meeting.

She lives in a collection of old, turn-of-the-century brownstones a few blocks over from the Prudential Building, one of the tallest skyscrapers in Boston's skyline. It's not the first apartment that she's rented here in the city—after her move from Hartford, she lived in a tiny studio in Dorchester—but it's by far the nicest. Round-the-clock concierge service, an elevator that keeps her from lugging groceries up five flights of stairs, and—her favorite amenity—access to a parking garage so she's not battling it out on the streets of Back Bay in the middle of a Nor'easter.

I can't help but wonder how long she'll last with rent. I'd offer to cover it for her, but I like my nuts exactly where they are—attached to my body.

When she merges onto Storrow Drive, completely bypassing the turn for the Pike, I let out a small groan. Only Daisy would be willing to sit through an obscene amount of bumper-to-bumper traffic to avoid driving on the highway. It's one of her quirks. Sort of like how she can't stomach the taste of milk when it's within three days of its expiration date—even though the smell hasn't gone sour yet—or how, whenever we watch a new show together, she spends half the time researching production instead of, you know, *enjoying* the show.

I know way more about *Lord of the Rings* lore than I've actually seen play out on the screen.

Which is why I know that something is off with her.

She walked out of that conference room without once glancing back, her posture stiff, her eyes downcast. If she could, I bet she'd hit up the rink in Watertown to get some skating in but since one of the employees sold us out to the tabloids, I doubt she'll risk turning up there again anytime soon.

Maybe it makes me overprotective, but I call her—or try to, at any rate. I'm intercepted by an incoming call, one that I'd prefer to send straight to voicemail. Unfortunately for me, the streets of Boston decide to fuck me over with a stray pothole. As my car bounces, I accidentally tap accept instead of reject.

My father's smooth, cultured voice immediately filters in through the car's speakers: "You've been avoiding me."

Yeah, no shit.

"And you've upset your mother," he adds stiffly when it becomes glaringly obvious that I have no plans to engage him in conversation. "She wants me to remind you that you've missed family dinner three weeks in a row."

"It's not really a reminder when I'm the one who made the decision not to show up."

"I won't tell her you said that."

"Maybe you should."

Though he falls silent on the other end of the line, I'm not naïve enough to think that I've won our little standoff. That's the thing about David Cain—he never raises his voice and rarely loses his shit, and yet there's no doubt in my mind that I've been pissing my father off since the second that I was born.

It started with small things as a kid.

Not wanting to go into the office with him on bring-your-kid-to-work day. Or showing very little interest in the activities that he rolled out before me on gleaming silver platters—piano lessons and tennis and fencing—while immediately shutting down any excitement I showed in hockey or even comic books.

I was too loud when I was meant to be quiet and too quiet when he wanted me to engage. The emotional whiplash put me on rocky ground from an early age. While I wasn't alone in the mess, Tory was always better at masking his emotions. When Dad said jump, my twin asked how high. Meanwhile, when he told me to sit down, I just left the room.

I'll give him credit where credit is due, though.

My father is really fucking good at turning on the charm. When I'm in the right mood, it's easy to see where I get it from—the difference being, of course, that I don't make it a habit of telling the people I love that they're wasting their lives away.

"What's the point of this call, Dad?" I ease off the gas as Daisy slows down in front of me. "Because we both know that Mom isn't exactly my number one fan right now."

"She's worried about you."

"Really? Because I didn't get that feeling when the two of you were telling me it was time to hang up my skates."

"Well, she—"

"Or when I had Sports 24/7 breathing down my neck last month because they received an anonymous tip that I'll be—how did they put it—oh, yeah—that I'll be *retiring* soon because I'm done with hockey and ready to get involved with the family business."

"Now, Weston, don't be pointing the finger at your—"

"She added her signature to the fucking email, Dad. I mean, come on. If you're going to start a rumor, at least make sure that it won't come back to bite you in the ass."

"I don't appreciate the way you're talking about your mother."

"Well, I don't appreciate the fact that my mother is trying to use the biggest sports network in the country to manipulate me." Holding the steering wheel in a death grip, I bite my tongue before I say something truly shitty. It would be so much easier to pretend that my parents can't stand me. That's the kicker, though. They don't hate me, they never have—they just don't *understand* me, and sometimes that feels like the cruelest fate of all. "I'm not even thirty yet. I have a few more years left in the tank before I need to worry about calling it quits."

"What about your hip, then? We know that you've been seeing your physical therapist again."

I resist the urge to bang my head against the wheel. "I'm a hockey player. I practically live at PT. They should be handing out frequent flyer cards or setting up bunkbeds so we can roll out of bed in the morning and just get on with it."

"And what about with your teammate—the old captain?"

Tension stiffens my spine at the mention of Jackson. "What about him?"

"Concussions are a big deal. I'm sure he wishes that he retired sooner, and I bet his family worries about him all the time. If he even makes it to old age, which is doubtful from what I've heard, he'll be—"

"Don't talk about him."

"Weston—"

"I said, *don't*." He won't like my tone, but I don't care. While we've been stuck in this vicious cycle of him wanting me to quit hockey and me telling him to shove it for years now, it's the first time that he's brought one of my teammates into our mess. And for it to be *Carter* of all people? Carter, who went through Hell and back over the last few years, and who will need to fight every day for the rest of his life? I'm so fucking angry that it takes physical effort to unclench my jaw. "You don't get to talk about him like that—as if he won't be here one day—just because you're trying to prove a point."

"I wasn't, son." He has the balls to actually try and placate me with that soothing tone. As if I might actually fall for it—I won't. "All I'm saying is that you should be grateful that you only injured your hip and not your head. Maybe next time it'll be worse, and you'll have to face the hard truth that hockey is running your body into the ground."

The world runs us into the fucking ground.

My brother sits behind a desk and suffers excruciating migraines. Before getting hired by the Blades, our equipment manager was putting herself through school by working ten-hour shifts at a restaurant—she said that the soles of her feet are still calloused from always wearing out her shoes. A buddy of mine from college ended up becoming a firefighter; when I talked to him last, he was worried about the long-term damage to his lungs.

We're all out here just doing our best, taking the shit with the good, living life the only way we know how—by facing it head on.

None of that is the point, though.

Because this conversation isn't really about my hip surgery or Carter, even. It's about the fact that my parents want a version of me that doesn't exist. My mom wants a son that she can tote around to all the fancy parties they attend in Connecticut, and my dad wants to feel like the Big Guy on Campus with both of his boys working for him.

They're chasing after a pipedream. In the process, they're pushing me farther and farther away.

"Good talk, Dad, but I gotta go."

When he doesn't answer, I let myself imagine that it's because he's trying to find a way to bridge the gap between us—but then I hear the insistent tapping of a computer keyboard, and reality slaps me clear across the face.

I bet he penciled this call in after a late lunch: *Don't forget to pester West about family dinner*. If I hang up, he probably won't even notice.

"Did you hear me, Dad? I have to go."

"Oh, right." The sounds of him typing don't even break for a quick pause. "We love you very much, son. You know that, don't you?"

It's taken me years to realize that I don't like their brand of love—it comes with too many terms and conditions.

"Weston?" His tone is expectant, and I grit my teeth.

"Love you, too, Dad. I'll talk to you later."

I hang up before he can say anything else and immediately call Daisy, who picks up on the second ring. After waving to me in her rearview mirror, she chirps out her usual greeting, "Stop stalking me, Cain. We've already talked about this."

Safe.

Home.

Daisy.

"How do you feel about takeout?" I ask.

CHAPTER 11
DAISY

"**S**o, is this officially our first date?"

Weston's question is so unexpected that I fumble the nacho on the way to my mouth and end up with guac and cheese smeared across my cheek. It's warm and kind of gooey. My stomach revolts at the sensation as I grab a spare napkin to wipe my dinner away from my face. "Ugh, warn a girl first, would you?"

Bathed in the cool tones of dusk, West's eyes crinkle with humor. "Thought proposing to you was all the warning you needed."

"Touché. But here I was thinking that all you needed was a little bit of time to realize that we really, really don't need to get married. I mean, it's *me* and it's *you*. We're friends, and friends don't—"

"If I'm marrying anyone, Hall, it's gonna be you."

Do you hear that? It's the sound of my stupid heart flopping around like a beached whale inside my chest.

It's dreadfully unfair that I didn't fall for an insensitive asshole who can't be bothered to even acknowledge my existence. No, I just had to fall head over heels for Weston

Fucking Cain, the single most romantic human being to ever exist—even when he's not even trying.

I shove another nacho into my mouth and chew grumpily.

After West called about takeout, he made a quick run to his favorite restaurant in my neighborhood—it's one of the few places that he feels comfortable eating from on the night before a game—while I headed home to grab my picnic blanket as well as a few odds and ends for our meal. The green space near my building isn't so much a park as it is a garden—it's narrow and winds down the street with benches and artfully arranged patches of grass—but we always make do.

Lifting my gaze, I take a moment to watch West while he's otherwise preoccupied.

He's beautiful.

It's not even his looks, exactly, which are more ruggedly handsome than anything else, but just *him*—his essence, aura, whatever you want to call it. Ask West and he'll say that he can be anti-social, which I guess is true, but it's only because he's not one to play games anywhere but on the ice. I've always figured that his blunt approach to life is a side effect of spending too many years trying to parse out his parents' intentions through all their bullshit. West is nothing like them. If he says something, it's because he believes it with his entire being.

Which means that he's not just blowing steam up my ass about the marriage thing. And that's a crazy thing to think about—that he actually wants to do this.

Softly, I ask, "What if you regret it?"

West stops twirling his pasta around with his fork to peer up at me through thick blond lashes. "I could never regret you, Daisy."

"You could, though." Pushing my takeout container out of the way, I bring my knees into my chest and wrap my arms tight around my shins. There's a crisp bite in the air tonight and I forgot to grab a jacket from my apartment. "You could meet someone a month from now. Really fall for them, you know? And then, whoopsie, suddenly you remember that you have a wife waiting for you at home."

West pushes his own container aside. Lifting both arms, he takes hold of the nape of his sweatshirt in one firm hand before drawing the material up and over his head. My heart thuds way too loudly in my ears when he offers me the hoodie. "Here," he murmurs. "You're cold."

He'll never get it back if I put my greedy paws on it.

My closet is spilling over with clothes that I've commandeered from West over the years. T-shirts. Sweatshirts. Even a pair of sweatpants that I need to triple-roll at the hips. Because he's not a dick, he never mentions the fact that I'm a desperate, little thief. And yes, fine, I admit it—sometimes I like to pretend that he lets me keep whatever I want just so he can see me wearing his clothes.

Still, I hesitate for a beat. "Are you sure?"

His gaze is unwavering when I tentatively dance my fingers over the soft fabric. "Take it, Hall. I know you want to."

You have no idea what I want.

With a tight swallow, I accept the offering and drop my knees into a cross-legged position. The moment I draw the material down over my head, I'm enveloped in his woodsy scent. Clutching the neck of the sweatshirt in my palms, I bury the lower half of my face in the fabric, breathing him in. We can pretend that the shiver twining its way down my spine is from the chill in the air, can't we? Only I need to know the truth.

Looking none worse for wear, despite the fact that he's now in only a thin T-shirt, West leans his weight back on his hands and stretches out his long, jean-clad legs beside our food. Dark blond hair falls messily across his forehead as he gets comfortable. "Back to the conversation—I would never say *whoopsie*."

I roll my eyes. "Okay, fine. I take it back."

"Also, I would never need to think about my wife waiting at home because she'd be right there with me."

"Are you really suggesting a threesome right now, West? We're not even a twosome yet."

It's his turn to roll his eyes. "You know the problem with marrying your best friend? I know all of your tells, which means that I know you only revert to sarcasm when you're feeling off-kilter about something."

My throat goes dry. So okay, yeah, he's not exactly wrong about that. Pathetically, I try to move the conversation along. "But I'm always sarcastic? If you think about it, it's kind of my natural habitat."

"Daisy."

I bury myself in the depths of his hoodie. "Yes, Weston?"

"Don't hide from me." The fading light slides over his frame as he shifts his weight, his knees falling open as they press into the blanket, his ass in those well-worn jeans resting back on his heels. His big hands drop onto his spread thighs. With him kneeling like that, he's suddenly taller than me again and I have to lift my chin to meet his gaze. "We're in this together—have *been* in this together—and there's nothing I won't do for you. You want me down on one knee? I'll do it. You want me to never mention this again? I won't. But you've got to give me something. Tell me what's running through your head."

I love you.

I love you so much and the idea of you down on one knee for a proposal might end me.

"We need rules," I blurt out.

He tilts his head. "Rules for what?"

"Marriage. Because it's not real, you know?"

His brow furrows in confusion. "If we get to the part where we say, 'I do,' then it's pretty fucking official."

"Yes, but . . ." Releasing my grip on West's sweatshirt, I reach for my phone. I have no idea what the plan is until I'm pulling up my reading app and typing "marriage of convenience" into the search bar. Satisfied with the results, I thrust the device at him. "Think of it like a prenup."

"We don't need one of those. Whatever is mine is yours."

I don't know whether to laugh or cry, and the end result is a weird bubble of sound that gets stuck in my throat. "It's not really a prenup about money or possessions, it's more like . . . Like a contract that protects our friendship." Worry winds itself into a knot, and I swallow, hard, to make it disappear. "If we do this, that comes first. It has to or I won't—I won't say yes, West. You mean too much to me."

"You mean everything to me, too." With his head still bent, he scrolls through the list of romance novels. I'm not sure if he actually stops to read any of the blurbs but after a minute or so, he sets my phone down beside his abandoned pasta bowl and folds his arms across his chest. "Okay. Fine. Rules to protect our friendship. What's first?"

"No kissing."

Somehow, his brows tick even higher, arching toward his hairline. "You came up with that one fast."

A furious flush creeps into my cheeks. "I thought—I mean—I just think that we shouldn't blur any boundaries."

His gaze drops to my lips . . . and he doesn't look away.

No, he watches as they part on a shivery breath, and he gives me his undivided attention when I subconsciously bite down on the plush cushion of my bottom lip. I want to pry into his mind and unravel all of his thoughts because for the life of me, I can't tell what he's thinking—if he's wondering what I might taste like or counting his lucky blessings that he won't ever need to press his lips to mine.

But then he murmurs, "A kiss on our wedding day," and my pulse somersaults into overdrive. In the failing light, his mossy green eyes look nearly black as they meet mine. "Rule number one—we kiss on our wedding day but not again after that."

I can barely feel my fingers they've gone so tingly with shock.

Kissing West.

One kiss. Just one. And then never again.

"Should I be writing these down?"

He doesn't acknowledge the new rasp in my voice, just lifts one shoulder in response. "Depends on how many rules you think we need."

"Not that many."

He gestures to my phone. "Those books said something about 'only one bed.'"

Yes, they probably did, and now I would like nothing more than to fling myself off the nearest cliff. With any luck, I'll die from fright before I even hit the water. "We'll sleep in separate rooms."

"Hate to break it to you, but your place doesn't have separate rooms. It's got one room with one bed—unless you want me sleeping on that tiny loveseat you call a couch."

The banter is familiar, and I grab onto the olive branch as if it's a lifeline. "It *is* a couch. Just because you're too tall for it doesn't mean that it isn't part of the couch family tree."

"A good friend would have bought something bigger."

"A better friend wouldn't make me feel guilty that the *couch* I purchased is as big as I could fit in my living room."

His dark, husky laughter sinks into my bones. "You'll stay with me, then? So, I don't need to sleep on the floor since sharing a bed is off the table?"

"Yes. I'll stay with you." I won't be giving up my lease,

though. Not anytime soon. "New rule—we set an end date."

More than the kiss, more than the one bed, it's this rule that seems to shake something loose in him. He reaches up to adjust his ball cap. Only when his palm collides with the top of his head does he seem to remember that he took it off before we sat to eat. With a self-deprecating chuckle, he ends up raking his fingers through his hair, his gaze pinging everywhere but landing on me.

Knowing what I know about how he deals with eye contact, I place a careful hand on his leg. "Or not," I say softly, squeezing his knee once before pulling away. "Maybe we take it day by day, feel the situation out as it unfolds. Make that decision whenever it seems right."

"What if it's never the right time?" His voice is strangely hoarse, reminding me of when we first met and discussed the terms of our friendship. He cracked open the door to his heart that day and let me peer inside. In nine years, he's never once locked me out. And sometimes . . . Sometimes I wonder if I'd be this hopelessly in love with him if he wasn't so determined to always be an open book. It's that openness that guides him now, that instinctual need he feels to share everything with me, even when it exposes the soft underbelly of his soul. "What if getting married to you just feels right, and I don't want to let you go?"

Would I stay in a platonic marriage with West over a sexual one with some random, faceless stranger?

Yes.

Always.

Forever.

Marrying West will hurt, but maybe the pain will fade one day. Or maybe it won't. Maybe the hurt will grow like the gnarled branches of a tree, old and weathered by time but stronger from the roots buried deep beneath the soil. And maybe one day, years in the future, I'll look back on this moment and know that I made the right choice in marrying West—because even when I'm in freefall, I know that he'll always catch me in the end.

"So, we stay married, then." Rolling his sleeves down over my fingers, I let my hands hang between my splayed thighs. "I mean, you did sort of promise me that we'd end up old and gray together."

"You're right, I did."

My breath catches as he leans forward to rest his weight down on only one knee, and then I stop breathing altogether when he reaches for my hand. The soft glimmer of moonlight slants across his handsome face as he carefully pulls back the sleeve of his sweatshirt to expose my wrist, my fingers, my palm. Our fingertips meet in a gentle brush of skin against skin.

"If our one kiss is saved for our wedding day, should we shake on it?" he asks. "To seal the deal?"

I nod jerkily. "Yeah, okay."

He slides his hand into mine. "Daisy Daisy-belle Hall, in the name of hockey and friendship, I promise to only kiss you once, to never share your bed, and maybe—it's currently undecided—to let you go at some undetermined date in the future. Will you marry me?"

As far as proposals go, it could certainly be better. But I'm laughing, and my heart is racing, and I'm holding the hand of the boy I love. Most of all, it feels like *us*.

"Yes, Weston Cain, I'll marry you."

"Giving away your heart is a terrifying prospect.
In hockey terms, it's a bit like rushing down the ice on a
breakaway when the clock is running out. You either make
the play and win one for the team or you trudge back to the
dressing room with the knowledge that you failed."
—*Confessions of a Puck Bunny*

CHAPTER 12
DAISY

I'm thigh-deep in a wedding dress when Sally, one of the shop's bridal consultants, leans forward to give me a hand. As in, she puts one hand on my butt, the other on the fabric, and like a pig in a blanket, I'm shoved directly inside two-thousand-dollar casing.

I barely manage to stifle a grunt of discomfort as she steps back to admire her handiwork.

"We're lucky that we had this one in your size from a return." Hands poised on her hips, Sally circles me like a shark scenting blood in the water. "Though you'll need enough time before the wedding to have the hem lifted. It's too long on you."

That's an understatement.

Though the bodice fits almost perfectly, my legs are swimming in fabric. I'm pretty sure that if I try to walk, I'll end up tangled in satin and face-down on the floor.

The good news is that West and I have decided to go to the courthouse next week as soon as he's back from his upcoming road trip. Assuming I walk away with a dress today, I'll have enough time to get it altered—with a little extra cash to compensate for the fast turnaround, of course.

I mean, there's no reason why I can't just wear a pair of jeans and call it a day, but I can't bring myself to act like I don't care. I *want* to wear a dress. I want to pin back my hair under a pretty veil and pick out something blue to wear.

Call me a hopeless romantic, but I'd like to at least pretend that it's not only a matter of convenience that's leading us down the aisle.

Sally hovers by my elbow. "What are you thinking?"

That I should have taken the few extra minutes to slather on some lotion after my shower this morning. Everyone knows that a dry Slip-n-Slide is objectively a bad experience, and I can still feel the imprint of Sally's diamond ring on my backside from all the pulling and tugging. As for the dress itself . . .

With two fistfuls of satin, I shuffle over so that I'm standing in front of the floor length mirror. Right. Well. Here goes nothing. As I lift my gaze, I find myself hoping for the best while preparing for the—

I physically wince at my appearance.

"Well?" Sally leans down to fluff the train. "Initial thoughts?"

The color, the fabric, the cut—all of it is horrendously wrong on my body.

Instead of reading the room, Sally gives a rather enthusiastic clap. "I'm sure your dad will love it!"

I'm sure he will since he's the one who picked it out.

"C'mon, let's show it off." Before I can utter an effusive *thanks but no thanks*, Sally draws the velvet curtain back with a dramatic tug. "Voila! What do you think of your daughter in this dress, Mr. Hall?"

He's seated alone on a sofa that could easily fit ten happy family members, and just like that, I regret not asking Tory to take off work and come along. Sure, he busted out laughing when I told him about the plan to marry West, but he also stopped laughing entirely when he realized that I wasn't joking around. That's when he cursed under his breath and threatened me with bodily harm: "Fake wedding or not, if you get hitched to my brother without me there, I will bury you both where you stand."

Friendships are weird.

Still, it's hard to see my dad sitting there by himself. In another life, maybe Mom would be here, too. Maybe she'd comb through the racks of sample dresses and instinctively know that satin is too heavy a fabric for my petite frame. Maybe she would save a smile for me when we found the right dress, exclaiming, "That's the one!" like in all those reality shows where the bride is surrounded by piles of discarded gowns only to end up walking away with the first one that she tried on.

Maybes are hard.

Especially when reality is particularly cruel.

Dad gives the dress a quick onceover, his expression growing panicked at being put on the spot. I almost feel vindicated when he hedges, "I don't know. You look like . . ."

"Like I should be running around with Casper the Friendly Ghost? Agreed. I'm practically translucent in this thing."

He grimaces. "You are rather . . . pale."

That about sums it up, yes.

I turn to Sally. "Do you have anything with lace?"

TWO HOURS LATER, Dad and I step out into the brisk autumn day.

The door to the bridal shop has barely swung closed before he's reaching into his shirt pocket for a pair of sunglasses. With a steady line of cars idling in the street before us, all waiting for the stoplight to turn green, he has to raise his voice to be heard over the low hum of engines. "You should have let me pay for the dress. Or at least the alterations."

"It's not a real wedding."

"But it is a real dress, and you just lost your job."

"I quit my job," I correct for no other reason than it feels necessary to mark the difference. Arthur wouldn't have fired me yet. He would have suffocated me like a snake does with its prey, cutting off all hope of oxygen, until he finally showed me mercy and sent me packing with all of my belongings. "And I have savings." I slip on my own sunglasses against the bright midday sun. "Don't worry, all is not lost."

He jerks his chin toward me in question. "*Mighty Ducks*?"

"Edgar Allen Poe, Dad."

"Don't know him."

The fact that he can make me laugh when there's enough awkwardness between us to fill its own zip code says everything—Sam Hall is still one of my favorite people even if we haven't really talked in days, not since the meeting with the team. A text here, a quick call there, all of it so incredibly impersonal that I can't keep the hope out of my voice when I ask, "Do you have time for some coffee?" I point to the bakery across the street. "I'll even let you pay."

Dad's mouth pinches under his mustache. "Can't, kid. I'm sorry."

"Oh." Smile slipping, I force myself to swallow my disappointment. "Yeah, sure. No problem. I know that you're busy."

"It's not that I don't want to, Dais." Lifting one arm, he passes his palm over the back of his neck, his pale skin already turning pink under the surprisingly warm sun. "We've got the upcoming roadie with Colorado up first, and you know that Colorado is a pain in the—"

"I know, Dad. I get it."

"I know you do, kid." He backs up a step, using his hand to shield his face even though he's still wearing sunglasses. "Hey, keep an eye out for a call from Gwen, would you? She said that she'd reach out to talk to you and West about doing some sort of Tell All. Obviously, not a *complete* Tell All. Think about it. Also, let me know if you want to come to any of the games while we're away— might look good for you to be seen at one. Show West some support before news breaks about the wedding, and all that. Just trying to think outside the box."

Is it really a marriage of convenience if your dad is pushing for it? Because I'm starting to feel like I'm stuck inside the pages of an arranged marriage romance instead.

I lift a hand in a wave. "I'll keep an eye out for Gwen, and I'll think about the game."

"Good, good. Okay, I gotta take off." After waiting for a break in traffic, he hoofs it across the street to where he parked his car, offering me a harried wave over his shoulder before yanking open the driver's side door and disappearing inside the vehicle.

Like a loser, I stand there waving until he's gone.

It doesn't occur to me until I'm on my way home that he never asked if I'm doing okay.

CHAPTER 13

WESTON

I'm starting to think that Joe Morley has best friends on every fucking team in the league.

Limping my way toward the visitor's dressing room after our game against Colorado, Kasey comes up beside me. In his goalie gear, he takes up twice as much space and accidentally knocks his elbow into mine when he leans close, his voice lowering to a worried murmur. "You good, bud?"

"Never been better." It's a lie. My hip is hurting like a motherfucker and I'm going to have a bruise the size of Texas tomorrow on my thigh. How we pulled out a win is beyond me; Colorado played with a roughness that said tonight's game was personal.

As if reading my mind, Kasey says, "Victor Nilsson is a dick."

"Joe Morley is a dick," I mutter grimly, "everyone else is just jumping on the bandwagon."

It started out innocently enough. A push here, a shove there, before becoming increasingly more pointed—and this time, I wasn't the only one catching the heat. Nilsson pinned Bjorn to the boards in the second period, somehow managing to jab the rookie in the soft, fleshy part of his throat with his stick. While Bjorn gasped for air, Nilsson played it cool, gloved hands lifted above his head in the universal sign for *it wasn't me*. He got sent to the sin bin for high sticking, and we scored twice on the power play, but still, the damage was done.

Tonight, we're the walking wounded, and I'm not just talking about our physical injuries. Morale is low as we start getting undressed.

Dragging my duffel bag close, I riffle through it for my phone. I have three missed texts: one from my dad that I ignore, another from Daisy that I'll check in a second, and the last from Tory. I open up my twin's first and crack a smile at the meme he sent of Daffy Duck with the tagline, "You're despicable." Only, he's replaced Daffy's face with Victor Nilsson's ugly mug.

I type out a quick reply:

> Your Photoshop skills are terrifying.

Within seconds, a new text from him pops up. This time, it's a picture of The Big, Bad Wolf from the movie *Shrek* decked out in the pink dress of Little Red Riding Hood's grandmother. My face is overlayed on top of the Wolf's, and Tory has added the line, "I'll Blow Your House Down, Motherfucker."

Laughter fights its way up my throat. It feels good after the night I've had.

TORY

> I've been saving this one for a while. Enjoy

> You are grossly unpaid working for Dad.

TORY

At least I'm paid. Imagine if I had to live with them still.

Don't worry, big bro. You can always be my assistant.

TORY:

shivers in horror

No thanks

Hey, I'd be a great boss.

TORY

No doubt

...said no one ever

Asshole.

TORY

You love me

By the way, you're welcome for keeping your little secret

Technically, you're in on the secret if you plan to be at the wedding. Which you will be since you're our witness.

TORY

Mom and Dad are finally getting hitched.
I'd never miss it

With a chuckle, I exit out of the thread. He's been calling me and Daisy that since college. I'm not even sure what prompted him to start, but it's been "Mom and Dad" this and "Mom and Dad" that for years now. Thankfully, Daisy doesn't seem to mind, and I've certainly never cared one way or another.

I open her message next and feel my lips tug upward in a soft, affectionate grin.

DAISY

Be safe please

I'm not trying to roll you into the courthouse next week.

My thumbs are flying over the keyboard to reply before I can even properly formulate my thoughts.

A little worse for wear but still walking on two legs so…

::ring emoji:: ::wedding chapel emoji::

You can't get out of marrying me that easily.

DAISY

Lucky for you, I've already accepted my fate

Oh, good.

I'd hate to have to drag you to the altar.

DAISY

…this isn't a dark romance, Cain.

Are there different levels of Hallmark? Like, fluffy ones with very kind, very respectable best friends? And others with bondage and kink?

DAISY

Hallmark would never.

> And stop trying to pretend that you're respectable

She follows that up with a zoomed in screenshot of my comment about dragging her to the altar, and I bark out a laugh loud enough to attract the attention of my teammates. Playfully, Beaumont points a finger in my direction. "Finish up, Cain. The rookies need us, and we're taking them out."

WE END up at a hole-in-the-wall bar about a mile away from the airport hotel where we're staying. The floors are sticky, the lights are wonky, and Bjorn is slow dancing all by his lonesome near the jukebox.

"Should we rescue him?" Hunt asks.

"Nah." Beaumont cracks the cap on his water bottle. "Let him be. He's not hurting anyone."

I pick at the label on my beer. I've barely taken a sip, but the repetitive motion keeps my hands busy, which soothes the restless part of my soul.

If you asked me ten years ago whether I'd be content playing babysitter to the youngsters on the team, I would have laughed in your face. Corralling Connie and Felix always felt emotionally draining, and even during my first few seasons with the Blades, I never let my guard down on nights like these. It was exhausting, always trying to be what other people wanted. There was the constant pressure to fit in; to say or do the right thing so my new teammates didn't think that I was completely awkward; to work up the interest to casually flirt with someone even though all I wanted was to go back to the hotel and give Daisy a call.

The harder I tried to be like everyone else, the worse I felt.

More pre-game rituals. Fewer nights of good rest. Anxiety was a thread that wound around me like a noose, growing tighter and tighter until I thought that I'd die from overexposure. And always in the back of my mind was the reminder that my parents were just biding their time, waiting for my dream to crumble down around me.

I'm not really sure when it shifted. Maybe around the time of my surgery when I realized that my teammates only cared about getting me healthy again.

I haven't managed to kick my pre-game rituals to the curb—and, anyway, they're a hockey thing and I'm nothing if not a hockey player—and anxiety is still my constant companion when a situation feels particularly out of control, but otherwise . . . I feel good in my skin. Relaxed. Like I can sit here with the boys, holding a beer that I don't have any plans to drink, and not care if I get any sideways looks.

Although, to be fair, the only one getting side-eyed right now is Bjorn.

"We really should stop him," Hunt says as we watch the rookie drunkenly back his ass up against a very unwilling bystander—the jukebox. "But I also can't look away."

"It's a trainwreck," I agree.

"Alarik is filming it," Beaumont says, pointing his water bottle toward the other Anders brother, "and I should put a stop to it because you know he's going to lord it over Bjorn's head for the next month, but also . . ." He shrugs. "Their sibling rivalry is not my problem."

"It will be if Bjorn murders Alarik."

Our captain tilts his toward me with a wry grin. "Can you imagine the headlines? One Cup under our belt and suddenly we're cursed."

Because I know he's only fucking with me, I don't take

the jab personally. "I don't know, imagine what they'll say when me and Daisy announce that we're married."

Hunt turns a curious glance my way. "So, you two are definitely going through with it?"

I raise a brow. "Gwen didn't tell you? She's got us booked for three interviews the moment we let her know that we've tied the knot."

"Aw, does that mean we're not invited to the wedding?" He presses a hand to his heart. "I'm fucking crushed, man. I thought we meant something to you."

I toss a crumpled napkin at his head. "Fucker," I mutter, laughing. "Besides, we're thinking that we'll hit up The Box in our finest that night, let everyone know that there's a round on us for anyone wanting to say congratulations."

"Romantic," Beaumont teases, and I know what he's thinking—that an unofficial reception at the private bar that the Blades have made our own is anything *but* romantic.

I don't know how to tell him that I want to give Daisy the world. I'd book us a stay at some fancy hotel in the city or a wooden lodge buried deep in the heart of Maine, if that's what she prefers. We can sleep in separate rooms and never kiss again, and I'll—

I'll be the happiest man alive.

Happy because I'd get to call her mine, and something about that—something about knowing that we're bound to each other by law—scratches an itch inside my brain that I didn't even know existed.

For years, I've thought that having Daisy as my friend is all I've ever wanted, but *marrying* her? I want it. I want it so fucking badly, and I have no idea what to do with that revelation, so I tuck it back inside that hidden corner of my heart that I rarely let people see because it makes me feel weird and vulnerable, as if I'm always two steps out of sync with everyone around me. It's easier to brush it off and give

Beaumont shit than it is to uncomfortably peel back the layers of my own confusion.

"It's not a real marriage, man." The words hang heavy in the air. Shaking off the wrongness of them, I press onward. "And anyway, after what happened tonight with Nilsson, something has to change."

Beaumont frowns. "And you think that getting hitched to Daisy will fix everything?"

"Fix Morley and others like him?" I shake my head. "No shot. The way Nilsson went after Bjorn was fucking uncalled for."

"He knew what he was doing," Hunt says, his blue eyes troubled. "It feels over the top, though, doesn't it? I get that Daisy pissed people off, but it's been almost two weeks since the story broke, and it hasn't died down at all."

"Gwen thinks that the wedding announcement will quiet the fans down. Well, at least divert their attention to something else." With the edge of my fingernail, I pick at the peeling label a little more. "And if the fans aren't egging on guys like Morley, hopefully everything else will calm down, too."

Beaumont meets my gaze across the table. "And if it doesn't work?"

"Then we fight our way to another Cup the old-fashioned way."

With our fists.

CHAPTER 14
DAISY

"**G**o ahead, Hall. Claim a room."

I'm exhausted and sweating from every orifice of my body after hauling boxes of crap into West's house, but apparently not tired enough to resist sneaking a peek at my soon-to-be-husband's ass as he bends over to set down the last of my boxes on his kitchen floor.

For the record, it's the perfect hockey bubble butt. High, tight, and thick enough to make even the most devout drool. You could stick West in a lineup, strip him down to only a pair of well-worn jeans, and I'd still be able to pick him out from the crowd.

Hello, my name is Daisy Hall, and I am a connoisseur of all things Weston Cain.

Pretty sure no one would find that addition to my resume impressive but me.

Their loss.

"Water first, room second." After collapsing on top of the closest cardboard box, I make a grabby motion with my hand. "Please take pity on me, good sir."

With a low chuckle, West picks his away around stacks

of my belongings to open his commercial-grade fridge. Everything in Weston's house is oversized—the rooms, the furniture, the appliances. Does he need it? Probably not. Then again, he once told me that he only bought the waterfront property for the view of Boston's skyline. Everything inside the place was simply a secondary bonus.

And now it's all mine.

Half-mine.

Okay, not really mine, and to be honest, I can take or leave the décor, but the view really is to die for. Without meaning to, I find myself straining sideways to get a glimpse of the water beyond the massive glass doors that lead from the living room and out onto Weston's deck. Even from here, I can see the city's tallest skyscrapers shimmering under the late afternoon sun.

A water bottle appears in front of me. "Need me to carry you out to the deck?"

Accepting the water, I lift my gaze past West's drawstring shorts, and the damp T-shirt clinging to his rock-hard chest, to meet his soft green eyes. "I can walk."

"Can you?" His mouth curves in a grin. "Because it looks like you're in danger of becoming one with that box."

I wriggle my butt a little. "It wants me to stay but I'm ready to go."

"Sounds like my relationship with my parents."

I laugh, but only because I know that he meant it as a throwaway joke. "Okay, yeah." I lift my arms. "I'll take the ride."

West turns around, presenting me with the broad expanse of his shoulders and the narrow width of his waist. He bends his knees so that I can loop my arms around his neck, the water bottle still clasped in my right hand. I hop up onto my toes to give him enough time to hook his big hands under my thighs. Blood rushes to my head as he stands up straight, bouncing me in place to put me in a more comfortable position.

I might as well be on top of the world.

Hoisted six-plus feet off the ground, I swear the air is a little thinner up here. Or maybe that's thanks to the fact that I'm tangled breathlessly around Weston, clinging to him like a koala, never wanting to let go.

To my surprise, he doesn't immediately put me down once he steps outside onto the deck. Instead, he positions us so that we both have a view of the harbor, with me sitting on the porch railing and him standing in front of me, his back still flush with my chest. We're both sweaty and a little gross, but—

My breath catches at his closeness.

At the realization that he has no intention of pulling away.

Would it be okay if I tuck my chin into the crook of his neck? Would it be weird if I link my legs around his waist instead of letting them dangle listlessly on either side of his thighs? Would it—could *we*—pretend, for just one second, that we're something more than friends?

West tilts his head to the side. "Is this okay?"

It takes me a moment to find my voice, and when I do, it's scratchy with desire. "If you wanted to be the little spoon, you could have just asked."

I feel the reverberation of his laughter all the way down to the tips of my toes. And then he shatters what's left of my self-control by gripping my thighs and encouraging me to wrap my legs around his lean waist. He drops one hand to the porch railing for balance and keeps the other linked around my ankles so I can relax into his hold.

"Now I'm the little spoon," he says, and his tone isn't smug, exactly, but . . . satisfied, I think. Pleased. As if having me wrapped around him is all he's ever wanted in life.

Oh, fuck. I won't survive this.

Not the marriage. Not the emotional devastation of unrequited love.

I'm going to pass out on the spot, and one day someone will discover my grave and realize that my epitaph reads: *Died from Sexual Combustion. May She Rest in Peace.*

It takes every ounce of concentration to focus on the horizon and direct the conversation elsewhere. "Have you talked to them?"

West doesn't ask for clarification, but beneath my crossed ankles, I feel his flat stomach expand with a sudden breath. "Yeah. Briefly."

"With your mom?"

"Dad, this time."

I don't let myself think too hard about it, simply lower my chin to the top of his shoulder so he knows that I'm here with him and that I'm listening.

Without further prompting, he murmurs, "Is it wrong that I don't want them at the wedding? I know it's not real, that we're not . . . Anyway, I know that if I don't tell them, they'll find out online with everyone else. It'll be so much worse that way, but . . ."

I stay quiet to give him time to untangle his thoughts.

"But I want them to understand that the harder they push, the closer I am to walking away for good." A rough sigh slips past his lips. "I'm tired, Hall. I'm so fucking tired of walking on a tightrope around them, just holding my breath, waiting for the moment that it snaps."

"Are you worried they wouldn't catch you?"

"I'm worried that they would. That I'd be stuck in the prison that they call a life, caring more about appearances than they do talking with their own kids to find out what we want, what *we* care about. I mean, Tory—"

"Is doing his own thing," I say. "He processes his relationship with them differently than you do. Not worse, not better, just different."

"Yeah." His fingers flex against my ankles. "Yeah, you're right, he does."

I turn my head and let my gaze travel over the familiar lines of his face—the delicate, blond lashes that are shades lighter than his hair, the crooked bridge of his nose and the perfect, sensual curve of his mouth. He hasn't shaved in a few days so dark blond scruff is growing in, and I can't help but wonder what it might feel like against my skin.

With a rough swallow, I blink those dangerous thoughts away.

"Do you want me to tell you what you want to hear?" I ask to the backdrop of waves crashing against the shoreline not even twenty yards away from the back steps of Weston's house. "Or do you want me to play tough guy?"

"Fuck, I hate it when you play tough guy."

At the acute misery in his voice, a wicked smile quirks my lips. "You're the one who introduced me to him."

"Yeah, for when *you* needed advice," he mutters, readjusting my limbs so he can sink deeper into me, "not so you can turn it against me."

I click my tongue to mime the ticking of a clock. "What's it gonna be, Cain? Make your decision and let me pass judgment."

He hisses through his teeth. "You're a menace."

"And in forty-eight hours, I'll be legally yours. Careful, hide your excitement now, I can't handle all of the enthusiasm. It blinds me!"

Shoulders shaking with husky laughter, he gives me more of his weight. Enough, actually, that I let out a surprised shriek, halfway convinced that he might send me toppling over the porch railing into his hydrangea bush. The water bottle clatters to the deck as I plaster myself against his back, heels digging into—

Weston grunts in pain. "Feet up, please," he croaks.

"Oh, oh shit." Dropping my legs from his waist, I hide my face against the warmth of his back, trying to stifle howls of laughter in his shirt. "Not so tough now, are you, Little Cain?"

He goes still in my arms.

And then slowly—so slowly, in fact, that I almost miss how tension sparks like a livewire between us—he steps forward and lets me slide down his back. His eyes are narrowed when he turns around to face me, his chin set in that same arrogant tilt he gets whenever he's playing hockey and has his sights set on the enemy. He opens his mouth, and with just one word, sends my world tilting on its axis:

"Run."

Stunned, I blink at him. "Sorry, repeat that please. I could have sworn that you just said—"

"Run, Hall." He takes another step toward me. This time, I have the good sense to skitter away on the balls of my feet. "Run far, run fast, because as soon as I catch you, you're going straight into the water."

My gaze slips past him to the glistening blue harbor.

It's October in Massachusetts. Not as bad as a dunk in the middle of winter but still, it's going to feel like an ice bath. And, you know, when I do choose to go swimming, it's generally summertime vibes only. Like, with water-melon margaritas, SPF 100 slathered across my vampire skin, and a really good book.

I tiptoe backward. "I'm fast, you know."

"I'm faster."

"You've got a bum hip."

"And you've got a bum leg," he counters.

"So, you're saying that we're a match made in Heaven, then."

Mirth dances in his gaze. "Soulmates."

"Partners in crime."

"Husband and wife," he says.

"For now."

"Maybe forever."

"Yes," I whisper back, feeling my heart trip over itself, "maybe forever."

Then I run, the wind in my hair, my laughter loud and wild and free. He catches me around the waist and throws me over one shoulder, and it's not until he's marched us halfway down to the beach, with me kicking and screaming with the promise of retaliation, that I pause long enough to catch my breath, and say, "Invite them, West. Just in case this never ends."

CHAPTER 15
WESTON

"How are you feeling?" Tory asks as he helps me straighten my tie. "Because if you don't mind me saying, you look like shit."

I feel like shit.

I tossed and turned all night, desperate for sleep that never came. It's been a while since my midnight hours were plagued by stress-induced anxiety, but I quickly recognized the signs and rolled out of bed at half past four. Since sleep was elusive, I finished prepping the house for Daisy.

We're getting married in . . .

"What time is it?" I ask again. He took away my phone earlier so I wouldn't be tempted to text Mom and Dad that I've called off the wedding. Although, to be fair, they drove in with Tory from Hartford this morning so I doubt that exit plan would get me very far before they called my bluff.

Tory finishes with my tie and steps back. "We need to head out in five."

"Or we could leave now."

Green eyes the same shade as my own stare back at me, unwavering in their intensity. Then his brows shoot up toward his hairline. "Holy fuck, you're nervous."

"What? No way." My cramping stomach makes a liar out of me. Turning away, I reach for my wallet from the entryway table and slip it into the back pocket of my slacks. "It's all for show, remember? Fake. A scam. Not real."

Tory scampers out the door after me. "But you want it to be?"

Maybe.

Yes.

Fuck.

After I finish locking up behind him, my twin follows me down the short length of my driveway. We pile into my car with me behind the wheel and him playing passenger princess. True to form, he puts the seat back all the way and extends his long legs out in front of him. Some things never change.

And some do.

"Can you text Daisy and let her know that we're on the way?" I ask.

"Already did."

"Right, okay." My chest feels tight. I let out a slow, calming breath. "Good."

Tory side-eyes me. "Have you seen her dress yet?"

"It's bad luck."

"But you said that the marriage is all for show, remember? Fake. A scam. Not real." I want to punch his smile right off his stupidly smug face. It's a wonder we survived to adulthood, honestly. "By that logic," he continues cheerfully, "there's no reason to hide behind silly superstitions."

"I'm set, thanks." No point in risking it.

"So, I shouldn't tell you that she sent me a picture of her in the dress?"

I take my eyes off the road just to glare at him. "Do you *want* me to make you walk?"

"We both know that I'd get lost. And then I'd be late to your fake wedding, which would leave you to deal with the parentals all on your lonesome, and you'd probably lose your shit, cuss in front of the priest—"

"It's a courthouse wedding, Tor. There's no priest."

"—Potentially get caught on camera by some secret journalist camped out in the bushes, who would, of course, air out all of your dirty laundry. Daisy would clearly see the error in her ways, abandon you on the steps of the church, and leave you to your tears of misery."

My jaw is actually on the floor by the end of his tirade. "What the fuck is wrong with you?"

"Everything," my twin says with a little finger wave, "and nothing."

"That doesn't make any sense."

"Were you entertained?"

"I'm speechless."

"So, you were entertained." He links his fingers together over his stomach and turns his head to look out the window. "My job here is done. You no longer look like you're about to puke up a week's worth of food onto Daisy's pretty dress. You're welcome."

There's so much to unpack there, and yet all I can think to ask is, "Her dress is pretty?"

Out of the corner of my eye, I see my brother's smile reflected in the passenger side window. "Yeah, West. It's beautiful."

As it turns out, we're the last ones to arrive.

The good news: being late leaves little time for me to chat with Mom and Dad aside from thanking them for dropping off Tory this morning so he could help me get ready. The fact that they think this wedding is real is not lost on me; neither is the fact that they aren't trying to talk me out of marrying Daisy. By some miracle, they've always adored her. So much so, apparently, they aren't even putting up a fuss about a courthouse wedding.

The bad news: I'm pretty sure that I left my house without my vows.

"Fuck," I mutter when I slip my hand into my pocket and come up blank. The curse earns me stern glares from my parents, never mind that this isn't actually a church and neither of them is particularly religious. Grimacing, I turn to Tory, elbowing him in the gut to snag his attention while we wait for Daisy and Coach. "Did you by any chance grab the sheet of paper that was on the entryway table beside my wallet?"

My twin shakes his head. "I was too busy plotting a plan to erase that constipated look from your face, and—oh, joy, it's back again. Great timing, bro." He claps me on the shoulder. "Look sharp, here she comes."

Whipping around, my gaze moves swiftly past Coach, who's wearing one of his familiar game day suits, to Daisy, and I—

I lose every train of thought.

All gone in the span of a second.

She shines so bright, it hurts to look at her, and yet I can't bear to look away. I remember this feeling—it was the same as when I stumbled into her at that gala all those years ago. It was the sensation of a fist clutching my chest, whispering, *She feels like home.* It was delight and surprise, my heart racing wildly when she traded banter for banter. It was holding out my hand when I had no reason to stick around except for a gut feeling that said: *She's special. Don't let her go.*

And I haven't, not in all these years. I'm not sure that I can.

Daisy Hall is burned into my soul.

Her long hair is pulled back and partially hidden

beneath thin, gossamer material—*a veil*. The word registers dimly but I've already moved on, sweeping my eager gaze over her upturned face, taking stock of every little detail as if I'll be quizzed on it later. Her lips are shiny with gloss, her eyelids shimmering with a dusting of champagne shadow. Amber eyes peer up at me, nervous and hopeful, as those shiny pink lips tilt sideways into a trembling smile.

I breathe her name.

She whispers mine.

Happiness fucking frolics through my chest as the justice of the peace instructs us to step forward and face each other. My gaze dips down. Intricate lace as far as the eye can see. The floor length gown is held up by two delicate straps. On her left hand is a silver bracelet that catches the light as she passes her bouquet of pink and purple flowers to Tory. Then her hands are in mine, and the permanence of the moment clicks into place.

This feels right.

It feels *real*.

Not for show. Not a scam.

If the JP recognizes me as one of the star D-men for the Boston Blades, he either doesn't let on or doesn't care. Instead, he casually flips through the thin book he's holding and begins to read. I follow all of it, word for word, but especially when he asks, "Weston, will you take Daisy to be your wedded wife, to love her, to comfort her, honor her, and keep her, for so long as you both shall live?"

Yes.

Always.

"I do," I vow.

Turning to Daisy, he repeats the same question. She holds my gaze, her voice ringing out clear as bell, when she vows in return, "I do."

"Do you have rings to exchange?" we're asked.

"Oh, shit, that's me. Sorry, coming through." After slapping Daisy's bouquet against Dad's chest, Tory reaches into his suit jacket and pulls out a black, velvet ring box, which he pops open with such flare, I know that he's been practicing that move all morning since I handed him our rings for safekeeping. After all, he's both my best man and Daisy's man of honor. Clearly, my brother gets around.

Plucking a plain, silver band from the cushioned bedding, he carefully places it in the center of Daisy's upturned palm. "One for you, brat, and"—he pinches the remaining diamond ring between two fingers and offers it to me—"one for you, little bro." With that, he salutes us both, tucks the jewelry box back into his pocket, and returns to his place beside Dad.

Looking utterly flabbergasted by Tory's antics, the JP visibly shakes off his confusion before carrying on with the civil ceremony, encouraging us to exchange rings when prompted and repeat after him, "With this ring, I thee wed."

The weight of silver feels unfamiliar but welcome on my finger.

Meanwhile, the sight of Daisy's diamond ring has my chest swelling with pride, the feeling so much more potent than all the times I've seen her in my clothes. Daisy Hall wearing my jersey number? That shit does something crazy to my heart. But seeing the ring that I carefully chose for her nestled at the base of her fourth finger? It feels like nothing short of possession.

A primitive claiming that says *you're mine.*

Clearly unaware of the emotions practically short-circuiting my brain, the JP continues, "By the authority vested in me by the Commonwealth of Massachusetts, I now pronounce you husband and wife." Closing his book, he aims a friendly glance my way. "Weston, you may now kiss your bride."

Our first and last kiss.

Remember rule number one.

I should stamp a brief, impersonal peck across those shiny lips. I shouldn't stall, shouldn't care to make this something that we'll both remember for the rest of our lives. I shouldn't lift my hands and gently cup her face; shouldn't step forward so I feel every curve of her body against the hard, straight lines of my own.

I shouldn't kiss her.

Not a real, *this-is-fucking-happening* kiss.

But I do.

I let myself linger in the rising swell of anticipation. Let myself tease her—tease us both—with the possibility of more. I cradle her face and lower my own. Catch her wide-eyed stare for one brief second before my lips are on hers, and I'm drawing a short, helpless sound from the back of her throat, and nothing—fuck, *nothing* has ever felt so right as kissing Daisy.

As kissing my *wife*.

Still cradling her face, I find myself leaning in, pressing deeper. Her hands are frozen mid-air for a series of heart-pounding seconds, and then they're gripping my biceps, her nails digging in almost viciously as she holds on tight. Our lips slip apart. Come back together. Gentle, so fucking gentle, and yet I feel like I'm climbing out of my skin. And maybe she feels the same way, too, because suddenly she's lifting onto the balls of her feet, and I'm circling my arms around the small of her back to keep her there, plastered against me from chest to thigh, our mouths moving tentatively through uncharted waters.

She tastes of sunshine and hope.

And I feel like I'm drowning.

Reality crashes over me in a wave of obnoxious applause. The sound of my parents cheering us on drives Daisy back with an audible gasp, her cheeks stained the same color as one of the blooms in her bouquet. In the awkward lull that follows, neither one of us breaks eye contact to look away. It's not until she's squeezed an arm between us to press two fingers to her swollen lips that I realize I don't want to let her go.

I *haven't* let her go.

Fate takes matters into its own hands when someone drags me away for a hug—*Tory*. I recognize the shape of him immediately. His forehead touches mine, his green eyes sharp and missing absolutely nothing when he cups my face in his hands, the way we always did when we were kids and about to tell each other a secret. "Pull your shit together, little bro."

I'm not sure what he means but then . . .

Then it hits me that I'm panting, hard, as if I've just done hours of bag skates. And my face feels hot like I'm running a fever. Every muscle in my body is wound so tight, I can barely think beyond the building pressure of—of—

Almost helplessly, I glance past my brother to where my mom is hugging Daisy. Her veil sits askew on the crown of her head. As she reaches up to fix it, her gaze meets mine over my mother's shoulder. Her amber eyes are wide in her heart-shaped face. Her cheeks haven't lost their color yet, and her lips . . . Her lips are still that warm shade of pink, but the shiny gloss is gone, kissed away by yours truly, and I taste strawberries on my tongue.

Sunshine. Hope. Strawberries.

The flavor of Daisy Cain.

"You're so fucked," Tory grunts as he lets me go, and he's right.

I am fucked.

Because as I stand there watching Daisy be passed around for hugs and well wishes, I can't ignore the fact that I just kissed my best friend—and I *liked* it.

CHAPTER 16
DAISY

I *kissed West.*

It doesn't seem to matter how many hockey players come up to give me a hug at The Box later that night, my brain is rudely focused on only one thing: West, our kiss, and the fact that I've been a resounding hot mess ever since.

In front of me, Joshua Kammer is gesticulating wildly as he tells me a story, but my eyes are held captive by the sight of my husband—my *husband*—across the room. He ditched the suit jacket and tie hours ago, leaving him in a pair of leather suspenders that emphasize the width of his shoulders. I can't help but drag my gaze over the rest of him— the cuffs of his shirt that he's rolled up to his elbows to reveal inked skin, the casual way he stands with his hands tucked into the front pockets of his gray slacks. Even the column of his throat catches my eye thanks to his unbuttoned collar.

He's so stupidly handsome that my heart actually aches.

I can't believe that we *kissed.*

Movement beside me ends my ogling, and I peer upward to find Kammer positioning himself so we're standing side by side. He slips his hands into his pockets, just like West, but it doesn't have the same effect on me. As in, I don't want to jump the rookie's bones.

"What are we looking at?" he asks.

My cheeks burn. "Um."

"Not the Anders brothers." He nods his chin toward where Bjorn is clearly trying to convince the bartender to refill his cup with something besides water. "So, maybe Cap?"

Despite the embarrassment eating me alive, I can't help but smile at the way Kammer still refers to Jackson Carter as the captain of the Blades. It's no shade to Andre, just a leftover habit formed on the road to Hell and back after last season's Cup win. Jackson currently has his wife, Holly, perched on his lap while they talk with Duke Harrison, who retired over the summer after a longer-than-average career of killing it between the pipes. Beside him is his new bride, Charlie, who flashes me a bright smile when she catches me looking their way. I smile right back.

Everyone has come out to celebrate tonight.

The players, their significant others, even some of management. I'm trying not to think too hard about the fact that none of them are in on the fake marriage scheme. They genuinely believe that West and I decided to randomly tie the knot after years of friendship, and they've all been incredibly supportive despite the recent upheaval of my alter ego—I'm talking hugs, excited high-fives, and about a million and one variations of, "I knew this day would come."

West has laughed it all off in good fun.

Meanwhile, I'm stuck in purgatory—feeling guilty over all the lies while still flying high on the memory of finally *kissing Weston Cain*.

Kammer dismisses Jackson and Holly with a shrug. "Nah, not them." As if he's got a homing beacon strapped to him, he lets his gaze skim over the rest of the crowd before settling in on West. "How long have you been in love with him?"

Just like that, the world crumbles to ash beneath my feet.

"I d-don't," I stammer, "I mean, I'm not—"

The rookie bumps his elbow with mine. "It's cool, we don't need to talk about it."

My tongue untangles itself long enough for me to get out, "It's not like that with West. We aren't—" *Lovers. Partners. Soulmates.*

Kammer lowers his chin to peer down at me. "But you are."

That's all he says.

That's literally it.

But. You. Are.

I swear, the fight goes right out of me, my shoulders drooping in defeat as I awkwardly avert my gaze. "Does everyone know?" Even to my own ears, my voice sounds pathetically small.

He waves a hand. "Nah."

"But you knew."

"I pay attention." I don't mean to laugh, because it's not even remotely funny, but thankfully, Kammer joins in. "I know, right? Not exactly my M.O. I'm like . . . Like, really chaotic almost all of the time so I sorta manage to slide under the radar." He bites his lip as if he's thinking hard on something, and then adds, "I'm like you that way—I think so, at any rate. Maybe I'm wrong. Sometimes I am. Okay, *loads* of time I'm wrong but, yeah."

I don't even realize that I'm staring until he fidgets and starts to blush.

"When I say that I'm like you, I just mean that you're— you come across as a sweetheart but—"

"Are you saying that I'm a bitch?" It's meant to be a

joke, but it goes right over his head. The poor kid stumbles over himself in his haste to apologize.

"What? No! No, definitely not a bitch. Did I say bitch? I'm sorry, I just—"

"Josh," I say, cutting him off. "Can I call you Josh?"

He blinks down at me. "Everyone calls me Joshua."

"Okay, that's fine. Joshua—"

"But I actually kinda hate it." He palms the nape of his neck, his expression losing that panicked edge. "Josh works. Hey, do you think if I tell the boys, they might stop calling me 'rookie' all the time?"

"Not a chance," I tell him.

"Fuck. Yeah, you're probably right."

He looks so miserable about it that I can't help but return his earlier elbow nudge with one of my own. "Calling you 'rookie' is their way of showing you affection. Imagine if all they said was 'hey, you.' Or worse, if they never spoke to you at all."

Josh physically shivers. "Yeah, I'm all good on that." Returning his hands to his pockets, he rocks back onto his heels. "I didn't mean to call you out on the West thing."

"No worries." I force sunshine into my voice even though I'm cringing so incredibly hard on the inside. "Everyone likes to be told that they wear their heart on their sleeve. It's good for the ego. Keeps us humble."

"And I wasn't trying to make you sound like a bitch, either," he goes on, sounding totally morose. "I only wanted to let you know that I appreciate what you've done with *Confessions of a Puck Bunny*."

My stomach swoops. "Oh."

"Yeah. My sister, she had a bad hand dealt to her a few years ago. Got in with this guy that really messed her up here." He touches his hand to his heart. "She's all good now, though, did some time in therapy or whatever."

"I'm glad." And I really, really am.

"Thanks." The small smile he gives me fades to a somberness that looks wrong on his perpetually happy face. "Anyway, after all that stuff about Bunny got leaked a few weeks ago, I know it's probably been hard for you, but I thought . . . I thought you should know that my sister would have been really lucky to have you on her side."

The rookie's face starts to blur.

I press my palm to my belly and attempt to breathe through the swell of emotion.

"See, you are a bit like Robin Hood, right? Giving people hope when maybe they were feelin' really alone. And I'm sorry if some of the fans can't see that, Daisy, but I hope you know that there are way more who feel grateful that you care."

My throat is thick with unshed tears.

I open my mouth to speak but nothing comes out.

Josh's brows draw together. "Did I say something wrong?"

No, not at all.

Shaking my head, a single tear slips past my defenses as I place a hand on the rookie's arm in gratitude. "Thank you," I choke out. "I just . . . if you don't mind, I need to— the bathroom."

"Yeah, sure." Clearly unaware that he's just turned my world upside down, Josh gives me one of his trademark golden retriever smiles. "Congratulations, by the way. I really hope you guys make it work—for real, I mean."

Right. My fake marriage to West.

Everyone is watching you.

I squeeze Josh's arm and then twist away, hightailing it to the bathrooms so I can have what is sure to be a messy meltdown in private. I'm stopped at least three times along the way with more hugs, more offers of congratulations, more "I knew this day would come" comments that should appease the desperate corner of my heart that wishes West loved me back but only serves as a crystal-clear reminder that all of this is a lie.

The wedding.

The reason for the marriage in the first place.

Pretending that I feel remorse about *Confessions of a Puck Bunny* when I don't. Deep down, I don't feel any remorse at all, and I wish that there was a way to keep her alive—keep that part of *me* alive when it feels as though—

The door to the bathroom swings open.

I barely have the time to turn my face away to keep the truth of my tears to myself. Crying in the bathroom on your wedding day? Not a good look.

"Sorry!" I chirp as I make a quick dash for the paper towel dispenser. "My allergies, they're just"—*dammit, Daisy, stop crying*—"I should have brought some meds with me, but I totally forgot."

"Daisy-belle."

That voice.

That deep, whiskey-smooth voice that I hear even in my dreams. The unexpectedness of it feels like a hand wrapped around my heart, increasing the pressure on my emotions until they're boiling over. A harsh sob pushes out of me against my will, and I press the back of my wrist to my mouth, suddenly wishing that I took the time to hide in one of the stalls.

Behind me, the lock on the bathroom door turns over.

I don't know what comes over me, but I hear myself say, "They're going to think we're fucking in here."

West's shoes clip quietly over the tile floor. "Let them. We're a newly married couple, aren't we? And newly married couples fuck."

"Yes, but—"

"But, what?"

I'm coming apart at the seams and this marriage is going to be the thing that pushes me right over the edge.

I sense his presence directly behind me right before I feel his warmth. To my surprise, he doesn't . . . He doesn't touch me or pull me into his arms for one of his signature hugs. He doesn't even press his hands down on my shoulders, the way he does sometimes, so that I feel the weight of him like an anchor keeping me grounded when I might otherwise float away. Instead, his arms come up on either side of me and he plants his hands against the wall. Inches separate my back from his chest, but still, I'm cocooned. Shut off from the rest of the world.

Safe.

"Let it out," he rasps from behind me, his breath warm where it ruffles the hair on the top of my head. "You need to cry? I'm not gonna let anyone see you. The door is locked, and it's just you and me in here."

My chest tightens. Tightens and twists like someone has stabbed a knife directly into my heart, bleeding out another ragged sob against my will.

"I know, sweetheart." His voice is a low, steady force. "You've been strong for weeks. Putting on a brave face. Trying to keep everyone happy. You did good, Hall, so fucking good, but I've got you now, and I'm tellin' you . . . Let it out, okay? Just let it all go."

I don't know what I did to deserve Weston Cain, but as fresh tears spill down my cheeks, the distance between me and my best friend grows smaller and smaller until I'm wrapped so tightly within the band of his arms, I swear he's trying to absorb the grief pouring out of me in waves.

Because it is grief, I think.

Maybe it's stupid, and maybe no one else will understand, but I gave everything of myself to Bunny. Five years of helping others, of taking a stand for what's right—all gone in the blink of an eye. I miss the community that I built from scratch, the kindness and understanding that filled the comment section, the friends who popped into my

DMs just to say hello. I've been carrying on for weeks, so busy with trying to keep my head above water with my dad, and the Blades, and even West, that I haven't stopped moving long enough to realize what I've lost.

Losing Bunny feels like I've lost a limb.

She's there, sort of, buried under the heavy weight of damage control. Soon, I won't feel her presence at all, and I'll be just Daisy Hall again—failed figure skater and the idiot teenager who hated herself for years.

Sniffling, I stay within the circle of West's comforting arms for another second before gently prying myself free. Roughly, I yank a few paper towels from the dispenser before, with my head lowered in shame, I return to the row of sinks where I turn on the tap and wet the towel. One glance at my face in the mirror, though, and I'm pretty sure there's no point in bothering.

"Shit." I look awful. Puffy eyes, swollen face. My cheeks are streaked with wet mascara. No chance anyone believes that we've been in here getting busy. We'll be lucky if they don't think that we're already heading straight to divorce.

West bumps me aside. "Here, let me." He takes the damp paper towel from my hand and motions for me to turn toward him. "Tell me what to do."

"Give me a new face," I joke weakly.

"I like this face." He slides his palm behind my nape to cup the base of my skull. Then he presses the paper towel to my overheated skin and begins to carefully wipe away my ruined makeup, his brow furrowing in deep concentration.

My sinuses are all kinds of stuffed right now, and I sort of feel as if I've just come down from a massive adrenaline crash. Still, I force myself to open my heart and let him in, the way that he always does so freely with me.

"I don't know if I can do this."

His movements still. "Marry me, you mean?"

"Everything else that comes with marrying you," I answer honestly. "The PR statements, the Tell All special that Gwen wants us to do. Pretending that I'm ashamed about what I've done when I feel so . . . so very *strongly* about it. I don't know how to put on an act like that, West. I'm no good at it."

He pulls back to re-dampen the paper towel. "You're better than you think."

I scrunch my nose. "Should I be offended?"

"No. Now close your eyes for me." When I do, he gently rubs what's left of my eyeshadow from my lids. "You've been putting on a performance for your entire life. Every routine you've performed, every time anyone ever said shit to you about your career after you got hurt—you dug down deep and put on a smile."

My heart tumbles into freefall. Breathlessly, I ask, "Have you watched me perform, Weston?"

"Not Worlds but everything else I could get my hands on, yeah. Had to see how good my girl was. As it turns out, you were the best."

I was the best—and then it all fell apart.

To make myself feel better, I think about the endearments he's showering me with—sweetheart, my girl. Both are new and both do funny things to my heart. Like a lead in a Hallmark movie, I want to swoon.

"How many times did you want to tell Arthur Phister to fuck off?"

At West's unexpected question, I choke out a laugh. "I don't know. Too many to count, probably."

"Exactly. But you never let it affect your job." His knuckles graze my temple as he moves the paper towel up to my hairline. "And every time you posted something for *Confessions of a Puck Bunny,* or answered a message from someone who needed your help, didn't you ever stop to think about how Bunny might respond?"

"I . . . I, yeah. I mean, yes."

West steps back, and immediately, I miss the feeling of his hands on my skin. Opening my eyes, I find him standing a foot or so away with a look of contemplation on his ruggedly handsome face.

"What?" I press a hand to my cheek, to my throat. "What is it?"

"Truth or dare."

My shoulders jerk in surprise. "What are you talking about?"

He tosses the paper towel into the waste bin before leaning his weight against one of the sinks. His suspenders dig into his shoulders but lay flat across his chest. The expression on his face says that he's not playing around. "What's it gonna be, Hall? Truth or dare."

I fight the urge to glance behind me, knowing that no one is there and feeding him lines. "Um, dare?"

"I dare you to stay married to me."

I swallow, hard. "Oh?"

"Because I'm a safe place for you," he says, as if I'm actually about to argue otherwise, "and we both know that I won't let anyone fuck around and find out—not with you." He lowers his hand to rest on the lip of the sink, his feet crossing casually at the ankle. "And while we're at it, I dare you to find out who Daisy Daisy-belle Cain really is."

My lips part on a sharp inhale.

"Because you've been in survival mode for years." His green eyes focus on the space right beside me, but I'm not offended, not even a little bit. "And I get that, sweetheart, I do, because most days it feels like I've just been surviving too. But for every performance that we give the world with this marriage, I need you to promise me that you're gonna think real hard about what *you* want. And then I want you to grab it, and make it your own, and not give two fucks about what anyone else says—not if it makes you happy. Can you do that for me?"

I love you.

I love you.

I love you.

"Yeah," I utter hoarsely. "Yeah, I can do that."

Finally, his gaze lands on me again, this time in a lazy sweep from the crown of my head down to the white Converse sneakers that are peeking out from under the hem of my wedding dress. He opens his arms without fanfare, and I dive into the warmth of his embrace, my ear pressed against the steady rhythm of his heart.

He lowers his chin to rest on the top of my head. "Don't let go, right?"

"Don't let go," I whisper, and I don't.

Well, not until Andre Beaumont starts banging on the bathroom door, that is.

CHAPTER 17
WESTON

"I promise this will be as painless as possible." Gwen tells me and Daisy as we ride the elevator up to the tenth floor of the John Hancock building. "And for whatever it's worth, I'll be glued to your side from start to finish. If they ask anything shady, I'll put that shit to bed so fast their heads will spin."

Daisy laughs. "That sounds pleasant."

"Doesn't it?" The elevator dings open and Gwen waves us past her. "All right, game faces on. Also, hold hands, please."

Holding hands with Daisy isn't a problem. The same, however, can't be said for our new living arrangements.

You're a filthy fucking liar.

Fine, living with Daisy isn't a problem either. In the two weeks since getting married at the courthouse, we've entered the land of domesticity with the same ease that we've handled everything else in our almost decade-long friendship. We don't bicker about doing the laundry or cooking dinner—although the latter might be because Daisy can't cook for shit. She's now happily partaking in the meal service that I've been subscribed to for the last few years. Honestly, playing house with my best friend feels *too* easy.

Except, of course, for when we linger awkwardly in the hallway each night before bed.

"You okay?" Daisy asks as she slides her hand into mine. "You look . . . something."

Something pretty much sums up the state of confusion I've been living in since she moved into my place and officially filed paperwork to take my surname.

I send her a reassuring grin. "All good. Let's just get this over with."

Up ahead, Gwen ushers us beyond a set of double doors and into the offices of Bar Down, a sports-centric media company that covers everything from trade deals to athletes announcing their upcoming nuptials. Although I've never had a reason to visit Bar Down's headquarters, they usually have one or two content creators present at all of our home games. More often than not, they're shoving tiny microphones in our faces and asking us obscure trivia questions about our teammates—like whether or not Henri Bordeaux had a pet parrot as a kid.

The answer is no, but his parents did give him a plushy version when he was seven. Apparently, he spent the next five years bringing it to every one of his games for good luck. We teased him mercilessly about it for months afterward.

Before Daisy and I can take a seat in the waiting area, a tall woman enters the office from a connecting hallway. Her brown hair is tied back in a severe knot, and she immediately moves in for a handshake, pumping my arm up and down with the sort of vigorous enthusiasm that threatens a dislocated shoulder. "I'm Jenna. Jenna Burke," she says before turning on Daisy and latching onto her hand for an equally firm greeting. "And you're Daisy. We've met once before—I'm sure you don't remember. It was years ago now. Worlds?"

Looking visibly flustered, Daisy produces a smile that doesn't quite reach her eyes. "Wow. It's been a really long time."

"You can say that again. Hope the leg is okay these days?"

Daisy's smile wavers. "It's fine, thank you for asking."

"All part of the gig." Turning on her heel, Jenna motions for us to follow her down the hall. "When you have a job like mine, you tend to remember way too much about way too many people. For example, I can't tell you my niece's birthday, but I can recite every time you made it to the Frozen Four, Weston." She flashes me a quick look over her shoulder. "That was a joke—UConn only made it once while you were there."

I don't even crack a smile.

Undaunted, Jenna chatters away about her predictions for this year's Division 1 finals—she has her heart set on Cornell, apparently—until she's pushing open one final door and letting us into a big, empty space with floor-to-ceiling windows and gray, concrete floors. There are a slew of staff already present, some of them working with camera equipment while others sort through racks of clothing. The arrangement of studio lighting around a raised platform carves out a designated area for our interview.

"Makeup. Clothes. Photos. Questions. In that order." Jenna wheels around to face us with her arms linked across her chest. "It's going to be a time crunch. We have less than five hours to get everything done unless . . ." She shoots Gwen a hopeful glance. "What do you say? Think that we can have an extra hour maybe?"

Gwen, bless her heart, doesn't budge from the plan to get us in and out of here as fast as possible. "Wish we could, Jenna. Really. But we've got another interview lined up in Medford after this, and you know we're going to get caught in traffic if I don't get us out of here on time."

"Fuck. Traffic," Jenna mutters. "All right, let's get cracking then. Hey, Nathaniel! Get these two into something pretty, will you?"

It says a lot about my current state of mind that it doesn't even occur to me that they expect newlyweds to feel comfortable disrobing around each other until Daisy and I are standing in a makeshift dressing room forty minutes later with only a curtain to separate us from the crew.

She shifts her weight.

I stare at the clothes they've left out for us.

"Should I just—"

"Yeah," I rush out, "yeah, that works."

Her eyes narrow. "You don't even know what I was going to say."

Fuck.

This shouldn't be a big deal. It's *not* a big deal. After spending half my life in locker rooms, I'm not one to feel embarrassed about getting naked in front of an audience. A body is a body, and I've never really cared to dwell on the details. Plus, friends change in front of each other, don't they? It's a thing that happens. Sort of like how I've seen Daisy in a bikini more times than I can possibly count. The girl practically lives at Revere Beach during the summer.

Only, the jittery feeling in my gut says that this is something new. Just like our wedding kiss was new. Just like how every night before bed, I can't help but wonder what it might be like if we ditched our separate rooms to—

Don't dwell on it.

Don't even think about it.

"I'm just going to . . ." Daisy snatches the lavender dress from where it's hanging on the portable rack. With the material clutched in her fist, she spins around to give me her back. "Don't look or whatever."

She's wrongly assumed that I have even a shred of morality in my bones. Because instead of waiting to make sure that I am, in fact, not looking, she promptly kicks off her Doc Martens and loose-fitting jeans, leaving her toned legs bare to my gaze—and I *can't* look away. Not when she slides that lavender dress all the way up to her hips. Not when she pulls her sweater over her head, moving carefully to avoid messing up her hair. Despite the cold day outside, she's not wearing a T-shirt or tank top underneath. After tossing her sweater onto a nearby chair, she slips her fingers under her crooked bra straps to lay them flat over her shoulders, and then she tugs the bodice of the dress up and over her chest.

Though the back gapes open, she doesn't ask for help with the zipper, and I—I can't tear my gaze away from the new tattoo peeking out from under the band of her bra.

When did she get that?

Down at my sides, my fingers twitch with the sudden craving to trace the flower's delicate petals.

"You two almost ready in there?" Gwen asks from the other side of the curtain.

"Almost!" Daisy calls back.

The reminder that we aren't alone is a much-needed kick in the ass. With a rough swallow, I wrench my gaze away from Daisy's tattoo and start stripping, first my jeans and then my Henley. I'm not sure what's so important about switching out one pair of Levi's for another, but I learned a long time ago that it's best to not question the professionals.

By the time I'm shoving my feet into a pair of brown Oxfords, I've done so much mental gymnastics to try and forget the sight of Daisy's inked skin that it feels like my brain is one giant fucking cramp. And yet, all it takes is one glimpse of her face to bring the flood of craving back.

Oblivious to my inner turmoil, Daisy thrusts out her arm for me to take. "Ready?"

I nod. "Yeah, let's get it done."

OVER THE NEXT TWO HOURS, we return to that makeshift dressing room three more times.

They dress Daisy in high-waisted shorts and knee-high boots. They put her in a skirt so fucking short, you can see the curve of her ass every time she so much as breathes. They doll her up and dress her down, and my heart should be racing when the photographer tells me to place my hand on Daisy's bare stomach for a picture. Hell, it should be running a goddamn marathon every time Jenna instructs me to pull Daisy closer or sink my fingers into her hair; to press my lips to her temple, and close my eyes, and look "in love."

Under all the lights, I barely break a sweat.

But then we decamp for another outfit change, and like the flick of a switch, my palms grow clammy with the nervous anticipation of being alone with my best friend—as if we haven't spent years together, just the two of us. This marriage, that first and last kiss. Her *tattoo*. I'm twisted inside out, making something out of nothing.

It's a total mindfuck.

Burying the feelings deep, I don't let myself look at Daisy again, not when we're alone behind that curtain. I keep my gaze respectfully averted and go through the motions of switching out jeans for slacks and then slacks for a pair of comfortable, drawstring shorts and an exclusive, Bar Down-created Boston Blades hoodie.

"Oh, I *love* this."

Before I can second-guess myself, I turn around to see Daisy twisting this way and that in an attempt to peer over her shoulder. She's wearing a matching Blades sweatshirt with my name and number plastered across the back.

Cain.

73.

Her wedding ring peeks out from under her left sleeve.

Eagerly, she meets my gaze. "We're matching, look." And then she lifts the hoodie up to reveal a nearly identical pair of navy-blue shorts that cling to her hips.

Between the oversized sweatshirt and those drawstring shorts, which just barely brush the tops of her knees, there's nothing remotely provocative about the outfit—and yet, my heart is cranking into overdrive all over again, pounding so goddamn hard that I can hear the blood whooshing in my ears.

It feels intimate, this quiet moment with Daisy.

It feels like it belongs to only *us*.

"You look good in my name," I hear myself rasp.

"You'd look even better in mine," she quips with a teasing wriggle of her brows. "Come on, let's go expose all of your deepest, darkest secrets."

"I don't have any secrets." Before today, before our one and only kiss, it would have been the truth—but as I follow Daisy back to where Jenna and Gwen are waiting to get the interview underway, I struggle to come to grips with the fact that I may have just lied to my best friend for the first time in my life.

CHAPTER 18
DAISY

"To get started, I'm going to field you both some softball questions," the editor of *Athletica* informs us after we finally make it to Medford a number of hours later. Outside the lone office window, the sky is already turning a bruised purple. "Sound good?"

West and I are both bone-tired, but we nod anyway. No rest for the wicked, and all that.

Brian Murphy gives us a pleased grin. "Perfect."

From the moment we walked into *Athletica*'s offices, it was obvious that we were in for a completely different experience than with Jenna Burke and Bar Down. For one, we haven't been put through a series of wardrobe changes. Secondly, the atmosphere is so incredibly laid back, I felt comfortable enough to stay in the shorts and Blades hoodie combo that Bar Down insisted that we keep as a gift. Weston's X-L set is currently folded in a neat little pile in his car, and he's back in his street clothes.

Tucking one ankle behind the other, I curl into West's side. Without missing a beat, he lowers his arm around my shoulders, silently encouraging me to snuggle closer. I'm so exhausted from Jenna poking and prodding us during our interview that I don't even think about how couple-y West and I must look until Gwen shoots me a subtle thumbs up.

For the sake of the cause, I sink deeper into his side.

I'm altruistic like that.

"All right. Let's get started. If you need to me to stop the recording for any reason, let me know. Otherwise, on the count of three . . ." Murphy makes a comedic show of inching his finger toward his phone. "Three, two, one—welcome to *Athletica,* Mr. and Mrs. Cain, it's fantastic to have you both here with us today."

The deep pitch of West's voice rumbles through me as he murmurs, "Happy to be here, Brian."

Murphy nods his approval. "I've got to ask, what is it like to be married to the coach's daughter?"

"About the same as being best friends with the coach's daughter," West answers dryly, "except for the fact that I'm somehow shown even less favoritism. Let's just say that Coach Hall likes to see me sweat."

"I can believe it. We see a lot of guys dating their team-mates' sisters, friends, cousins, that sort of thing—but marrying the coach's daughter? Some might say that you have a death wish."

Feeling West stiffen against me, I place my hand on his leg in warning. "Dad has a scary reputation in the league, but he cares about me, and he definitely cares about his players." I lift my shoulder in what I hope comes across as a careless shrug. "He's happy to support us." Probably happier than most would think considering that he helped orchestrate this entire marriage.

I don't say that part, though. For obvious reasons.

Murphy's pen slashes across a blank page in his note-book. "Daisy, despite your fall from grace years ago, you're no stranger to the life of an elite athlete. Do you think that your career in figure skating prepared you for marriage to a pro hockey player?"

Beneath my hand, West's thigh turns to stone. "That's not—"

"I knew West before he was a pro hockey player," I cut in smoothly before he can say something off the cuff and get us in trouble. "At home, he's not some superstar athlete —he's just a regular guy who makes sure that I'm always fed before I get hangry."

Murphy doesn't take the bait. "Regular guy?" He huffs out a laugh. "Weston, didn't I read somewhere that you attended Northwood in Lake Placid?"

Wait, what?

I jerk my gaze away from *Athletica*'s editor to stare at Weston's familiar profile. He attended *Northwood?* As in, one of the country's top prep schools? Tuition alone is over fifty thousand bucks a year, and their hockey program is notorious for pumping out NHL prospects. Truthfully, I can totally see West training at the Olympic Center as gangly teenager, but I thought he went to school in Hartford . . .

Jaw tight, West clips out, "I was only at Northwood for my freshman year."

Murphy's pen goes back to work scribbling in his note-book. "Couldn't hack it?"

"My parents wanted me closer to home."

"Your mother is the one who attempted to anonymously contact Sports 24/7 last month, wasn't she? Something about quitting hockey to join the family business?"

"Brian," Gwen murmurs with a tightly lipped smile, "stay on topic, please."

"Sure, yeah, no problem. We'll leave that one alone, then." Murphy's hazel eyes dart to his notebook before fixing unerringly on my face. "Daisy, you've mostly stayed out of the limelight since retiring from figure skating, but we've recently learned that you're the mastermind behind the now defunct account, *Confessions of a Puck Bunny.*

Would you say that your marriage to Weston is a convenient match to avoid online backlash—"

Gwen moves so fast, I almost don't register that she's left her chair until she's already ended the recording on Murphy's phone. With one hand planted on his desk and the other coming *this* close to jabbing him in the nose, she hisses, "I don't know what game you're playing, but these questions are not on the pre-approved list."

Athletica's editor merely leans back in his chair. "You know how it goes, Gwen—sometimes we throw in a little something extra just to see how it plays out."

"This interview is about their *wedding*."

"And it is," Murphy drawls. "But see, there's also this thing called journalistic integrity. Long-time friends decide to finally get hitched two weeks after a scandal breaks loose? Cut me some slack here. I'm curious. Fans are curious. You're telling me that *you* aren't curious, too? Unless, of course, you're in on the scheme."

"Are you *kidding* me right now?"

"Gwen, it's okay."

Her red hair sweeps over one shoulder as she turns to stare blankly at West. "What?"

"Sit down. Please." Every muscle in his body is coiled tight with tension—I can practically feel him vibrating against me—but his tone is deceptively easygoing. And when he smiles, there's no indication that he's really fucking pissed off. His eyes are hard, though. As frigid as the ice he plays on. "We don't mind you asking questions about the wedding. Right, sweetheart?"

"Sure." My own smile is all teeth. Meanwhile, I'm digging my nails into Weston's thigh hard enough to draw blood. "Do you want to hear about the legalities of changing a surname? Because I can tell you right now, it's a total pain in the butt."

"Speaking of surnames . . ." Hazel eyes flick between

me and West. Just as he taps his phone screen to start a new recording, he asks, "I had the chance to speak with Alice Hall today. Your mother, Daisy, am I right?"

Like I've been caught in a predator's sights, the hair on my nape stands on end, and I go utterly still.

Murphy continues, unfazed. "She mentioned receiving an invitation for the wedding, but one glance at her socials reveals that she was in Maui at the time?" He glances down to comb through his notes. "Apologies, she was actually in Lanai. My question to you is—do you suppose there's some sort of psychological correlation between your fractured relationship with your mother and your bid to remain anonymous behind the faceless logo of *Confessions of a Puck Bunny*?"

I open my mouth to speak but nothing comes out.

Not a word.

Not a sound.

Brian Murphy's upper lip curls. "Your mother was shocked to learn about your secret identity. She seemed relatively disappointed by the news."

Disappointed?

In a flurry of movement, I launch to my feet, almost tripping over West in my haste to stand. I've stayed professional for weeks now—in quitting my job, while accommodating the Blades, even in this sham of an interview—but there is absolutely nothing professional or dignified about the way that I run from *Athletica's* offices.

I run like I'm scared.

I run like I'm angry.

I don't stop running until I'm outside on the sidewalk, dragging the cold, October air into my screaming lungs.

A pedestrian catches sight of me and makes a quick beeline across the street. I don't even blame her. I'm a volatile, trembling mess as I tear my purse from my shoulder and fumble around for my phone. The irony is that I don't even have my mom's number anymore. I deleted it years ago when she never bothered to visit me in the hospital.

But Dad never got rid of her number.

He calls her like a pathetic, lovesick teenager every few months, praying for scraps of attention, hoping that one day she'll come back around. As I wait for him to pick up the phone, I summon every bit of hurt and rage from my bleeding heart so I can unleash all of it on him as soon as he answers.

Only, he doesn't.

Answer the phone, that is.

I call again.

No answer.

I call *again*.

Nada. Zilch. Nothing.

On my third attempt, he sends me straight to voicemail. And the real kicker is? The stupid fucking thing is *full*.

I want to scream at the top of my lungs or kick something or just—just—

Gwen appears before me, her blue eyes heartbreakingly somber in her drawn face. "Hey," she says gently.

How embarrassing.

"Shit, hi. I'm sorry." Using the sleeve of Bar Down's Blades hoodie, I wipe at my wet eyes. "I didn't mean to run out of there." A borderline hysterical laugh scratches at my throat. "Granted, it wasn't really a conscious decision, either. It just sort of . . . happened."

"It's okay." Catching me totally by surprise, Gwen steps close and uses her own sleeve to dry my tears. I'm pretty sure that she's wearing cashmere, and I'm pretty sure it's now stained with mascara, but she doesn't seem to care. "You had every right to get yourself out of there. I'm—" Her lips press into a thin line. "I've worked with Brian on and off for years, and I've never seen him pull a stunt like that."

Weakly, I tease, "I clearly bring out the best in people."

"You don't need to apologize—you didn't do anything wrong. Trust me, my boss will be having a meeting with Murphy ASAP." Belatedly, she tacks on, "If there's anything left after West is done with him, that is."

Remembering what happened with Douglas North, my stomach lurches uneasily. "I don't think leaving him up there alone with Murphy is a good idea. He's, um, a little protective of me." Understatement of the year. He broke North's nose. I saw the medical reports after New York released them.

Gwen lets her hands fall to her sides. "West said that he's only going to talk."

"With his fists, maybe."

"Have a little more faith in me than that, Hall." The woodsy scent of his body wash envelops me a second before his arms do. Without a word, he tugs me back into a hug that I instantly welcome. Over the top of my head, he says to Gwen, "That was fucking bullshit up there."

Wincing, she fidgets restlessly with her wedding band. "I'm really sorry. Trust me, I feel awful about—"

"This isn't on you, Gwen," West cuts in. "We went over the questions he emailed you. He went off-script and that's not your fault. But if Murphy is taking shots on whether or not we're in this for real, we probably need to consider the fact that fans are questioning everything too."

"Which would put us back at square one," I mutter grimly.

Is that why Dad didn't pick up the phone when I called? Have the Blades benched him, so to speak, and now he's taking his frustrations out on me? It wouldn't be fair, but then again, we're all stuck in this rapidly sinking ship because I made an anonymous account that's no longer anonymous. Whoever hacked me can honestly get fucked.

"Can we call it quits for tonight?" I ask, feeling the weight of exhaustion tugging me down. "Pick it all up tomorrow again?"

Gwen cracks a tiny smile. "Call me. We'll do brunch, okay?"

"On a weekday, too." I try to answer her smile with one of my own. I'm not sure that I succeed, though. "Daisy the Accountant would never."

"That's the spirit," she says before pulling me out of Weston's arms for a quick hug. "Text me when you guys get home."

Home.

As in, Weston's house in Winthrop.

"We will," I tell her. "Say hi to Marshall for us."

Neither West or I move from that spot on the sidewalk until we watch Gwen safely get in her car. Only then does he reach down to hold my hand. "Home?" he asks softly.

"Home," I whisper back.

CHAPTER 19

DAISY

By the time I shower off the day and change into a pair of comfy pajamas, it's past eleven. If I still had my accounting job, I would have been in bed hours ago for an early wakeup call, but being jobless does have its perks—as in, if I want to eat my feelings in the middle of the night, there's no one around to stop me.

The floorboards creak under my feet as I pause outside West's bedroom. His door is closed and the thin strip of space between it and the hardwood floor is completely dark. He must be in bed already.

I swallow my disappointment and head for the stairs.

Living with West has come with its own set of adjustments. Mainly, my new husband thinks nothing of strutting around the house without a shirt on. I mean, he doesn't even bother with putting one on when he's whipping something up in the kitchen. It's a serious health hazard— to his perfect body and to my own sanity.

Downstairs, the living room is drenched in creepy shadows. I flip on every switch that I come across. By the time I get to the dining room, almost the entirety of the first floor is beaming with light. Then I step into the kitchen, fumble for the switch on the wall, and let out a bloodcurdling scream when a gray streak moves directly in front of me.

West doesn't scream but he for sure jumps a foot in the air.

"Fuck, Daisy," he growls, gripping my biceps, "what is wrong with you?"

"I thought you were in bed!"

"I texted you an hour ago to say that I was heading out."

"Oh." Sheepishly, I readjust my glasses from where they slipped down my nose. "I might have—maybe—buried my phone in my underwear drawer so I'm not tempted to keep checking if Brian Murphy has decided to put us on blast. He hasn't, by the way. Not yet at least." I tip my head back to look up at West. "Where'd you go?"

With a small sigh, he steps aside and waves a hand at his kitchen island. "Made a run for you."

It's like Christmas morning exploded in the form of all my favorite snacks. There are bags of Cape Cod chips, M&M cookies approximately the size of my face, and boxes upon boxes of SweetTarts. Awed, I whisper, "Did you clear out every corner store in a five-mile radius just for me?"

West snorts. "Well, I didn't do it for me."

"But you'll have a cookie with me?" I follow him deeper into the kitchen. "It's practically tradition."

"It's not a tradition if we haven't done it in years. Like, since college."

As I drop onto one of the bar stools, I am not above batting my lashes at him. "*Please*? One cookie, West. A bite. A nibble. A crumb, even."

He rolls his eyes. "You can be such a brat, you know that?"

"I am clearly in my feelings right now. Here I was, planning a nighttime excursion to snack on some of that Laughing Cow cheese that you always forget is in your fridge, but I ask you this—why eat alone when my favorite person on the planet can keep me company instead?"

"Maybe because it's almost midnight." Despite his grumbling, he claims the stool opposite mine. "And unlike someone else I know, I've got practice bright and early tomorrow morning."

"Hey, no need to rub my temporary retirement in my face, thanks." Popping open the plastic container housing the M&M cookies, I select the best looking one out of the bunch and silently—but with loads of eye contact—slide it toward Weston. "For the sake of tradition."

True to what he said, it's been years since we last had a late-night session like this—easily since our college days— but there's something kind of wonderful about pushing all of Weston's buttons while he reluctantly accepts the chosen cookie. It's easily the size of his hand. Instead of taking a massive bite, he breaks off what probably amounts to a few crumbs and pops them into his mouth. With a low moan, his eyes slide shut in appreciation.

Ducking my head, I hide a smile behind my hair. "You really didn't have to do all of this."

"I wanted to," he utters without hesitation. "Today was kinda shit. That stuff Murphy said about your mom—"

"Yeah." Inelegantly, I tear open the closest bag of chips only to set it down when my attention veers back toward West. "Well, what about Northwood? I had no idea you went there for a year."

He lowers his gaze. "I begged my parents to let me go when recruiters started coming around. I was the only one in my grade getting scouted at that point, and it did crazy things for my self-confidence. Not that it mattered in the end. Mom and Dad pulled me out of Northwood before the season was even fully wrapped."

"I'm so sorry."

"Nah, don't be. It all worked out. As Fate would have it, I ended up at UConn a few years later and met this girl."

I preen. "I hear she's very kind, very respectable."

Ignoring my sass, West finishes, "She can be a real menace, sometimes, but I'd be lost without her."

"Wow, so sweet."

That sensual mouth of his curves wickedly. "I thought so when we kissed."

"Oh my God, you did *not* just say that." Except that he totally did, the jerk, and his mossy green eyes are still glittering with humor when he carefully breaks off another tiny section of his cookie. From beneath his dark blond lashes, he watches me closely. Almost in unison, we speak at the same time:

"I was thinking while I was out—"

"In the shower, I couldn't help—"

We break into awkward laughter, urging the other one on with a wave, until finally, I give in first. "He was right," I admit begrudgingly. "Murphy, I mean. Getting married out of the blue like we did *is* pretty suspicious."

West dips his chin in agreement. "Yeah, it kinda is."

"I'm not really sure if there's a solution. I'll be—can I be honest with you?"

Sensing a serious turn in the conversation, his voice deepens to a husky pitch when he vows, "Always, sweetheart."

There he goes dropping that endearment again.

I like it. I like it so much that it takes every ounce of self-control to streamline my suddenly chaotic thoughts into something hopefully more coherent. I push my glasses back into place. "I don't really care what anyone has to say about me online. I know how that sounds—no, stop. Come on, West, don't make that face. I'm being serious!"

"And I'm being serious when I say that no one gets to talk shit about you." When he drops his elbows to the island and leans forward, the fabric of his sweatshirt strains across his broad chest. "They don't get to make you feel bad about yourself, Daisy. No one does—not Brian Murphy, not your dad, and definitely not some random stranger on the fucking internet."

"Brian Murphy doesn't matter to me."

"Good. He shouldn't," West mutters grumpily, this time tearing off a whole chunk from the cookie he's still eating. He offers the piece to me between his forefinger and thumb. "Here."

Issuing a quick thanks, I pluck the baked treat from his fingertips and take a small bite. "What did you say? When you stayed behind, I mean?"

"It's more about what I made him do."

My brows lift. "Should I be calling a lawyer?"

"No. Just made sure that he deleted every trace of our visit from his records. Didn't want him getting any bright ideas."

"Oh. That's not too bad—"

"And I told him that if he ever makes my wife cry again, I'll shove my hockey stick so far up his ass, he'll be coughing up splinters for weeks."

I open my mouth.

Clamp it shut.

Okay, so, violence is never the answer but tell that to the swarm of butterflies taking up residence in my stomach. I polish off the M&M cookie, seeking to replace the emotional rush from West's declaration with an artificial sugar high. Both are bad for my health, but here I am, swept right off my feet by my temporary husband whom I've only kissed once.

God, I have it so bad for him.

I clear my throat. "What were you going to say? Before, I mean."

West passes me the rest of his cookie. "We need a more

hands-on approach." I'm not sure what my face says in response to that, but he forges on with renewed determination, his dark blond hair slipping into his eyes. "Think about it. Right now, we're surfacing every few weeks with some big new headline. Hey, we're married. Oh, look, here's this interview we did. It all feels contrived."

"PR sort of *is* contrived?"

"Exactly." Slipping his fingers into his hair, West pushes the strands back from his face. "But Murphy went off-script, didn't he? And it worked for him because it caught us by surprise. Like the opposing team making a break-away when you're still thinking your slap shot made it between the pipes. What if we take Murphy's approach?"

Smoke and mirrors.

The more I turn the idea over in my head, the more it makes sense. "Giving fans content around the clock could work," I muse out loud. "On the other hand, giving them, well, more of *me* might blow up in our faces. There's no way to tell how it'll play out until we're monitoring the comment section and analyzing the data." Popping the last bite of the M&M cookie into my mouth, I shamelessly lick the crumbs from my fingers. "Lucky for us, that was always one of my favorite parts about *Confessions of a Puck Bunny*. Nothing makes me nerd out faster than a breakdown session with numbers and some wine—West. Hey, Earth to West, are you even listening?"

His cheeks are flushed.

His cheeks are flushed and he's *staring at my mouth*.

My heart starts beating in double-time. No, triple. Actually, I might be having a heart attack.

Instinctively, I dart my tongue out to delicately trace the seam of my lips, seeking any last remaining crumbs. I don't do it to torment him—then again, besides our one and only kiss, when has West ever seemed particularly tormented by my proximity? Literally never—but his expression shutters with some inexplicable emotion that I can't quite put my finger on, and then he shocks me completely by rasping, "We need an amendment."

"To our rules?"

Though his gaze flits away, his chin jerks in an almost imperceptible nod. "If we want to be believed then we need to be convincing. Daily content from the Cain household."

Faintly, I hear myself say, "We don't need to amend the rules for that."

It's a blatant taunt, a chance to see what he might do—

West doesn't disappoint.

He reaches into his sweatshirt pocket for his cell, which he sets down on the island halfway between us. I stare at the phone. He stares at me. "We don't have an end date," he says gruffly, "that rule doesn't change. But unless we want people prying into every corner of our lives the way Murphy did, we need to give them more than what they've been getting."

"Like kissing after a game or something?"

Green eyes flit down to my mouth before being wrenched away. "Yes."

Pushing my luck, I ask, "Or a kiss shared over some late-night snacks?"

Maybe it's all in my head, but I swear West shivers.

I have no idea what's going on right now—are we flirting? Is *he* flirting? I wouldn't know. In all the years that we've been friends, I've never actually seen West hook up with someone. When he first signed with the Blades, there were a few late-night texts where he mentioned talking to girls with his teammates, but those pick-ups never seemed to last long, and West always made it a point to stress how happy he was to get back to his hotel room and call me.

I'm not sure what changed. I'm not sure if anything *has* changed. There's a very good chance that all he wants is to keep the heat off my back as Bunny, and he's willing to sacrifice his own lips for the sake of the cause.

I glance at his phone again.

From somewhere deep, I pluck out a thread of courage. "Truth or dare."

His answer comes on a swift, ragged breath: "Dare."

Here goes nothing.

Baby steps.

"I dare you to kiss my cheek on camera."

CHAPTER 20
WESTON

The picture of me kissing Daisy's cheek goes viral. Within twenty-four hours, it has more comments than the photo we shared from our unofficial wedding reception at The Box. Within forty-eight, it's trending on more than one social media platform. And within seventy-two, well, the trolls start to creep in through the woodwork, but I barely notice their existence—especially now that I don't need to open Instagram anymore just to look at the picture.

Yesterday, I set it as the wallpaper on my phone.

As the team's private jet inches closer to the clouds, I find myself staring down at our happy faces squeezed into the narrow frame. Thanks to the way I angled the phone, you can see that the kitchen island is littered with all of Daisy's favorite snacks—but the focus remains on her, on me, on the way her eyes are squeezed shut in laughter from my attempt to feed her an M&M cookie while pressing a soft, gentle kiss to her cheek. It's silly and awkward—not to mention the fact that the camera's flash isn't doing us any favors—but Daisy said to trust her, and fuck it if she doesn't have the Midas touch.

It worked all right. Maybe too well.

At last count, we've received over a thousand new interview requests. The number, frankly, is staggering. Even Gwen is having trouble keeping up, and she's started forwarding us only the ones that she thinks are viable contenders. After our run in with Murphy at *Athletica*, though, I'm wary of anyone looking to do a Tell All on me and Daisy. I'd be more than happy to never do another one again.

With one last look at Daisy's smiling face, I shove my phone into my pocket so I can ignore the rest of my notifications until we land in Toronto.

A few of the guys are taking the opportunity to get more shut eye but some are still up, including Beaumont and the rookie, who I'm pretty sure are fighting over an alleged "illegal" Battleship move a few rows back from me. Leaning into the aisle, I cast my gaze past where Hunt is sprawled out toward the middle of the plane.

"Just get it done," I mutter under my breath.

I wait for Matt, our resident flight attendant and sarcasm king, to give us the thumbs up that we can move about the cabin, and then I'm pushing to my feet and angling my too-big frame down the narrow aisle. If I wait any longer, there's a pretty good chance that I'll talk myself out of it. I already know that this isn't going to be a fun conversation.

I ruffle Carter's hair as I pass him, nod good morning to our equipment manager, and then pause beside the man camped out in the very first row. "Hey, Coach, you got a sec?"

Sam Hall looks like he hasn't slept in weeks.

"Sure." Plucking his reading glasses from his face, he tucks them into his shirt pocket. "Yeah, of course, kid. Here, just let me—" With a tired groan, he hoists himself up, shuffles over, and drops into the window seat, leaving the middle one empty.

That works for me.

Lowering down into Coach's vacated seat, I'm suddenly grateful that the Blades GM always opts for us to fly private—the extra leg room makes it feasible for me to angle myself so I'm not spilling out into the aisle or, worse, eating my kneecaps for breakfast.

Coach's blue eyes are weary when I meet them. "What's up, kid? Your hip feeling all right?"

"Yeah, the hip is fine." *Just gotta rip it off like a Band-Aid, that's all.* After taking a deep breath, I bite the proverbial bullet: "It's about Daisy."

In close quarters like these, there's nowhere to hide, which means that I'm privy to Coach looking vaguely nauseous. Shit. That does not bode well. I bite the inside of my cheek, fully intending to wait him out, but as the seconds tick by, I find it increasingly harder to sit still and keep quiet.

Fuck it.

"We both know that I'm decimating every professional boundary there is right now," I utter in a low, careful voice to avoid being overheard by other the coaching staff seated directly behind us. "And trust me, I'm fully aware that it's in my best interest to keep my mouth shut. I love playing for the Blades. Hell, I love playing for you, too, Coach, but you gotta know—I mean, really, you *have* to know how much your silence is killing her, don't you?"

I'm not sure what to expect, honestly. Maybe an apology for dropping the ball where his daughter is concerned, or at least some sort of visual cue that his hands are tied and he's doing all he can with the limited resources at his disposal. But aside from scrubbing his hand across his mouth—a nervous habit that he picked up years ago—Sam Hall doesn't give me much to work with.

That's fine, though. I came prepared with a Plan B.

"Is something else going on?" Dropping my shoulders, I speak urgently into the empty space between us. "I get that there's probably a lot that you can't tell me, but if there's anything we can do to make sure that Daisy is—"

"Do you know the first thought that I had when I met you?" The abrupt subject change catches me off guard, but the question must be largely rhetorical because Coach doesn't wait for me to fumble my way around to an answer. "I thought you were too nice to be a D-man."

I'm . . . not sure that's a compliment—to anyone, actually.

Coach pins me with an inscrutable stare. "You can be a real bastard on the ice when you want to be, Cain, but you still have the softest fucking heart out of everyone I know—including my daughter." As if feeling the weight of exhaustion, he tips his head back against the closed window shade. "One of these days, you're going to wish that you'd hardened it some."

The comment sounds like an echo chamber of every insult my dad has ever flung my way, and I feel my bones stiffen with the need to defend myself—but this conversation isn't about me. It's about Daisy. His daughter. My best friend. My *wife*. And I can't deny that my tone gets real damn sharp when I bite out, "That's all you have to say? Really?"

"No, it's not."

Frustrated, I drag my fingers through my hair. "You know what? I'm done with the mind games. Just say what you mean or—"

"You're going to *wish* that you'd hardened your heart," Coach says plainly, "but I hope to God you never do, kid. I hope you stay exactly how you are, how you've always been—a good soul with a heart of gold."

Just like that, the fight drains right out of me.

"Coach, you're speaking in riddles and that's never—that's not my strong suit." Feeling flustered, and confused, I shake my head. "I don't understand what the hell is going on."

"My little girl is the strongest person I know." Cutting eye contact, Hall reaches for his laptop from the seat back pocket and props it open. With his head lowered, he adds, "And I need her to be strong for just a little longer. Can you tell her that?"

Emotion lodges in my throat like a boulder. "She thinks that you've abandoned her."

"She's not that lucky, unfortunately."

"Coach—"

"You're good for each other, you and Daisy. I've always thought so." Blue eyes flick toward me and then just as quickly dart away. "Now if you don't mind, kid, I've got to get some work done."

"Yeah, sure. No problem."

But as I make my way back to my seat, I can't help but feel like the entirety of that conversation just went over my head.

WE LOSE to Toronto that night.

And then we lose to Calgary, Ottawa, and St. Louis in one fell swoop, too.

CHAPTER 21

DAISY

Who is Daisy Daisy-belle Cain?

"Well," I mutter to myself as I mindlessly scroll through a series of job listings, "she does not enjoy retirement, that's for sure."

No wonder Arthur Phister would rather croak at his desk than deal with the alternative—aimlessly wandering around for days on end with no direction and absolutely zero motivation to do, well, just about anything.

Ugh.

"Maybe you all need a step-pet—a foster friend? Whatever." I turn my head to direct the question at the lineup of potted plants bathing in the late afternoon sun on West's kitchen counter. "What do you all think about that? Comments? Concerns? I'm all branches."

Not even a leaf tremor.

"Wow, tough crowd." Then again, the fact that I'm having a full-blown conversation with my neighbor's plants probably says it all. I highly doubt Anita imagined this particular scenario playing out when she called yesterday to ask if I could lend a hand while she's out of town for the next few weeks.

It does feel kind of nice to not be alone in Weston's house, though.

Sighing, I close down my laptop and hop off the bar stool.

The problem with job hunting is that I don't actually have any sense of direction right now. The prospect of returning to another accounting firm is unappealing. Thanks to managing Bunny's accounts over the last five years, I could probably net myself at least an entry-level marketing position somewhere, but every time I stop to think about working my butt off to grow someone else's online presence, it feels like I'm withering away inside.

"No pun intended," I mutter to the plants, who are, most definitely, *not* withering in any capacity.

I may lack whatever chef DNA turns mere mortals into cooking sensations, but I've always felt the nurturing bug in other ways, which is probably why I miss *Confessions of a Puck Bunny* so much. It was a community. One with roots that stretched far and wide. And now it's just me and whatever punishment inevitably gets doled out to me by the big wigs.

On silent feet, I make my way into the living room and collapse on the couch. West won't be back from his week-long road trip until tonight, and if the Blades' losing streak is anything to go by, he's not going to be a happy camper when he does.

In the past when he's lost a game, I've always been a phone call away. For the first time since college, I'll be in the same house with him. The realization sends awareness zipping down my spine. It feels . . . momentous. Important that he knows how deeply I care, and that I'm here for him, whatever he needs.

Before I can talk myself out of it, I grab my keys, put on a jacket, and walk out the door.

MY PHONE PINGS with a notification while I'm standing in line at Dunkins an hour later.

Almost immediately, my stomach starts to roll with unease.

Unsolicited messages with West out of town can mean a wide variety of things, but of course my brain decides to fixate on the worst possible scenario. It's like choosing to drink milk close to the expiration date. Has it gone bad? Not according to the date stamped on the jug. But then, is that lingering smell just my brain pranking me or is the milk actually sour?

Receiving a text or call from an unknown number isn't all that different except that it's socially irresponsible to drop it in the trash.

As the checkout line continues to move forward, I force myself to look at my phone—the notification winking back at me is an email with the subject line: HI THERE BUNNY.

Tell me why that could be either a threat or the title of a children's book.

"Next, please."

Lowering my phone, I step up to the counter to place my order. "Medium sweet cream cold brew, please, and two donuts. Chocolate and apple cider. Also, say you got an email with the subject line *Hi There Bunny* in all caps. What do you think—serial killer vibes or the next Eric Carle?"

The teenage girl behind the cash register smacks her gum. "Wasn't he the one who wrote that kid's book? *The Very Hungry Caterpillar* or whatever?"

"Yup."

"Dunno, could go either way, I guess. *The Very Hungry Bunny*." While I pay, she dumps my donuts into a white paper bag along with a few napkins. "And then, like, everyone gets murdered at the end."

Sounds like I'm not the only one with intrusive thoughts.

I take my coffee and donuts from the counter. "Good point. I'll think on it some more." I've barely moved aside before she's shouting, "Next!" at the customer behind me, so I pick up the pace and get out of the way.

The world beyond the storefront window is gray and rainy. In another month, it'll be cold enough to snow, but early November is always hit or miss, so I draw my jacket tightly around me and step out onto the sidewalk. I have one last stop before I can head back to West's house, but as I pile into my car and crank the heat, I can't help but think about the email. *The Very Hungry Bunny* one.

"Fuck it."

With a sip of coffee for fortification, I grab my phone from my bag and click through to the email. My hands are a little sweaty from nerves and the heat from the car is rapidly thawing out my cold nose. I glance quickly in the rearview mirror to make sure that no one is waiting for this parking spot, and then settle in to read—or rather, I decide to spoil the ending first by checking out the signature at the bottom of the message.

Amber Conners.

Oh.

I suddenly feel very overheated. Overwhelmed. Over-everything.

Tearing off my jacket, I toss it on the passenger seat besides my Dunkins order. Only, the upward tilt of my hips has my phone slipping right off my lap to land down near my feet. With a curse, I duck and contort myself around the steering wheel to awkwardly fumble around for it. By the time I'm rightly seated again, I'm sweating.

It's fine. I mean, it's not every day your real life and secret one collide, but it's *fine*.

I open the email and read:

Hi there Bunny—or should I say Daisy?

It's funny to think of you having a face. I know that's weird. Like, OBVIOUSLY you have a face. Obviously, the person who consoled me and made me feel like not all hope was lost <u>would</u> have a face.

But for some reason, it feels weird.

It's weird to know that you're in your twenties.

It's weird to know that you have blonde hair, and that you retired from figure skating the same year that I met Joe. It's weird to know that every time we DMed, I always found myself thinking after how you felt so familiar—so I guess that makes it not weird at all since we've actually met in real life. I mean, it was just one time, and only in passing, but still, I know you.

I don't know if this means anything, but I'm glad to know you, Daisy Hall (or is it Cain now?). I'm writing this email from my office, in the house that I live in on my own, with not a single worry besides what to eat for dinner.

(And wondering whether M&M cookies are a sufficient choice.)

Anyway, I hope you don't mind me reaching out. I could have gotten your number from the WAGs—the hockey world is way too small sometimes—but I thought it might be more appropriate to reach out to you the way that I first did—

Through words.

I'm going to leave my phone number here for you. If you ever want to talk, just give me a call.

Love,

Amber

Before I lose my nerve, I call her.

Maybe I shouldn't. Maybe including her number was

just a friendly courtesy. People do that all the time—they say what they don't mean and offer things while having no intention to ever follow through. But for the first time since everything went to shit, I've been offered a bridge back to Bunny instead of being handed an axe to cut her down. I'm strong enough to admit when I'm weak, and I'm weak enough to be honest, at least with myself: Amber Conners reaching out to me feels like I've been given a lifeline.

With my heart in my throat, I wait for her to pick up. Finally, on the third ring, the dial tone clicks, and a vibrantly cheerful voice says, "Hello?"

"Hi. It's Daisy." Wait. *What if she knows multiple Daisy's?* In a rush, I add, "Daisy Hall, I mean. Or Daisy Cain. Technically we're just waiting on paperwork, which hopefully won't be too much longer but who really knows, honestly. I swear dealing with the government is like existing in purgatory—you know that you'll get out at some point, but you may die a thousand deaths before that day finally comes."

The other end of the line is so quiet, I can hear rain pinging off the hood of my car.

With a mortified groan, I drop my forehead onto the steering wheel. Talking online is so much easier. Nothing says true, everlasting friendship like editing everything you say before you hit send.

"Sorry," I mumble when the silence starts to feel like a crime scene, "I bet you're wishing that I came with a muzzle."

And then she laughs.

Laughs.

Soon, I'm laughing, too, practically bent over the steering wheel with my hand pressed to my mouth, wheezing, "I'm sorry. I panicked and then I couldn't shut up."

"I literally can't believe I thought you were old enough to be my grandma."

That sets us off all over again.

"Your *grandma?*" When I tell West, he'll never let me live this down. "What made you think that?"

"Your emoji usage was questionable," Amber says between giggles, "and you used so many literary references in your posts that I constantly had Google pulled up to figure out what the hell you were talking about."

"First, emojis are the bane of my existence. Like, is it two people hugging or is it a video camera? Nobody knows. And hello, nice to meet you. My name is Daisy, and I'm obsessed with books so complex that they give you migraines."

"Wine achieves the same results."

"Oh, I love wine, too."

"So, you *are* human, then."

Even though she can't see me, I press my fingers to my pulse. "Still human, still kicking. I can't say that I'm thriving but, you know, there's always room for improvement."

"You just married your best friend, didn't you? Sounds like thriving to me."

Slowly but surely, reality creeps back in.

My fake marriage to West. The lies we've told and will continue to tell. None of it should make me feel bad when it wasn't even my idea, but guilt still writhes like a snake in my gut.

If Amber notices the shift in my mood, she doesn't call me out on it. "And here I thought you hated all hockey players," she teases when I'm too lost in my own head to keep the conversation flowing naturally. "But I guess that's not the case if you've married one."

"I don't hate hockey players."

"But it's not like you started an account called *Confessions of a Cleat Chaser*." She doesn't sound angry, just curious. "It's always been about hockey, even from the beginning."

Slumping back in my seat, I stare at the car parked in front of me. The rain is coming down harder now and steam is gathering on my windows.

I'm at a crossroads—I could lie some more. Really just dig my feet in, bury my head in the sand, and say whatever it takes to divert the conversation back to Amber. Or I could reveal a fragment of the truth. *And risk her thinking the worst of you.* Which wouldn't be the worst thing ever, I guess, because there's nothing that she can say about me that I haven't already said about myself.

"Daisy?" she prompts softly. "You still there?"

As if it belongs to someone else, I stare at my finger as it traces the raised logo on my steering wheel. "There was this guy . . . when I was younger, I mean."

"How old were you?"

"Sixteen? Seventeen?"

"And how old was he?"

I drop my hand into my lap and curl it into a tight ball. "Older. Late-twenties, I think. Maybe early thirties."

Amber falls silent, and I choke down my embarrassment long enough to hear her whisper, "Okay. Keep going. So, he was older?"

"Yeah. He, uh, worked with my dad at one point. When I was in high school, I mean. Although saying that I was in high school is a bit of a stretch because I was home-schooled, you know, because of how involved I was with figure skating."

She makes a small, encouraging sound. "That makes sense."

"So, I saw him sometimes. Whenever I went to one of my dad's games. He was . . ."

"Nice?"

My nails are biting into the meat of my palm hard

enough to make my skin throb, and I flatten my hand against my thigh. "He was, yeah. Really nice. And I didn't —I didn't think too much of the way he always made a point to mention the figure skating program at the school he'd just taken a coaching job at. College wasn't even on my radar. But then I . . . but then Worlds happened." Restlessly, I pluck at a loose thread in my jeans. "Everything I'd worked for just gone in a second."

"I'm so sorry, Daisy. I can't even imagine."

"You can, though, can't you?" I twirl the loose thread around my finger. It pulls, lengthens. I tug at it even harder. "You gave everything to your marriage with Joe, and then one day, it was done. Years of your life just circled down the drain in a heartbeat."

The other end of the line is quiet. Then, almost introspectively, she murmurs, "I hadn't thought about it like that, but yeah. I know exactly how that feels."

Emotion swells in my throat. The loose thread winds tighter around my finger. "There was a long recovery period. I couldn't walk for ages let alone skate. All my peers . . . I mean, everyone just carried on without me. Which is normal, honestly. Unless you're competing in pairs, it's a very solitary sport. So, I started to think, maybe —maybe college might be an option? I worked really, *really* hard in physical therapy. I wouldn't be good enough for the Olympics again, but I was . . . I was still good, still better than most."

The thread tears from my jeans, leaving a tiny gap in the fabric. I close my eyes. "It wasn't even a conscious thing at that point, but I was working my butt off, and I kept thinking about the figure skating program. Over a year had passed since he last mentioned it to me—since I last saw him, even. And he wasn't . . . he wasn't one of *my* coaches at school—he coached hockey, you know? But he was still really nice whenever our paths ended up crossing on campus, and he was still very encouraging. And I—I liked that, I think. I liked that he didn't make me feel bad about myself because everyone . . . Well, to my own coaches, and everyone else, I was a disappointment."

"Oh, Daisy."

"I know," I whisper roughly, "I know." Lifting my hand, I pinch the bridge of my nose, trying desperately to keep myself in check. "Anyway, yeah. You can probably imagine how it all went down. Stupid, naïve girl gets crush on nice, older guy. I fell for him pretty quickly. I was easy, you know. Like, I'm not even talking sexually, but that, too, I was just . . . *easy*. I believed everything he told me. I ignored every red flag—including the wedding band he wore. He said that him and his wife were separated, headed for divorce, and I was stupid enough to believe it until—"

"Until what?"

"She caught us."

"Oh."

"Yeah." My throat clicks with a dry, audible swallow. "I transferred to UConn right after that." Met *West* right after that. I look down at my wedding ring. The weather is pummeling my car even harder, the sky gone bleak and gray, and yet the diamond sparkling on my finger seems to capture every stray ray of light. "So, that was probably more info than you ever wanted, but to answer your question—I don't hate all hockey players. I don't even hate *most* hockey players. So many of them are good guys, you know? But there are some bad eggs in the bunch, and I guess that I took it upon myself to weed them out."

With my heart thudding loudly in my ears, I wait for Amber to shut me down or call me names—I mean, how am I any different from all the girls that her ex-husband slept with behind her back? They aren't at fault for the lies that Joe fed them, but still, Amber must be harboring *some* sort of resentment, right? It only makes sense that she'd be upset to find out that I'm no better than—

"Daisy, have you . . . I don't know how to ask this so I'm just going to say it, okay?" She takes a deep breath. "Have you ever told anyone this story? Even your dad, I mean, when you transferred schools?"

"No. You're the first."

There's the distinct sound of a couch cushion deflating as if she's sat down heavily. "Do you know who I told first about Joe?"

My brow furrows. "Your parents? A friend?"

"My therapist, Daisy. I told my therapist that I knew he was cheating on me."

"Oh."

"And I'm not going to sit here and tell you that I love therapy because honestly, it can get fucked, like, ninety-nine percent of the time. It's uncomfortable and awkward, and you feel like you want to crawl out of your skin for pretty much the entire session."

I grimace. "That sounds lovely? I guess?"

"It's not. It's really, really not, but it also sort of is." She huffs out a self-deprecating laugh. "My point is, you make it sound like this was some sort of harmless teenage crush when it wasn't—he manipulated you."

"Maybe, but I was also—"

"You were also *what*? Sixteen? Seventeen? *Eighteen?* He was like—like some fucking *creep* in a van, luring you in with sweets, giving you attention when everyone else was shitting on you, and you're surprised that you took the bait? It's called *abuse*, Daisy."

A short, sharp breath gets stuck in my throat. "He never hurt me."

"He put your back against the wall and made you feel like he was the only one who cared enough to listen—he hurt you, Daisy. He's hurt you in so many more ways than you probably even realize, and I want—oh my God, my blood is boiling so hot right now, I could scream."

"Please don't scream."

"I won't. But I could. I really, really want to."

Slowly, awareness falls down upon me. My shoulders are hunched, my knees drawn up as far as they can with the steering wheel in the way. Simply put, I'm as close to being curled up in the fetal position as is possible while stuck in the driver's seat of a car.

I force my feet back down to the floor.

"I'm sorry," I manage to say past my itchy throat. "You didn't expect any of this when I called, and I'm just—"

"I'm not," Amber says shortly. "I'm glad you called. I mean this—you can call me whenever you want. I like that you have a face now."

I choke out a watery laugh. "Thanks."

"I have to go, but I want you to ask yourself this—are you okay? With everything that's happened with *Confessions of a Puck Bunny*, and with everything that came before . . . Are you okay? Don't answer that now. Just think about it."

I feel heavy, emotionally drained. Still, I whisper, "I will. Promise."

"Good."

"Bye, Amber."

I swear that I can hear her smile through the phone when she says, "Bye, Bunny."

CHAPTER 22
WESTON

After coming off a Cup win, I didn't necessarily think that this season would be completely smooth sailing, but I never anticipated ending a roadie with one of our worst losing streaks either.

When it rains it really pours. Literally, in this case. Our flight home was delayed by more than two hours thanks to the weather.

As we circle over Boston, I press my forehead to the window and stare out into the city. Through the dense cloud coverage, I can just make out the Prudential with its top floors lit up with purple lights. In contrast, the harbor down below is pitch-black; if there are any sailboats bobbing in the water tonight, you definitely can't see them. Another plane passes into view and then lowers to descend before us. And somewhere in the midst of all that gloom and doom is home—

Daisy.

Under my balled fist, my knee bounces anxiously as we finally prepare for landing. Beside me, Beaumont is fucking around on his phone; he's been playing Tetris nonstop for the last three legs of the trip. Except that his headphones died last night in St. Louis—fitting, honestly, because so did we—and instead of pawing through his shit to find his charger or, you know, asking to borrow someone else's, he's decided to blast the game's theme song to fuck with everyone's mood.

Our captain may be a reformed bad boy with a kid on the way, but sometimes he's still a raging dick.

In the row in front of us, Kammer tells Alarik, "I'm going to Mickey D's on the way home. No, for real, I'm gonna order everything on the Dollar Menu. Just eat my feelings to the fullest until whenever Andre texts me that I need to leave my condo."

Over the sound of Tetris, Beaumont drawls, "Maybe I'll text you at six in the morning tomorrow."

Kammer's head pops up over the seat to glare down at our captain. "Wow, rude. That'd be a dick move, Cap."

Beaumont doesn't even lift his head from playing his game—though he does let out a long, tired sigh. "Rookie, how you've remained this gullible, for *this* long, is seriously beyond me."

The rookie's brows lower. "So, you aren't going to text me at six in the morning?"

"Let me put it this way." Andre sets his phone down on his thigh. "I'm not waking up on our one day off to call you, text you, or even say hi to you. I'm going to be wrapped around my wife, oblivious to the world, and if any of you fuckers disturb me before noon, I will haunt you for the rest of my life."

Kammer sends me a quick sideways glance before directing his attention back to Beaumont. "To haunt me, you'd have to be dead first."

Swear to God, Beaumont doesn't even blink.

Despite my shit mood, I turn my back on the boys and try to smother a laugh without either of them noticing. In the window's reflection, I watch the rookie lean one forearm against the back of his seat. "So, like, is that an invitation for us to murder you?" he asks with a straight face. "Because normally I'd say tough luck, but you *have* made us listen to that fucking song for the last ten hours straight, and so I volunteer as tribute. I'll kill you and you'll haunt me, and we'll be one big, happy family."

Across the aisle, Hunt audibly chokes, and soon, everyone around us is snickering, too. Except for Beaumont, who really does have a resting bitch face when he's in the right mood. He just blinks up at the rookie, dark eyes slightly narrowed, and growls, "You're a dead fucking man, Josh."

The rookie's expression freezes—

And then he smiles so wide, so brightly, at Andre's use of his first name, it's actually blinding. He plops back down into his seat, chattering excitedly to Alarik.

Beaumont nudges me in the arm. "Think he'll realize that you told me what Daisy said?" he asks in a low voice. "About him being upset that we only ever call him 'rookie'?"

"Nah. He'll never connect the dots."

But even if he does, there's no harm in the rookie realizing that we think of him as one of us—even if giving him shit is our favorite sport. Besides hockey, of course.

By the time I make it home, it's well after midnight.

Disappointment sits heavy in my gut as I quietly shut the front door behind me, careful to make as little noise as possible. The only thing that's kept me going over the last few days has been the anticipation of seeing Daisy, but I'm not about to wake her up from a dead sleep just to—just to *what?* Say goodnight? Go in for a hug? Tell her that we should put up another post online, see if this one catches more steam than the last?

In the middle of my foyer, I slam to a halt and squeeze my eyes shut.

I have no idea what I'm doing. Not with hockey—we'll grind away at it until we're back on the upswing again. I'm talking about with Daisy, my best friend, my *wife*. I don't know what to do with the fact that I can't get the memory of her inked skin out of my head. I don't know how to put into words that knowing she's somewhere in this world, with my ring on her finger, feels so fucking right, it's a wonder that I haven't proposed to her before now.

I don't get why it all feels so different.

And yet, nothing feels different at all.

Because it's still just *us*, isn't it? Just us, as we've always been, but living under one roof. Just us, as we've always been, but holding hands all the time. Just us, as we've always been—but I'm losing my goddamn *mind*.

Groaning, I kick off my shoes and feel my way along in the darkness to the staircase, the strap of my duffel bag slung over one shoulder. The material scratches along the wall, echoing like a high-pitched whine in my ears, and I yank my bag fully behind me with a curse. In the weeks since we've moved in together, I've learned that Daisy is a very light sleeper.

On the second floor, I drop my bag off in the laundry room to deal with tomorrow, and then make my way down the hall. Daisy's bedroom door is closed, the light inside switched off from what I can tell. I hover there a second, torn between knocking lightly and doing the right thing by not waking her up out of pure, selfish need.

I end up sending her a quick text:

> Home safe. Night.

Night? Really, *that's* the best that I can come up with? God, I'm such a loser. Biting down on my lip, I stand in front of Daisy's closed door for another straight minute, wracking my brain for something better—*anything* better— to say. So, we kissed. That doesn't erase almost ten years of friendship. Who cares if my hands are clammy as shit right now? Nobody, that's who.

Refusing to stress anymore about it, I send one last text:

> I know this marriage isn't real, but you are —and coming home from a shitty week, knowing that you're under the same roof as me? It settles something in my chest. Makes it not feel as tight. I'm gonna find a way to let you go one day but for now, I'm just happy that you're here. Sweet dreams, Daisy-belle. See you in the morning.

Warmth burns in my cheeks, but I ignore it, fully, as I head one door down to my own bedroom. Silently, I turn the knob and push the door open, only to come to a full stop at the sight of the woman splayed out on my bed.

Propped up against my pillows, Daisy pulls her gaze away from her phone. She's smiling, her amber eyes lighting up behind her glasses at the sight of me.

I dart a glance to her phone.

Drag it back to her face.

Daisy smiles even harder, creases popping in her cheeks.

"Don't," I warn.

"But—"

"Don't. Please." *Fucking take mercy on me, sweetheart.*

Daisy shuffles forward onto her knees. "But you missed me, West. You just said so." She holds her phone in front of her face, reading out loud: "'I know this marriage isn't real, but you are.' My God, it's poetry."

I want the floor to open up and swallow me whole.

"And here—this is my favorite part." She clears her

throat to mimic the deep tenor of my voice. "'It settles something in my chest. Makes it not feel as tight.'" Eyes crinkling with humor, she presses one hand to her forehead and pretends to swoon right there on my comforter. Pillows fly off the bed and land on the floor. Going full-Shakespeare, she cries, "Be still my heart!"

My cheeks are on fire.

And my dick is actually hard.

I want to die.

"You're a fucking menace," I mutter, choosing to ignore her theatrics because if I don't, well, I don't know what I'll do but I'm pretty sure it will mark the end of our nine-year friendship. "I should smother you with one of the pillows."

"But West, if I'm dead then you can't write me any more poetry." She scrabbles off the bed to follow me into my walk-in closet. "You'd be so sad without me. Look, you said so right here." Because she really is a menace, she proceeds to read more from my text, specifically highlighting the part where I mention how happy I am to be under the same roof as her.

With a pair of shorts and a T-shirt tucked under my arm, I head back to my room. "I take it back. We're divorcing tomorrow."

"You can't do that."

"Watch me, Hall."

"Cain."

My heart thrashes wildly against my rib cage as I turn to stare down at her. "What?"

"Cain," she says again, chin lifted, shoulders straight, all that defiance not backing down a single inch. "Temporary or not, we're married, aren't we? Which means that you're mine and I'm yours, and that includes me taking your name. Or does it only count when I'm wearing your jersey?"

I want it to count all the time, I realize.

I want it to count *always*.

It's in that moment that it really hits me—I want Daisy Daisy-belle Cain. As in, I *want* her in a way that I rarely, if ever, want anyone. I want her smiles, and her laughter, and I want the way she makes me feel seen and heard and cared for. But the fact that I'm hard as a goddamn rock tells me that I want her in other ways too—the chance to see that flower tattoo up close, to watch her slip out of her clothes when it's only the two of us . . .

I crave that level of intimacy because it means having all of Daisy.

And I've been obsessed with her from the start.

"You can have every part of me, sweetheart." My voice sounds like gravel. Every word feels torn from my throat. "And that includes my name."

Her pink lips part on a shaky breath.

I don't always notice social cues—mainly because I don't care to, not these days—but there's no part of my best friend that I don't find endlessly fascinating, which means that I can't stop my pulse from quickening when her gaze touches lightly upon my mouth—the width of my shoulders—the narrow lines of my waist.

Slowly, she drags her gaze back up to my face. Her cheeks are tinged pink with a flush that I feel mirrored in my own. I'm burning up inside. Restless yet frozen in place. If I move—if I so much as *breathe*—the spell will break, and we'll be left scattered in the mess that's left behind.

I want her, and I think . . .

Fuck, I think she wants me, too.

I don't know how long we stand there in silence. Long enough that the empty space between us begins to dwindle away to almost nothing. Long enough that I know I'm gonna kiss her if she doesn't shoot me down. Long enough for me to realize that the sound of running water isn't coming from the rain rushing down the gutters outside but from my bathroom instead.

I tilt my head, listening. "Did you leave the faucet running?"

Daisy blanches. "Oh, shit." And then she's flying over fallen pillows and throwing open the door to my bathroom with me right on her heels.

The first thing I notice is the steam.

The second is that the marble floor is sopping wet.

And the last—there are lit candles everywhere. On the counter. On the windowsill. Even on the bench in the shower. My bathroom has been converted into a scene right out of a spa or an orgy, it's tough to tell which, but then I spot the comic books stacked neatly on top of the bath towels that I keep on a shelf beneath the sink, and swear to God, my heart feels like it's going to explode right out of my chest.

Daisy rushes to turn off the tap for the tub. "Crap, I'm sorry. What a mess. We got to talking and I completely forgot—"

"Did you do all of this for me?"

Her head jerks up. When her eyes meet mine, they're soft and appear slightly bewildered behind her glasses, as if she's positive the answer to my question is obvious. And it is—obvious, that is—but I want to hear her say it, anyway.

I take one step toward her. "Well?"

"Yes." She sounds breathless, curious. "Of course, it's for you."

I look at the flickering candles, the comic books, the water splattered across the floor. Down at my sides, my fingers itch to sweep her into my arms and never let her go.

Gruffly, I hear myself ask, "Why?"

Those lips that I've kissed only once tilt upward. "Because I missed you, too, Weston Cain."

CHAPTER 23
DAISY

There is no preparing for a shirtless West.

One second he's prowling toward me with an expression on his face that I've never seen before, and in the next, he's stripping off his shirt and tossing it on the counter. Just like that, I'm rendered speechless by the very sight of him.

It's not even my fault, really.

Candlelight flickers across the breadth of his chest, the hard slab of his stomach. The waistband of his slacks sits low on his lean hips, and with a bitten-off whimper, I watch helplessly as his big hands take hold of his belt.

The metal buckle clinks open. The soft leather slides free.

Pressure builds in my ears as West pushes his slacks down the length of his legs, exposing muscular, hair-sprinkled thighs and strong calves. I've seen him in swim trunks before. In theory, there's not much of a difference between them and the briefs clinging to his hips—only, the latter leaves very little to the imagination, and it's taking every ounce of self-control to keep my attention from drifting south.

He takes a single step toward me. "Truth or dare, Cain."

Cain.

It's surreal to hear him call me by his name instead of Hall. Then again, everything about this moment feels positively dreamlike—like lightning in a bottle. Rain lashes against the windowpane. Steam billows in the air. And West stands before me looking like a god.

I am so stupidly weak for him.

"I-I don't think truth or dare is a good idea."

His green eyes watch me steadily. "Why not?"

"You know why not."

"Tell me, anyway."

"Because we're on a razor's edge here. Because it's the mood, the close proximity. Because you've been gone for a week, and your teammates are right—we're entirely too co-dependent. And obviously—" Wetting my lips, I tip my head back on my shoulders to stare resolutely up at the ceiling. Anything to remove the temptation of dropping to my knees before him. "Obviously, we've let this whole marriage of convenience thing go straight to our heads."

"You know what excuse you didn't use?"

Feebly, I protest, "They aren't excuses."

"You didn't say that you don't want me."

"West—"

"So, go ahead, sweetheart. Say it."

I swallow a frustrated groan, refusing to even glance his way. "Why are you like this?" I slash a hand through the air. "You don't have a filter. Every thought you have comes right out of your mouth like ten seconds later."

"Here I was, thinking that you liked that about me."

"It's maddening. Do you hear me? *Maddening*."

"Oh, I hear you."

A growl crawls its way up my throat but still, I don't peel my gaze off his ceiling. It feels like a matter of life or death. As in, death to our friendship—death to *us*—if I fail.

I am entirely too worked up when I say, "You're using that tone. The one where I know you're laughing at me."

"Do you want me to stop talking? Would that make you feel better?"

"I want to know how you just made the leap from friends to—to whatever *this* is." I gesture between us. "I want to know what you're thinking. Not the off-the-cuff stuff that comes out of your mouth when you're just messing around with me, but what you're really, truly—"

"I want to kiss you again." His deep, whiskey-smooth voice rings out with startling clarity, leaving no room for error in translation. "I liked it. A lot. It caught me by surprise, but it felt right having you in my arms like that. It felt . . . inevitable."

Down by my sides, my fingers shake so hard, I curl them into fists.

"And I think about your—" He cuts off with a sharp breath. Then another, this one slow and measured, through his nose, as if he's gathering his confidence to admit the rest. "Been thinking about that tattoo of yours since we were at Bar Down and you put on that purple dress."

I must be dying.

This must be the Afterlife.

Because there is no way that very kind, very respectable Weston Cain just confessed to watching me undress.

My thoughts are scrambled, desperate to keep up. I think about our kiss, how natural it felt to push onto my toes and make the moment last a little longer. I think about how he didn't pull away, not once, until being physically dragged out of my arms by his brother. I recall that day at Bar Down, how scattered he seemed, his voice gritty like gravel while his anxious gaze landed everywhere but on me.

How long has he felt like this? As long as I've been in love with him? The thought alone is unfathomable.

Adrenaline careens through my veins. I can hear the blood rushing in my ears, I can feel my heart fluttering in my *throat*. And I'm trembling from my fingers all the way down to my toes when I say, "You don't even know if I feel the same."

Lush, dark laughter falls from his lips. "Oh, Cain. Nobody likes a liar."

The sound of water splashing onto the floor has me tearing my gaze away from the ceiling with a breathless gasp. It's not until I spy the quiet mischief glittering in his mossy green eyes, though, that I realize that I've just been played.

He knew that I'd look. He *knew*, and he's—he's—

Perfect.

Hours spent toiling away in the gym and on the ice have carved him from stone. As he grips the sides of the porcelain tub to fold his big body into the oversized bath, he's all raw, powerful muscle. Once seated, he skims the water with the palm of his hand. Sinks all that beautiful skin beneath the surface until water ripples against the column of his throat. From beneath his lashes, he watches me steadily. "Do you know one of the reasons why I've always felt safe with you?"

Struck mute, all I can do is shake my head.

"Because everything you feel is right there on your face. Not with everyone," he murmurs when I try to correct him otherwise, "but with me, Daisy, you never hide."

Except that I've hidden so much from him.

Bunny. About what happened at Dartmouth. *My love for him.*

"You've always made me feel like I don't need to be anyone but who I am," he continues, flaying my heart open wide with his brutal honesty. "I can be vulnerable or petty or so excited about something, I'm barely coherent, and you give me the space to talk out how I feel without passing judgment."

Pressure burns behind my eyelids, and I dig my teeth into my bottom lip.

"I've never had that with anyone else. I can't even imagine—" His eyes slam shut. When they open again, the green of his irises appear brighter, somehow, in the flickering light. "I try to imagine feeling this way about some other person, and I can't. I truly, fucking can't. Because it's not even about sex, it's—" As if he's mirroring me, he bites his lip and tilts his head back against the tub, turning his gaze up to the ceiling. His pulse flutters in his throat. "It's about getting to have every part of you. And that's what I want most—to have you, Daisy-belle. Whatever that means, whatever that looks like, so long as I get to keep feelin' like this, as if you're the reason my heart exists."

In short, hard breaths, I pant, "I hate you."

The air is fraught with tension as he slowly returns his gaze back to my face. He must see everything I'm feeling— the hesitation, the fear, the longing—because he licks his lips and nods to the water with a jerk of his chin. "You can hate me some more after I kiss you again."

Fuck.

Fuck this, and fuck him, and fuck me, too, because I'm slipping all over the place in my haste to tear off my shirt and kick off my sweats. I leave my bra and underwear on because there's only so much courage I have riding in my veins.

"Daisy, wait—"

Heart racing, I pause with one leg lifted over the side of the tub. "Wait, what?"

He grins broadly at me. "Truth or dare."

"You're the worst," is my mulish response right before I climb into the lukewarm water and land with my knees on either side of his slightly bent legs. "You don't get to give a romantic speech like that and then follow it up with a game of truth or dare. It's not allowed. I can't even believe that we're doing this. Obviously, this is a fever dream. Tomorrow, I'm going to wake up, and I'll spend the whole day wondering how we even—"

"C'mere," he rasps quietly.

Breathing fast and hard, I stare at him, wide-eyed. "I'm scared."

"I know, sweetheart." His throat works with a tight swallow. "I'm scared, too."

"Because you're not sure about it?"

"Because I already know that I'm never gonna want to stop."

Oh.

Heat coils in my gut as I awkwardly walk on my knees toward him. Water sloshes over the side of the tub. Fragments of candlelight burn in his gaze. The moment I'm close enough to touch, his hands grip the outside of my thighs, and he guides me the rest of the way. Then I'm straddling him, technically, anyway, but without sitting down in his lap.

The water licks at my waist.

"What if you regret this?" My hands curl over the tops of his shoulders, nails biting into taut muscle. "What if we ruin us?"

West's hand slides from my thigh to the small of my back. He urges me to sit, so I do. A whimper tears from my throat when I feel his hardness pressed against my core.

"*Weston.*"

His other hand cups the back of my neck. His eyes flick over my throat, my lips. "I could never regret you," he husks out, and then his mouth comes down on mine.

Sunshine. Hope. Strawberries.

Her flavor bursts across my tongue as I pull her flush against me. Water splashes across my chest, droplets landing on my throat and clinging to the jut of my chin. I tug her even closer. Like every piece of furniture in this house, the tub is large enough to accommodate my big frame, but it's not just me in here now—I've got *Daisy* sprawled out in my lap—and so I sink a little deeper into the cooling water, propping her up high on my lower abdomen so she can sit more comfortably with her knees coming to rest beside my hips.

The position puts my dick right up against the curve of her ass.

A feral little moan slips out of her, the sound reverberating against my lips, and I feed her a groan of my own. Latch my arm like a tight band around her waist and push myself up against her, needing friction, wanting more.

This kiss is nothing like the one we shared on our wedding day.

That one was soft and innocent, a gentle inquisition rather than total possession. It was carefully crafting a map through uncharted territory, kept tame by heightened nerves and the general awareness that we were being watched.

No one is watching us now.

There's no one around to see how Daisy bites my lips when I don't part them enough for her, and no one to judge when I rear back in surprise to stare up into her hungry gaze, my lungs seizing with each hard breath. It's just her, just me, just us, and I drag her back down with my fingers linked together at the base of her skull, barely giving her any reaction time at all before our mouths collide again.

I have Daisy in my arms.

Daisy, who is gripping my shoulders hard enough to draw blood. Daisy, who is ripping her mouth already from mine. Protest sounds in the back of my throat but then she's nudging my chin aside with the tip of her nose to press a damp kiss to my equally damp skin.

Oh, *fuck*.

Her teeth sear my flesh. Lust sweeps across my skin in a flash of fire and ice, the sensation so polarizing that my hands break their hold on her to grip the sides of the tub the way that a dying man clings to life. Water spills onto the floor. My knees come up in a knee-jerk reaction, inadvertently pushing her higher above me. Undeterred, she presses back down with a swivel of her hips that has me seeing stars.

Desperately, I dig my fingertips into the porcelain. "Daisy."

Another scrape of her teeth over my bobbing Adam's apple. Another feral little moan that I feel like a vibration against my skin.

Her hips are moving, grinding down. She's lost in a rhythm of her own creation while I'm a man swept up in the storm.

"Daisy." My voice is frantic. I peel my right hand away

from the tub to flatten it against her warm skin, right there in the shallow valley between her shoulder blades. It doesn't occur to me that I'm encouraging her to move faster, to push down harder, until my lips part on a silent, trembling gasp. "*Daisy*, I'm gonna—"

She pulls back far enough to meet my gaze.

But her hips don't stop moving—and I'm the one at fault for that. Helplessly, I grind up into her, settling my other hand on her waist, my fingers pressing divots into her soft skin. I'm lost in the moment, lost to the frenzy. Understanding flickers in her eyes but instead of pulling away in disgust, or pity, she places one hand on the flat planes of my chest and begins to roll her hips forward and back, forward and back, sending my blood pressure soaring through the goddamn roof.

Her bra is soaked through.

Her navel flashes in and out of the splashing water, every sensual rotation of her hips giving me another glimpse of her wet skin.

She's beautiful.

She's always *been* beautiful even on that first night at the gala.

But like then, it's her gaze that I can't look away from, that play of light and dark in those gorgeous amber eyes, still framed by her glasses, that see all of me and always have. They see me now, desperate and panting, and they don't shut me out.

Daisy never shuts me out.

"It's okay," she whispers. "Come for me, West."

It's permission that I didn't know that I needed. Not because I'm feeling submissive, but because even I know that it's too soon for me to let go. I haven't gotten her where she needs to go. I've barely fucking *touched* her and I'm already coming apart at the seams, my head tipping back on a guttural groan, exposing my throat for more of those biting kisses that make me feel out of control.

Panting, I utter, "Tell me what you need."

She presses a kiss to the underside of my chin. "It's okay, I promise."

My jaw firms. Every part of my fucking soul is demanding release, and yet I hold strong to the fact that I can't do this without her. Not our first time. Not after all these years.

"Tell me," I growl hotly. "Tell me what you need."

Her answer is a high-pitched whimper.

A second later, her fingers lock down on my hand, the one that's biting into her waist. She fumbles for a moment, frustration clicking in her throat, and then she circles my wrist and gives it a little tug. The water is cool, but her skin is feverishly hot as she slides my fingers under the waist-band of her underwear. Her lips come back to mine. In an open-mouthed kiss, she begs, "Touch me. *Please.*"

Fuuuuck.

The fabric of her underwear makes for a tight squeeze, but I rotate my hand to get the angle right—to get close enough to graze her clit. Daisy shudders above me, a keening cry slipping past her lips that I devour with a hot, frantic kiss.

There's no rhythm now. We're both caught up in the storm.

One messy kiss drags into another, my single finger on her clit becoming two, circling faster and faster until she's crying out with every pass. With my free hand, I drag her underwear down, shoving the flimsy material around her thighs. Through the mindless haze of lust, she catches on, and I feel her claw frantically at my briefs, parting the front so she can curl her hand around my length.

At that first touch, I throw back my head with a curse.

The *feeling* of her—

"Oh, fuck," I grunt, thrusting up at the same time that she pushes down, so that my cock slides through her parted ass cheeks. "*Fuck*, Daisy. You feel so good."

Her reply is lost in another meeting of our lips.

Pressure builds low in my gut as I tunnel my dick upward, my fingers still working her over. Water sloshes against the wall of the tub, the surface now lapping at our waists. Unable to resist, I glance down, and the sight laid out before me is one that I'll carry with me until the day I'm put to rest. My fingers rubbing my wife's clit, her underwear a tangled mess, the tantalizing glimpse of her hand gripping the base of my dick every time she lifts her hips again, only to come back down in an increasingly uncoordinated rhythm.

She bites my lips.

I suck on hers.

"West," she whimpers, "West, I'm going to—"

"Me, too." I tuck my face into the crook of her neck, inhaling the scent of her skin into my soul. "C'mon, sweetheart. Come all over me, I'm begging you."

With a shattered cry, her hips jerk under my hand as she comes, and fuck, fuck, *fuck!* Burying a groan against her throat, I follow right after her, pumping my hips faster and faster, shooting my load all over her soaked skin. Everything feels tight and achy, as if I've just spent hours on the treadmill, the same dopamine fog that I get after a game cluttering my thoughts as we fall into serene stillness.

She shifts some, pulling on her underwear, and then collapses against my chest with a sigh. It's only then, with air still pushing roughly past my parted lips, that I catch sight of our reflection in the standing mirror that's tucked away in the corner of the room.

"Fuck," I whisper.

"What?" Lazily, she lifts her head to follow the direction of my gaze. When she finds the source of my attention, another one of those feral little moans catches in her throat. "Oh."

Most of the candles have gone out, leaving the bathroom darker than before, but there's enough light left that the pools of water on the floor reflect their flickering yellow flames. Droplets of water speckle our flesh, and our faces are flush with exertion. But it's the sight of Daisy wrapped up in my arms that I can't look away from. Deep in my heart, hope tangles with conviction until, without even meaning to, I murmur, "Forever."

I feel Daisy's gaze touch upon my face. "Forever?"

"Yeah." I watch my reflection pull her closer. Her heart beats hard and fast against my own. "This marriage is forever, Cain. I can't let you go."

CHAPTER 25

WESTON

That night, after we spend an hour cleaning up the bathroom, Daisy crawls into my bed.

I curl myself around her like a king guarding his queen.

Forever, I think as sleep finally takes over, *this means forever.*

"Dais!"

Lowering my phone, I turn away from the ice to see Gwen and Holly Carter clambering down TD Garden's concrete steps toward where I'm standing in the row usually reserved for WAGs.

They're dressed up for tonight's game against Detroit in the standard gear—jeans and matching Blades sweaters—although I'm pretty sure that Gwen is rocking her husband's name while Holly probably wears Jackson's retired number. I can't say that I blame them. Plastered across the back of my NHL-issued jersey is the number 73. I say NHL-issued because I totally stole it out of West's closet. The hem is currently tucked into the front of my jeans, it's so big on me.

As soon as Gwen and Holly get close, I'm pulled in for tight hugs.

"Where's Zoe?" I ask, referring to Andre Beaumont's wife. The three of them, including Charlie Denton, are usually glued at the hip.

Holly winces. "First trimester is kicking her ass."

"Oomph," I mutter in sympathy. I try to imagine what it

must be like for her but the closest I can come up with is how it felt to be stuck on the couch for months after my injury. Being sedentary is pretty much my worst nightmare. "I'll send her a text."

Gwen reaches for my phone. "Did you want me to get a picture of you?"

"Sure. I was just going to . . ." I swing an awkward glance toward Holly. "Just going to send a selfie to West or whatever. He's a total caveman, you know. Loves it when I wear his jersey—like all hockey players do. It's almost stereotypical at this point."

Sliding her clear, TD Garden-approved purse onto her hip, Gwen holds my phone in one hand and motions for me to get into position with the other. "If you're worried about spilling the marriage beans to Holly, don't—she already knows."

Holly's smile turns sheepish. "Sorry, Jackson told me. I swear he knows how to keep a secret—but just not from me."

Sounds a lot like West.

With a light laugh, I tuck my hair behind my ear. "Okay. Fair. Then pass the phone to Holls, Gwen—why am I stuck with a B-grade photographer when we've got the real deal here?"

Gwen mock-glares at me. "Rude."

"But it's true," Holly chirps as she swipes the phone from her friend's hand. "One of us gets paid to babysit hockey players and the other gets paid to take pictures of them. One of us is winning at life, girl, and it's not you."

It's so brutally savage, but delivered with Holly's trademark Southern sass, that Gwen and I immediately burst into laughter. The sound attracts attention from the growing crowd, but thankfully, no one approaches. Not that they would. I've sat with the WAGs plenty of times over the years, and fans have always been incredibly respectful. At most, parents come over with their kids to ask about signed merch from their favorite players.

Holly motions for me to angle my head a certain way in order to make the best of the arena's trashy lighting. "I've been following your accounts. The pictures seem to be turning the tide—especially the one of you and West together in bed." She hands me my phone.

My cheeks heat at the memory of the impulsive photo that we took a week ago, right before West hopped on the team jet for another set of away games. We'd fallen into bed together again—literally and figuratively—for another round of hot-as-hell dry-humping that led to mutual orgasms and an epic cuddling session afterward.

I press a hand to my warm face. "That one was Weston's idea."

"I bet," Gwen laughs.

Holly winks. "The sheets covering y'all was a nice touch."

"Yeah, um. We thought so. Anything to get the heat off my back, right? And it seems to be working okay." I fidget under their watchful stares. "At least no one is telling me to go jump off a bridge or whatever. Shows some improvement from last month, I think."

Gwen's brows draw together. "Daisy?"

I shove my phone into my back pocket. "Yeah?"

"You're sweating."

"What?" Awkwardly, I pat my face again. "Is my makeup okay?"

"No," Gwen says with narrowed eyes, "I mean, you look like you're sweating heaps of mortification right now. Wait, are you—" With a quick glance over her shoulder, she leans in close enough that her long hair brushes my arm. "Are you *sleeping* with him?"

Just then, the national anthem starts to play, saving my

butt in the nick of time. "Oh, look! How fun. The game is starting."

Holly chuckles. "You are such a trash liar. How many times?"

I press my hand over my heart and lie, lie, and lie some more. "I have no idea what you're talking about."

She turns to Gwen. "My bet is three times. Minimum. But maybe one of those times they just fooled around with their clothes still on."

I can feel Gwen studying me with a critical eye. It takes everything in me not to react when she announces, "I'm voting twice—but not penetrative sex either time. They're working their way up to that."

"Guys, I'm literally standing right here. I can hear you."

Gwen slings an arm around my waist, her finger finding my belt loop and hanging on. "I think this is great news, actually. Now Marshall can stop placing bets on when the two of you are going to finally admit that you love each other."

The comment is eerily similar to what Kammer said to me at our reception.

After everything that's happened with West, I still don't know what to make of the fact that everyone seems to think that we've been falling for each other all along. Even in the weeks that led up to us tying the knot, not a single person batted an eye when we announced the wedding. Sure, there was asshole Brian Murphy—as well as some online chatter —who questioned the validity of the marriage, but everyone who knows us personally never doubted that the vows we took are a forever type of deal.

Not even West wanted to believe that our marriage of convenience will one day end in divorce, and that was long before we ever got naked with each other.

Down on the ice, Hunt meets Detroit for the face off. The Blades' losing streak is still going strong, and I hate to think that it's somehow my fault. They were reigning champions last year and now they're scraping the bottom of the barrel in the Eastern Conference.

"Do the guys blame me, do you think?"

Holly leans around Gwen to stare at me. *"What?"*

"They've lost the last nine games," I say, my stomach cramping with guilt. "And I can't help but wonder if all the noise surrounding *Confessions of a Puck Bunny* is responsible."

"No, Daisy." Holly's tone is kind but firm.

"But—"

"I'm telling you right now that the Blades sucking this season has nothing to do with you and everything to do with the fact that half their roster is a bunch of pimply-faced rookies who have exceptional talent but aren't ready to hack it in the Show yet."

Pressing my lips together, I turn my head toward her to listen.

Holly continues with a frustrated huff. "You thought that Jackson was intense on the ice? Imagine what he's like now that he's an assistant coach." Affection for her husband curves her mouth before she shakes her head. "Trust me, they're working overtime to fill those weak spots. You know, before the trade deadline starts looming in March, and they're stuck with their hands tied behind their back." Holly's brow furrows. "Hasn't your dad mentioned any of this to you?"

I don't know how to admit that my dad hasn't said a single word to me in weeks.

West did share the weird conversation that he had with Dad on the way to Toronto, but aside from that, there's been no other updates on the Sam Hall front. For the first time in my life, my dad has shut me out, and I have no idea how to handle that.

The worst part is that I should be way more upset than I

am about what Mom told Brian Murphy. Sure, in the moment it felt like an unexpected gut punch. Who wouldn't feel like crap after learning that their mother—estranged or not—chose to forego attending her own daughter's wedding for a vacation on the beach? Never mind the fact that I wasn't the one to extend the invitation in the first place, and I wouldn't have wanted her there, anyway.

But the thing is, I don't have a relationship with Alice Hall. I haven't *had* a relationship with her since I was ten years old, and she took off for greener pastures.

I don't wish her ill. I mean, I'd be lying if I said that I want the *best* for her, but I simply just don't . . . care. And maybe that means I'm broken in some irreparable way, if I can feel so little for the woman who gave birth to me, but my loyalty remains steadfast with the man that she left behind. The man who raised me from the ground up—who did homework with me, and who fumbled his way around the store for pads (with wings, thank you). The man who cried with me, and held me up, when I was stuck in that hospital bed watching my dreams fade away.

I love Dad with my whole heart, and it kills me inside that a choice I made has created such a rift between us.

Almost as if the universe is messing with me, the Jumbotron flashes to the bench and zooms in on his grumpy, pissed off face. I almost want to cry.

"Daisy?" A gentle hand touches my shoulder. "Are you okay?"

"Yeah." I'm cheerful when I turn to look at Gwen. Probably too cheerful, honestly, but it's the best that I can do given the situation. "Yeah, I'm great. I hope the guys kick ass tonight."

Gwen isn't the first one to ask me if I'm all right—Amber Conners came first.

As we watch the Blades lose yet another game, I can't help but wonder if I really am.

CHAPTER 27
WESTON

"**F**uck this." Across the weight room, Kasey angrily peddles on one of the bikes during our postgame workout. Shifting his weight off one hand, he strips off his ball cap and wipes his brow with the back of his forearm. "What is happening to us? Seriously. Ten *fucking* games?"

No one says anything.

Even our conditioning coach stays quiet—though he does tell me to up my incline on the treadmill.

Sweat beads across my nape as I keep my head down. It's not that I don't want to bitch and complain, I just don't see the point. We lost. We've *been* losing. And unfortunately, it's coming down to a lack of experience with the newbies. For what it's worth, it's not their fault either. Management made those deals. They decided to fork out less money by investing in new talent rather than pay out the nose for veterans already playing in the league, guys who would have no problem filling the holes left behind in our team from retirements and trades.

"Kase," Beaumont says firmly. "Enough, man. Okay?" The speaking glance he aims toward where Bjorn and

Alarik are grimly riding their own bikes at the end of the row, by themselves, says it all.

They already feel like shit. Don't make it worse.

With a huff, our goalie shuts his mouth and gets back to his postgame workout. The rest of us keep our mouths shut, too, though the room is rife with discontent.

By the time I'm walking out thirty minutes later, I'm so ready to get home to Daisy that it comes as a complete surprise when I enter the hallway and see her waiting. With her back toward me, she's looking down at something on her phone. My name and the number 73 are big and bold across her spine. The sight of her in my jersey makes me so damn happy that I don't even hesitate when I get close.

Dropping my duffel to the ground behind her, I sink my arms around her waist and crowd her from behind. "Hi, wife."

A shiver wracks her frame as she leans back against my shoulder to look up at me. "Mr. Cain. Fancy seeing you here."

My gaze falls to her lips. "Can I?"

"Yeah," she whispers.

Turning my Blades hat backward on my head, so the brim won't be in my way, I cup her face in my palms and lean down for a kiss.

The mood isn't frenetic the way that it was the other night in the bathroom. It's soft and searching, the pace languid as she presses up onto her toes. Her hands grip the front of my shirt for balance, and I kinda like it, the idea of her using me, so I don't do the very kind, very respectable thing by wrapping my arms around her to give her a helping hand.

Instead, I let her take what she wants from me—little nips of her teeth leaving bruises on my lips, her hands fisting my T until the fabric feels loose around my torso from her needy, possessive grip. I have no plans on pulling away, but then the door to the weight room slams open behind me, and I can hear the Anders brothers arguing in Swedish as they come down the hall.

With my hands on Daisy's waist, I put a little distance between us.

Her lips are puffy from my kiss as she waves at Bjorn and Alarik, who both keep their heads down as they walk by. In subdued silence, we watch them turn right toward the parking garage.

Daisy's mouth tugs to one side. "Are they okay?"

I sigh. "C'mon, let's head out and I'll fill you in."

As I grab my bag, I notice Daisy peering past me. She chews anxiously on her bottom lip, and then blurts, "Is Dad—?"

My heart sinks for her. "Nah, sweetheart. I'm sorry. He already left."

"Oh." Her amber eyes shine a little too bright in her face. "I figured, you know? I just thought . . . never mind, I don't know what I was thinking."

You're thinking that your dad loves you and you don't understand why he's acting like he doesn't. It's completely different from my own parents. The Cains are single-handedly great at proving time and time again that they don't care to know me and Tory, not unless we stay within the very specific lines that they've drawn. Sam Hall is made of different stock, and the fact that he's acting out of character is starting to feel like a bigger problem than I thought.

Looking disappointed, Daisy slips her hand into mine and squeezes. I squeeze back.

"LET ME RIDE WITH YOU," I say when we step into the

parking garage. "I'll call one of the boys tomorrow for practice."

Daisy peers over at me. "Are you sure?"

Am I sure that I want to spend as much time as I can with her, even when we're sleeping in the same bed these days? Yeah, I'm pretty fucking sure. The chaos of my schedule makes it feel like every second I have to spare should be spent at her side. If a miracle happens and we make it to the playoffs, it'll only get worse.

I wave her forward so she can lead us to wherever she parked.

It's not until we're on our way home, and I'm behind the wheel, that she asks, "What's up with the brothers? They looked really, *really* sad. Like, someone kicked their puppy sad."

With one hand on the wheel, I lift the other to scrub over my mouth, never taking my eyes off the road. It's already dark out and the highway is jampacked with weekend traffic. "We're obviously not doing well. The team, I mean." Out of the corner of my eye, I see Daisy nod. It's her signal that she's listening but giving me the floor to take whatever time I need. With a grateful sigh, I settle my right hand over her thigh.

She doesn't move it off her. Instead, she flips my hand over and threads our fingers together. My heart beats a little faster.

"It was easy to pretend even a month ago that we weren't doing well because of assholes like Morley, you know?"

At the mention of Amber Morley's ex-husband, Daisy's hand flexes in mine. "It was bad," she utters tightly. "All of it. The way that Morley, North, and the rest targeted you wasn't okay."

Chest feeling tight with how quickly she always comes to my defense, I lift our clasped hands to press a kiss to the back of hers. "It wasn't okay, but it's also hockey, sweetheart. You know that. Piss off one person and you piss off their friends, neighbors, and cousins-twice-removed. Shit happens. Bunny might have been the catalyst but those guys? They would have found one reason or another to pick fights with us on the ice."

I shake my head, letting out a rough laugh. "No, *we're* the issue. And that's—that's a hard fucking pill to swallow on the best of days, but considering where we were less than nine months ago? This season is starting to feel like a nightmare."

This past summer, I took Daisy and Tory with me for my Day With The Cup. We rented a small yacht—okay, it was more like a tiny fisherman's boat—and sailed the waters around Cape Ann. We drank out of Stanley. We danced *with* Stanley. At one point, I even kissed Stanley and promised to hold him in my arms again one day soon.

Soon is definitely not happening this year.

"Some of the guys aren't taking it well." Definitely the understatement of the year. "And instead of realizing that we win and lose as a team, they're pointing fingers at the rookies."

Daisy squeezes my hand.

"It sucks, you know? Hockey is my haven. It's work, yeah, and my livelihood depends on us not being total shit, but . . ." Biting the inside of my cheek, I blow out a frustrated breath. "I hate that guys like Kasey, they're stripping the joy out of it for the rest of us. I love the game. I love it when we're winning, and yeah, I love it a little less when we're losing, but when the alternative is not having it at all? I can't imagine that life, Dais. Honestly, I'm scared to."

Faintly, she says, "I can't imagine that for you either."

Something in her voice raises the hair on the back of my neck. Cutting my gaze away from the road, I try to get a read on how she's feeling, but her face is hidden in shadow.

"Daisy-belle. You good?"

Her hand is clammy in mine, her eyes fixed on the road in front of us. Only when I tear my gaze away to focus back on the highway does she whisper, "If I . . . If I said no, would that be okay?"

My gut reaction is to demand answers, to know who hurt her and how badly she'd like me to hurt them in return. But that will only make *me* feel better. It's not at all what she needs, which is a safe space to curl into a ball and nurse her wounds. It's a rare day when Daisy lowers her guard and asks for help. Like most elite athletes, it was trained out of her at an early age to never show any signs of weakness.

Only, I don't think she's ever been stronger than she is right now, with her hand trembling in mine and her breath shallow with nerves.

"Yeah, sweetheart," I say hoarsely. "It'd be okay if you were, and it's also okay if you're not."

Her fingers cling to mine. "Will you hold me?" Her voice cracks on the last word. "When we get home, I mean?"

"I'll hold you for as long as you need," I vow. *Forever, if that's what it takes.*

My new therapist's name is Karen, and she's *lovely.*

I tell Amber as much while leaving her a voicemail on my way home from my first session: "You're totally right. Therapy kind of sucks—I mean, wow, talk about seriously invasive. But I actually kind of loved it? Or maybe it's that I just really love Karen—that's my therapist. She asked to see me once a week for now, so I'll have more to share soon. Anyway, I should probably stop spilling my guts out to your voicemail. I'm just really grateful that you asked me to think about how I'm doing. Okay, I'll talk to you later. Bye!"

The second that I hang up, I immediately feel ridiculous over the barrage of word vomit that she'll need to suffer through whenever she gets around to my missed call. With any luck, she'll just delete it and call it a day.

Ugh.

Despite the lingering embarrassment, my mood is still flying high by the time that I pull into West's driveaway a short while later. It snowed for the first time last night, but it was such a light dusting that it's not even noon yet and the snow is completely melted. Boston in November is considerate like that.

After gathering my bag, I stomp my boots on my "Oh Shit, It's You Again" welcome mat that I brought over from my apartment when I first moved in, and head inside. Immediately, my senses are assaulted by the aroma of Thanksgiving, which is actually later this week. When I scamper into the kitchen, I find the counter teeming with takeout containers while West waters Anita's plants.

He doesn't notice me right away, which gives me ample opportunity to shamelessly ogle him. Wearing a pair of gray sweats slung low on his hips, as well as a faded UConn sweatshirt, he looks thoroughly rumpled as if he recently crawled out of bed and stumbled his way down here to get the day started. Maybe it makes me a hopeless romantic, but I feel so incredibly lucky that I get to see him this way.

I feel even luckier that when he does become aware of my presence, his mouth ticks into a grin so wide it creases the dimple in his cheek. He abandons the plastic St. Patrick's Day cup that he likes to use as a makeshift watering can, and prowls toward me with his arms already outstretched to drag me close.

His mouth comes down on mine a second later, and thoughts of Amber, Thanksgiving, and therapy all flee as I chase the taste of coffee on his tongue. We've gotten off together a handful of times now, and I know that West enjoys all of it—but kissing remains his favorite activity.

So, it's no surprise when he bends his knees to swing me up into his arms. He lowers me onto the massive island, away from all the plants and the food, and pushes my knees wide so he can stand in the cradle of my thighs. His big hands clutch my waist, his thumbs disappearing beneath the hem of my shirt to trace idle circles on my bare skin, while his mouth continues to ravage mine in a slow, delicious glide of his lips pressing mine open until he can lick his way inside.

I can't think when he kisses me.

There's nothing but fragments of memory and touch— my fingers biting into his shoulders and needy, little whimpers rising in the back of my throat. West is a complex blend of curiosity and possession, and I never know which side of him will win out until we're in the thick of it and I'm already drowning.

When his fingers slide upward, tracing a direct line from my belly to my flower tattoo, I swallow a grin and surrender myself to whatever itch West has in his brain this morning that he wants to iron out.

I'm putty in his hands as he draws my shirt up over my head and tosses it on the floor. His green eyes are sharp and bright when he stamps one last kiss across my lips before pinning my hands to the island within the shackles of his fingers.

"Thought about your tattoo again all morning," he grits out, his voice still husky with sleep. His lips follow a path down my throat, soft and arousing, the words a quiet rumble against my skin. "Couldn't stop wondering what it might look like bathed in sunlight."

He's set me down in a pool of autumnal sunshine. It's bright but not overly warm, and a shiver carves a path down my spine when he drags his mouth along my collarbone in a series of open-mouth kisses that have me squirming with the desperate need to touch him. But still, he doesn't let me move my hands. They're captured within his ironclad grip.

"Shit," I exhale raggedly, kicking out my legs to wrap around the backs of his thighs, if only to have a little leverage.

His teeth marking my skin scatters the rest of my thoughts.

When I've taken charge of our pleasure in the bedroom, things tend to get heated and messy very fast, but West manipulates my body with the same stubborn streak of patience that he shows his opponents on the ice. He plays with me, dangles hope and release like a reward in front of my face only to snatch them away in a move so deliberately orchestrated that I'm left floundering with the realization that he never had any intention to show me a little mercy.

Best friend West is silly and affectionate.

Husband West is a ruthless fucking tease.

Whimpering his name, I fight against his hold as he presses a wet string of kisses along my bra strap. His eyes are closed, blond lashes fanning his cheeks. There are more kisses littered across the inner swells of my breasts, sparking a tender ache in my core that has me mewling, tilting my hips, practically begging him to *give me more, please give me more.*

West continues undaunted.

In one smooth move, he pushes my hands backward, forcing an arch to my spine, while his morning stubble scrapes across the sensitive skin of my rib cage. My breathing turns shallow as his soft, damp lips find the petals of my tattoo. It's barely two inches tall. Something I got done on a whim during the summer. There's no hidden meaning, no heartfelt origin story. And yet, West treats it like it's worthy of worship, a man brought down to his knees by the flash of a little ink.

I have no idea why it turns him on so much, but I think —if I had to guess—it's the intimacy that he loves most, the feeling that he's been given a glimpse of me that I've given to no one else. And I get that on a deep, visceral level, because it's become pretty apparent—if you know which clues to look for—that West doesn't share his body with others very often, if at all.

I'm not sure if he's still a virgin. To be honest, I don't care, and I don't plan to ask.

I'll take West however he comes—inexperienced or not, shamelessly flirty or not. My only requirements are that he treats me with care—that he knows my worth—that he keeps me safe. My heart, I mean. Because I'm starting to realize that while I might brandish courageous words on behalf of others, I leave myself tragically exposed in the process, and I'm so tired of always bleeding out.

To my surprise, his lips trail south.

As in, away from the tattoo.

Wide-eyed, I watch as his dark blond head moves lower, his lips still pressing kisses every so often to my sternum, to my navel, to the soft part of my lower belly that used to be flat and toned from the constant pressure to exercise and diet every ounce of fat from my body. I suck in a tight breath as he lingers there; then his hands finally release mine to clutch my hips in big fists, dragging me forward until I'm nearly hanging over the edge of the waterfall island.

Those mossy green eyes lift to my face. "Can I?"

Can I? He asks me that before he kisses me. He asks me that every time he folds me into a new position. He asks me that when he damn well knows that I'll give him anything he wants, but still, he asks it anyway. He wants to drive me crazy in the same breath that he wants to make sure that we're on the same page. No person left behind. We're in this together or not at all.

I love it. I love him.

Oh, God, if he puts his mouth on me, I'm going to die. *La petite mort.* The little death. Whatever the French call an orgasm. That's for sure going to happen, and I'm bound to embarrass myself with how close I already am to begging.

"Daisy?"

"Yes," I chirp way too eagerly, "whatever you want, yes.

I mean, if you want it—if you want *me*—then you can have it. Me. Everything."

His lips quirk in a teasing grin. "Are you sure? Sounds like you might be on the fence."

Groaning, I kick him playfully in the side. "You're the worst."

"The best," he corrects, but his attention is already fixated on his hands peeling my jeans away from my waist. He encourages me to lift my hips off the marble, and I help him by grabbing a handful of denim once it's past the curve of my butt. Between him tugging and me pushing, we get the material down to my ankles. He whisks it away with a sweep of his arm.

Though I'm still in my underwear, I feel painfully exposed.

His hands return to my legs. I feel every calloused ridge of his palm as he glides them up my thighs. Wantonly, I tilt my hips, but if he appreciates my attempt to give him better access, he doesn't seem to notice.

He follows the path of his palms with the stamp of his lips, the heat of his breath. One hand skims past my stomach to settle on my chest, urging me to lay back on the island. The other traces the band of my underwear around the crease of my thigh—and then he pushes that leg up toward my chest so that I'm completely open to him.

"West," I gasp.

His brow furrows. "You'll tell me if you want it a certain way?"

At my sides, my hands curl into fists. "I'll like anything, I promise."

"I mean it." His stubborn gaze flicks up to mine. "Tell me, so I can make it good for you."

"Yes, okay, I'll tell you."

A wicked grin touches his lips. "Good girl."

Oh, *fuck.*

He's so big that his frame blots out the rest of the kitchen as he bends over me, his wide shoulders hunched as he slowly lowers his face to where I'm already wet. I'm torn between squeezing my eyes shut in embarrassment and watching everything unfold, but the moment he touches his lips to the damp spot on my underwear, I forget everything—including my own name.

The fingers gripping my thigh tighten to just this side of painful. With a low groan, he nuzzles the crease of my thigh before using a single finger to drag my underwear to the side, exposing the heart of me to his burning gaze.

Heat sweeps over my body, my pale skin betraying me with a splotchy blush. For every moment that follows where he just *looks* at me, I swear that I lose another thread of sanity. Dimly, I'm aware of my hips beginning to churn of their own volition, my back rising sharply off the island as I chant, "Pleasepleaseplease."

He licks his lips.

I cry out before he even gets his mouth on me.

Finally, he shows me mercy—I'm treated to the gentlest flick of his tongue across my clit. With a broken whimper, I dig my nails into my palms. It's not enough to quiet the storm rushing through my veins. It's barely enough to sate the hunger.

He must realize how far he's pushed me to the edge because he soothes me with more kisses on my skin, narrowly missing the place where I need him the most every single time. Helplessly, I thrash under the heavy weight of his arm keeping me pinned in place, so desperate to be touched by him that I feel like I'm losing my mind.

"Please." My hips flex upward. "*Please.*"

"Easy, sweetheart," he husks out, "I got you."

And then he applies the most exquisite pressure on my clit with his lips, sucking on the swollen bud hard enough to rip a tortured sob from my throat. "*West.*"

"Fuck, Daisy. God, look at you."

Looping his free arm under my other thigh, he urges me to plant my foot on the edge of the island. Wordlessly obeying, I grip my knee, pull it wide, leave him all the space he needs to play with me.

Biting off another curse, he takes full advantage—keeping one thumb hooked under the band of my underwear while his tongue moves sinfully over my clit. He flicks it faster, faster. Alternates that perfect pace of deliberate frenzy with slowing it all down, tugging on my sensitive flesh with his lips, rolling his tongue across the peak before starting my descent into Hell all over again.

I'm coming undone.

My legs are trembling where I hold them open, my head is thrown back with every ragged breath that I try to pull into my lungs. I'm splayed out shamelessly. The fact that I'm lucky enough for it to be Weston who has me pinned down like this is a total mindfuck that I'll need to properly freak out about later. Sometimes, I'm still convinced that all of this a dream.

If it is, I don't ever want to wake up.

Deep, throaty groans spill from his lips as he licks and sucks, driving me higher and higher until I reach down to thread my fingers through his messy hair. He hums—fucking *hums*—at the sensation of me touching him, and with a sharp cry, I shatter into a million little pieces, my hips twitching with each and every aftershock.

West doesn't pull away as I slowly come back down.

Soon, it's too much to take, though, and I push at his shoulder with a weak laugh. "No more. Please. Mercy. I beg."

His lips are shiny as he straightens his spine, and I'm hypnotized by the sight of them as he gingerly lowers my legs and stretches out his body over mine, elbows planted down on either side of me. "Kiss me," he growls.

I lick the taste of me off his lips.

Swallow it down, committing this moment with him to memory.

Just as I open my mouth to fully let him inside, the doorbell rings and he pulls back with a frustrated noise. "Fuck."

"Who is that?"

"The lesser twin—Tory."

CHAPTER 29

WESTON

Turns out that it wasn't just my brother at the door, which is how I end up at my dining room table an hour later with Daisy, Tory, my parents, and an assortment of Thanksgiving dishes.

The tension is suffocating.

Tory keeps shooting me apologetic glances while Daisy has adopted the role of peacemaker the way she always does with Mom and Dad—she praises their clothing, the new car that they rolled up in, a recent acquisition that my father apparently made. Daisy let it slip a few years ago that way back in college, she bookmarked my dad's real estate brokerage just to have something to bring up in conversation with him. To this day, I'm pretty sure that she still scans the site every once in a while, on the off chance that David Cain shows up out of the blue.

Today's surprise appearance is not the norm.

I suddenly find myself wishing that I hadn't thought to surprise Daisy with today's lunch. Better yet, I wish that tonight's game was suddenly pushed forward by four or five hours, so I'd have a convenient excuse to escape before the conversation inevitably takes a nosedive.

"The wedding was very nice," Mom tells Daisy as she uses her fork to push the sweet potatoes around on her plate. "Perhaps a bit understated but very nice."

"Oh." Looking startled by the compliment, Daisy's mouth kicks up in a genuine grin. "Thank you so much."

"But West, I did want to discuss with you about holding something better—maybe in the new year? We could rent out the Society Room, do you remember it? Your cousin Matilda got married there but you must have been . . . oh, David what would you say? Maybe eight or nine?"

"Six, I think," Dad says while pouring himself more wine.

"*Six*?" Mom's brows flash upward in surprise. "There's no way. That would have to mean that the boys are—"

My twin stabs his fork into a piece of turkey. "We're twenty-eight, Mom."

Her laughter is almost shrill as she holds out her empty wine glass for Dad to refill. "Yes, of course, you are. I swear, you get older and all the little details just—*poof*—disappear."

Beneath the table, Daisy's hand lands on my leg for support.

I fold my fingers over hers and hold tight.

"Speaking of details, West." Even just the start of that sentence coming out of my dad's mouth has me bracing for impact, and I force an expression of apathy onto my face. "What does your coach have to say about your losing streak?"

With our hands still linked under the table, I feel Daisy's flinch at the mention of her dad.

My own father either doesn't remember the connection between my wife and the head coach for the Boston Blades or he simply doesn't give a shit. "Seems like a fireable offense, in my opinion," he goes on, tearing a piece of bread from the loaf. "Would be in my world, that's for sure. You don't deliver results, you get shown to the door."

My jaw firms. "Dad."

"What? You don't agree?" Grabbing the butter knife, he proceeds to slather it across the bread with crisp, precise movements. "You're the one who won't walk away from hockey. I didn't think that you'd be happy to be losing while you're at it. Honestly, Weston, sometimes I have no idea what—"

"*Dad.*"

Lowering the butter knife, he stares at me blankly. "What?"

Beside me, Daisy chews on her bottom lip. This isn't at all how I planned for today to go. For one, we'll be spending tomorrow evening at Jackson and Holly's house for the official celebration of Thanksgiving. With the whole team invited, it'll be tons of fun but entirely too chaotic. I wanted to balance it out with a lowkey afternoon, one where me, Daisy, and Tory could kick back and hang out with enough time for me to squeeze in a pre-game nap before we face off against New York again tonight.

"Well, Weston?" Dad doesn't snap his fingers but with that tone, he might as well have. "What's the problem?"

"Apologize to my wife, please." My voice is eerily calm. Dad looks completely bewildered. I grit my teeth. "I'm gonna do you a favor and pretend that you came here today with the hope of finding some common ground, and I'm going to assume that you thought that I'd want to complain about my coach with my family, the way that employees generally like to complain about their bosses. Am I right?"

"I don't—"

"And I'm going to *assume*," I continue, speaking directly over his protest, "that in all that worry in trying to find something to discuss with your son, you forgot that Coach Hall is Daisy's father."

Dad's gaze flickers to Daisy.

"Please apologize to her." Gripping her hand in mine, I add, "No one likes to hear about how awful their parent is, wouldn't you agree?" It's a pointed remark but he doesn't even react. There's just . . . nothing in his gaze as he stares back at me. It's a brutal realization to have, that he can say things like "I love you" while never really meaning it at all.

My wife's voice is small when she murmurs, "West, it's okay—"

"It's not okay." I swallow past the hard lump in my throat. "Whatever is happening with us, it's not all on Coach. We win as a team, and we die as a team. And I know that concept is probably hard for you to grasp, Dad, but there are twenty-two other guys who are working their asses off to come back from a shit streak. And it's not just us, either. It's our equipment manager and our strength coaches and our nutritionist and the folks over in marketing—everyone doing their own part to make sure that we end up with another Cup at the end of the season."

"It's doubtful that you'll win."

"David," Mom hisses from her spot at the table. "That's not very nice."

"Would you like me to lie to him, Molly? Because I won't." Dad tosses his napkin onto the table beside his plate. "He has fans all over the country willing to blow steam up his ass, but that's not my job as a parent. I'm meant to guide him. And, yes, part of that includes showing him a little tough love when the situation calls for it."

My pulse is pounding so hard, I can barely hear my own raging thoughts. But just before I can open my mouth to tear him a new one, it's Daisy who is speaking up, Daisy who is defending me the way that she does best—with her whole fucking heart.

"That's not tough love, Mr. Cain." Her hand never leaves mine. "It's treating your sons the way that you do your business—with terms and conditions. You punish them when they step out of line, but you ignore them when they do what you want." Across from me, Tory lowers his head. "And they put up with it because the alternative is not having you in their life at all."

Dad's mouth thins in an uncompromising line. "Daisy, I would like to caution you against—"

"Did you wonder at all why my mom wasn't at the wedding?" Daisy angles her chin, exuding quiet strength. "It's because she walked out of my life when I was ten years old. She left everything behind, and I really do mean everything—her car, her clothes, even our dog, who she claimed to love so very, very much. For months after she left, my dad wouldn't let us touch any of her belongings. He thought that if we left them as they were, she'd come back—she'd *have* to come back, right? Because she *loved* us, he said.

"I don't know if she did. I don't even know if she *does*. For whatever reason, my mother made the choice to not have a daughter. But you know what I did?" That same defiant chin trembles with emotion, but then her jaw tightens with resilience, and she forges on. "I made the decision to move on in my life without a mother. She's out there somewhere, doing her own thing, but she is not my family. She's not who I run to when I need help, and she's not who I share all of my hopes and dreams with. I have my dad for that, and Tory, and most especially, I have West."

I can't tear my gaze away from her.

She's utterly beautiful, inside and out. Swear to God, this world doesn't deserve her. None of us do.

"I'm only saying this, Mr. Cain, because I think you're at a fork in the road. If you push, and you push, and you push, one day you're going to look around and realize that you don't have a son. He'll have made the hard decision to leave you behind because your brand of tough love doesn't work for him, and he has every right to make that call." Her fingers slip away from mine as she stands up. And just like the day that I met her, she holds herself like she's seven feet tall, her amber eyes entirely too forthright. "I'm going to have to ask you both to leave. My husband has a game tonight and this—this isn't good for him. I'll walk you out."

My parents look shell-shocked as Daisy escorts them through my house like a five-foot-nothing bodyguard.

I should get up and follow her but I'm shell-shocked, too. Slumping back in my chair, I fold my right hand over my left, digging my thumb into fluttering pulse. That girl is a storm. She caught me when I was just nineteen years old and I've been circling her ever since, helpless to the way that my heart yearns to be near her, to have her, however I can. She could order me to my knees, and I'd fall.

West and Daisy.

Daisy and West.

My *wife*.

The sound of my brother clearing his throat jerks my gaze up to his face. He's moved to Daisy's seat, and he knocks my knee with his. "Mom and Dad finally fell in love, huh?"

"What?"

"You and Daisy," he says, and there's a small, pleased smile lurking at the corner of his mouth that is totally at odds with the meltdown that just occurred at this table. "You love her."

I give a quick jerk of my head. "Of course I love her."

"No, West." That small smile on his face broadens into a heartfelt laugh as if he can't believe that he has to put up with my shit for the rest of his life. "You're *in* love with her."

Oh.

My chest grows tight. My hands turn clammy. I can hear her speaking quietly with my parents, holding firm at the door like some ancient queen barring her enemies from entering. Not that my parents are our enemies, exactly, but . . . Yeah, that vision of her ready to take on the world to keep me safe does something to my heart.

"I love her." It tastes honest on my tongue. It tastes real. Swallowing tightly, I press harder on my pulse point and let out a harsh, disbelieving laugh. "Fuck, Tor. I *love* her."

Eyes the same shade as my own shimmer with happiness. "Always knew you did, little bro. Always knew you did."

CHAPTER 30
WESTON

Fuck hockey.

Blasphemous, I know, and if it ever gets back to Stanley that I said that shit, I'm never going to get my hands on him again but—no, for real. Fuck hockey.

Thanks to the game against New York, I don't get the chance to tell Daisy how I feel before I head out to make it to the Garden in time for our pre-game workout. The irony is that while patience is what I'm known for on the ice, I'm slightly more chaotic when it comes to my interactions with my wife. She's right about me that way. I want to tell her everything and I hate the idea of keeping secrets.

Which is why it's killing me to stay quiet while we warm up on the ice. She should know how I feel. Maybe if Tory left my house a little sooner today, I could have—

"Cain, look alive, man."

Hunt bumps me on the back of my head with his glove as he skates past. I wonder when he knew that he loved Gwen. I wonder if he made her wait to tell her how he felt or if, like me, he's cursing the fuck out of the hockey gods for their epically bad timing.

W E'RE PLAYING SLIGHTLY BETTER than shit tonight.

I'm hesitant to give us any more credit than that because Bjorn is looking shaky and Kasey has already let in two goals by the end of the first period, but New York isn't looking all that hot either. We've lit the lamp twice, too, once with a filthy slap shot by Hunt and another with a sweet fucking assist from Kammer that rebounded off the pipes before making it in the five hole.

So, yeah, we're not winning tonight but we're not necessarily losing either.

It makes for a rough go in the second period.

If I shove Joe fucking Morley into the boards a little harder than I might have last season, none of my teammates call me out on it. Morley, on the other hand, has plenty of feelings that he wants to share with the class.

"Fuck off, asshole," he snaps when I thrust my stick between his skates, angling for the puck.

This whole scene feels like déjà vu. Last time we were battling it out one on one like this, it was the final game of preseason back in late September. It's been two months since I've seen his face, and yeah, I hate it just as much. My lip curls. "Nose is lookin' good, Joe. You pay a pretty dime for it?"

Mouth twisting in a snarl, he tries to shove me out of the way. "I'm telling you, Cain, you better watch it or I'll—"

"You'll what?" I growl. "Bitch some more to your buddies?"

His eyes narrow into thin slits behind his visor. "Yeah, well, me bitchin' causes problems for you."

"The only problem I see is that you're a waste of fucking breath, Morley."

With a smooth pivot, I turn on my blades and send the

puck skimming the base of the boards toward where Beaumont waits on the other side of the net. I'm gone before Morley can pop off again, bending low in the knees as I push off each blade, chasing my captain as he dekes one of Morley's linemates. Upon seeing me to his left, Andre flicks the puck my way. I feel the vibration run up along the length of my stick from the force of his wrist shot.

After Hunt's goal in the last period, New York has barely let him come up for air again, so I scan the ice with a fast, critical eye. Ultimately make the call to pass it to Bordeaux even though he's surviving tonight by the skin of his teeth. Literally. He took a puck to the lower half of his face in the first ten minutes of the game. A period and a half later, dried blood still clings to his jaw like a battle scar.

I let out a sigh of relief when Henri makes enough space for himself to hook the biscuit with his stick just before one of New York's D-men tries to swipe it away. With savage precision, Bordeaux dumps the puck deep in the offensive zone, sending Kammer and Hunt off on a high-speed chase before New York can claim the prize.

Twenty seconds later, the lamp lights as Bordeaux sinks the biscuit between the legs of New York's goalie. It's a thing of fucking beauty and we all swarm him with hollers and cheers. I get one gloved hand on the back of Henri's helmet, and Hunt grabs the both of us with his big paws, and then he pulls us in until our helmets all collide. We're laughing and sweating and telling Bordeaux that he's the best boy in our very limited French, and he's pretending to fight us off while sporting a massive, still-bloody grin.

3-2.

Fuck, it might not be a win yet, but it feels so good.

CHAPTER 31
DAISY

I've just finished returning Anita's plants to her apartment when my phone vibrates with an incoming call. As I reach for it in my bag, I spare my old front door a passing glance. It's been over a month since I've moved into Weston's house, and I'm no closer to figuring out what I want to do with my life than the day that I quit my job.

So far, rent isn't an issue, but—

Is rent *even* the issue? With the way things are going with West, I can't imagine returning to my place. And if I'm not planning on moving back in, what's the point of holding onto the keys? I'll talk to West about it. I mean, I already know what he's going to tell me, but talking things out is sort of our thing, and I'd rather he get a say in my living situation, too.

Although maybe I'll leave it for tomorrow. He has to still be reeling from everything that happened today with his parents. Even just thinking about it sends my heartrate soaring, and David and Molly Cain didn't even raise me.

When my phone starts vibrating again, I curse under my breath. Fumbling for it again in my purse, I take note of

Amber's name on the Caller ID as I press the device to my ear. "Sorry," I say breathlessly as I head for the elevator at the end of the hall. "I totally got distracted. Let me re-do all that. Hi Amber, it's so great to hear from—"

"Daisy."

As soon as the panic in her voice registers, my feet stop moving. I'm maybe ten feet away from the elevator. To my left, someone in their apartment has the volume set so loudly on their TV, I can hear that they're watching one of the Marvel movies.

"Daisy, are you home?"

I feel myself turn to glance back at the door to my apartment. I'm not *not* home. Only, Weston's house feels safer to me than my place ever has. I'm not talking about the locks on the doors or a concierge service. I mean, the fact that I share the house in Winthrop with *West* makes it feel safe—a place to ride out the storm.

"Is it Weston?" I ask. The game should still be on. One quick look at the clock on my phone tells me that they're somewhere in the second period and closing in on the third. There aren't any new notifications from Sports 24/7 from the last time that I checked, so it can't be an injury, I don't think. Gripping the strap of my bag, I force myself to ask, "Did Joe get hurt? Did the team call you?"

Because they're playing New York again tonight.

Because this is actually my nightmare, getting a phone call like this. No one who asks if you're home like that has anything but bad news to share.

I press a trembling hand to my heart.

Amber's voice is soft but stern in my ear. "Please sit down. Please, Daisy."

"You're scaring me."

"I know."

Grabbing my keys from my bag, I flip through them until I get to the one for my apartment. I shove it in the lock. Turn the knob. It's dark inside. Musty. I ask, "Should I be scared?"

Amber only says, "Tell me when you're sitting."

"Okay, hold on. I just—"

I hit the switch on the entryway wall, but the overhead light in the living room doesn't come on. Moving deeper into my apartment, I try the lamp that's perched on the end table beside my loveseat. It doesn't turn on either.

As I stand there in the middle of my old living room, it dawns on me that I must have forgotten to pay the electric bill. Not a problem, since I haven't been living here, except for the fact that I'm pretty sure Amber is about to drop a bomb on my little world while I'm drowning in darkness.

Fuck this.

I close the front door behind me and slide my key back into the lock. The hallway is overly bright after standing in the near pitch-black for a few minutes. "Tell me," I say to Amber as I head back for the elevator.

"But are you—"

"I can handle it." Because I can handle anything, can't I? I've had my world turned upside down more times than I can count. I'm not sure that I've always turned out stronger for it, but aside from some bumps and scrapes, I'm still whole. That's a lot more than some can say. "Amber, just spit it out. Please. You're seriously freaking me out."

The elevator takes forever in this building.

More than enough time for her to tell me whatever she has to say while I wait for the car to get up to the fifth floor.

I stab the button and watch it light up.

"Joe, he . . ."

"He, what?" Honestly, fuck that guy. I've never even met him, and I hate him. "Did he hurt you again? Did he say something to you?"

"No, no, Daisy, he—I think that he's been—"

It occurs to me in that exact moment that she's crying.

Not small little sniffles, but great, big heaving sobs. The elevator chimes with the arrival of the car, and the doors slide open to reveal an empty interior.

I don't get on.

Something like dread weights my feet to the floor. It crawls along my skin. Scrapes down my spine. With my heart thundering in my ears, I hear myself ask, "He's done what, Amber?" And somehow my voice doesn't waver although I don't know why it's not when a full-body tremble has taken hold of me from the crown of my head down to the tips of my toes.

"I think he put a camera in my house. Somehow. Maybe when I first moved in. I-I don't know but he must have, okay? He must have because otherwise—otherwise there's no way that he would know, Daisy. I promise you, there's no other way that he would know unless—unless he heard us."

Us.

Heard *me*?

The elevator doors close shut.

I'm frozen in that hallway.

The dread is in my belly now, and I think that I'm going to be sick.

Amber lets out another big sob. "I'm so sorry, Daisy. If I'd known, I wouldn't have emailed you. I wouldn't have taken your call. I wouldn't have—"

I sink to the floor right there in the hall. Better here, in the light, than tucked away in the darkness of my old home. I wrap my arms around my shins, tight, tight, tight, curling into a tiny ball where nothing can kill me if I don't let it.

And this won't kill me.

It will hurt. It will drag me to places where I'd rather not go, but it won't kill me.

It *won't*.

I can't let it.

"Who did he tell?" I ask, and again my voice is strangely calm.

And again, Amber lets out another sob, right before she says, "Everyone."

*"Sometimes you want to scream. Sometimes you want to fight.
When it comes to hockey, the good news is that you can do both."*
—Confessions of a Puck Bunny

CHAPTER 32
WESTON

I know something is wrong when one of the publicists from the Blades' in-house PR team actually enters the bench in the middle of the third period.

Beaumont and I both turn to stare as she shuffles behind the row of seated hockey players and coaches. "Excuse me, coming through, sorry, Kammer, sorry." Panic streaks across her expression, the sight of it so visceral that I actually rear back.

"What the fuck?" Beaumont grunts.

I don't say anything, just watch as she practically launches herself at Coach Hall. Grabbing hold of him by the arm, she tugs him down to whisper something in his ear.

All the color drains from his face.

"Andre," I start to say, voice tinged with worry, but then we're being called for our next shift. Muscle memory kicks in and I follow Beaumont onto the ice. By some miracle, we've managed to put another one in the net, bringing the score to 4-2 with less than eight minutes left in the game.

Beaumont sends me a pointed glance over his shoulder. The look on his face says to forget what just happened and keep my head in the game.

I do my best.

But by the time our shift is over and we're shuffling back onto the bench, Coach is gone, Jackson Carter is in his place, and everyone is talking over each other. The sight of me standing there, sweating from my shift, has my whole team clamoring up.

I feel my heartrate shift into overtime. "What happened?"

Hunt says, "It's Daisy."

NO ONE KNOWS ANYTHING ELSE.

I spend the last six minutes trying to get information out of Jackson and the other assistant coaches, but their lips are sealed tight. Then again, the worried looks on their faces tells me that they don't know anything either.

We win by two. It's by far the best numbers that we've put up in weeks, but I can't even enjoy the celly because Daisy.

Daisy.

As soon as the final buzzer sounds off, I'm tearing down the tunnel toward the dressing room. Fuck the post-game workout tonight. Fuck talking to the media. Fuck everything besides finding out what the hell is going on before I lose my mind.

Carter steps in beside me. "He's waiting for you."

"Where?" I bite off.

"Parking garage." He tells me where Coach is parked, and I give a curt nod.

I don't remember stripping out of my gear, and if I'm being honest, I don't even remember if I took the time to put any of it away. If there's one thing that I'm not worried about, though, it's that. My boys will take care of it all for me because we're family. With just my wallet, car keys, and phone, I jog all the way to the garage.

No missed calls from Daisy.

No missed texts either.

But there's something else—a notification that's popped up from Sports 24/7 has me slowing my steps. With my heart in my throat, I click on it:

Confessions of a Puck Bunny: Sinner or Saint? Daisy Hall's Past Marital Affair Revealed

Trembling, I briefly allow myself one moment to close my eyes, and then I shove my phone into the pocket of my jeans. The headline could be anything. Hell, it could be them coming out with some crazy spoof piece claiming that Daisy's cheating on me to be with Tory. I'm not gonna feed into the fear because if I know anything, it's that Daisy loves me.

Correction: she's *in* love with me. Just like I'm in love with her.

The rest we'll figure out.

When I turn the corner, I spot Coach pacing by his SUV like a man possessed. He takes one look at me, and says, "Can you drive?"

He thrusts a set of car keys at me. "Coach?"

"I can't, kid." His voice is a tiny thread of its usual booming tenor. His blue eyes are wide with terror and something else that I can't pinpoint. He gives the keys an emphatic shake. "I can't get behind the wheel. Not like this. Can you drive?"

He looks like shit. I'm sure that I look no better.

I take the keys anyway. "Yeah, I'll drive. Get in." And because he really does look like he might shatter in two at any second, I get the passenger side door open for him and help him in. When I climb into the driver's seat, I force myself to disassociate the way that I do when I'm on the ice. It's just me, it's just our destination. I grip the steering wheel in both hands, swallow down everything inside my soul that's screaming out for Daisy, and say, "Where are we going?"

"Back Bay. Daisy's old apartment."

We don't speak until we're on Storrow Drive.

"I'm retiring."

The pronouncement is so unexpected that I almost swerve us into the next lane. Righting the car at the last second, I spare a quick glance for the man sitting in the passenger seat. "What? *Now*?"

Coach stares straight ahead. "The plan was to retire at the end of this season, so I guess resigning is more appropriate. I'm heading out early."

I shake my head. "I don't understand."

"I love my daughter, Cain. That's what you need to know."

Three months ago, I would have let it go. But in the last two months, Sam Hall has done his very best to make his daughter feel like shit. Which means that I *can't* let it go, and if he's already one foot out the door with the Blades, then I don't really see a point in mincing words.

"Love her?" Incredulity drips from my tone. "You've got a funny way of showing it."

I hear his throat work with an audible gulp. "Okay, yeah. I deserve that."

"You deserve a hell of a lot more, actually, but Daisy would never forgive me. You've been utter shit to her, but she keeps you on a pedestal—lately, I can't even tell you why."

With that off my chest, we lapse into more awkward silence.

Hall's SUV crawls its way forward through traffic. When someone cuts me off, it takes every bit of willpower to keep from leaning my head out the window and shouting at them. We have all of two miles to go and yet we've barely gone half that.

"Her mother wanted me to go out to California with her," Coach says suddenly. "Can you imagine what that's like, having the love of your life basically imply that you're welcome to join her but the invitation doesn't extend to the child that you share together?"

Shocked, I slam too hard on the brakes. "What the *fuck*?"

"Drive, Cain."

"But—"

"What are you going to do? Sprint all the way to California to yell at the woman? Drive, please."

I ease my foot onto the gas again.

"Alice is a dreamer. And in the beginning, I loved that about her. There's something obscenely romantic about falling for someone who thinks that the two of you came together by Fate. It makes you feel special. Wanted." In my periphery, I see him tap his thumb against his thigh. "Soon, that dream became about more than just me—she dreamed about getting married, having babies, going back to school, taking a trip out West because wouldn't that be fun?" A harsh noise pushes past his lips. "Individually, none of those things are problems. Even collectively, they aren't. Until you start to put the puzzle pieces together inside your head, and you realize that when your wife says that she's dreaming, it's because she never feels satisfied. I spent almost seven years of our marriage clinging to her. And I still . . . It's still something I'm working on, let's just put it that way. I know better."

"Did she resent you for it? Back then?"

"Every day," he sighs. "So, then it became all about California. She was enthralled with Hollywood, and I was enthralled by her. I just never thought she'd come right out and ask me to go with her when she left. I had a job, bills—"

"What about Daisy?"

"Yeah, what about Daisy? According to Alice, Daisy was old enough to stay with extended family. Ten years old. Can you fucking imagine?" Shoving his hand into his pocket, Coach pulls out his pack of toothpicks. "I couldn't. That little girl owned my fucking soul."

I bite the inside of my cheek. "Does Daisy know? About how her mother feels?"

"Never saw the point in spelling it out for her in black and white like that. Daisy is smart. Too smart for her own good sometimes. She understood far sooner than I ever did that her mother was never coming back."

Today, she told my parents that she'd made the decision to move on in her life without a mother. She hadn't said it cruelly, just matter of fact. Even when her dreams didn't pan out with figure skating, she went and got a job in accounting. With a mother like Alice Hall, no wonder Daisy has turned out to be so pragmatic. It's incredibly rare that she allows her emotions to get the best of her, and lately, the only times when that brave mask of hers slips is when she talks about Bunny.

When the news broke about her alter ego, she asked me if I wanted to know why she'd created *Confessions of a Puck Bunny* in the first place. I didn't want to push, then. I still don't want to push now. But there's a niggling feeling in my gut that tells me I'm about to find out.

I end up in Anita's apartment again. This time, she's here with me.

Her luggage is parked by the front door and she's bustling about the kitchen to make me some tea. "You're lucky that I got home when I did," she tells me as she turns the stove on to heat the kettle. "No electricity? I've told you this once, Daisy, and I'll tell you it again. You don't move in with a man without some sort of contract." Her brown eyes pierce me with a hard stare. "And you never, ever let him throw you out."

I sigh. "Anita, I already said that West didn't kick me out."

"You were crying on that dirty floor."

"It's really not that dirty?"

She huffs. "And where is he, huh? Not here when you need him."

There's no point in telling her—again—that West won't have his phone for at least another hour. In an effort to quickly reach my dad, I ended up calling various staff members for the Blades until someone promised they'd be able to personally get him a message during the game. Normally, I would never bother him while he's working, but considering the *last* scandal that broke out in relation to Bunny . . . Well, I figure it's better to just get it over with.

Even if rehashing everything means making me feel like crap all over again.

As I sit at Anita's table, I can't help but feel like a kid about to be reprimanded. Until Amber, I've never breathed a word about what happened at Dartmouth to anyone. I didn't keep my silence out of a weird, sick need to protect him; I just wanted to forget that it ever happened at all.

Thanks to Joe Morley, the whole world now knows that I slept with one of Dartmouth's hockey coaches. A married one, at that.

"Here, take this. You will feel better." Anita plunks a steaming mug of tea down in front of me.

I tip my head back to smile up at her. "Thank you," I whisper gratefully.

She's somewhere in her seventies, I think. With gray-streaked hair and a big, wide grin, Anita sends most of the folks on our floor running the opposite way. She's always been very kind with me. While I drink the tea that she made me, she gently pets the top of my head like I'm a dog. I've always loved living across the hall from her.

When a knock comes on the door, she pats my head one more time. "That must be your father."

Show time.

Taking one last sip of tea for fortitude, I set the mug down and push to my feet. I've barely taken one step toward the door when a wiry pair of arms fold around me and bring me in close.

Dad.

I recognize the feel of his hug immediately. Despite what Anita said, I haven't cried once since Amber's call.

Truly, I've felt more empty and numb than anything else. But the moment that I wrap my arms around my dad, tears start to fall. They blur my vision and build pressure behind my nose. My dad whispers something in my ear but I'm crying too hard to make sense of anything beyond the comfort of his arms around me.

It takes minutes, maybe longer, for my tears to finally taper off. When they do, it's to the realization that Anita has left us alone in her apartment—and that West is sitting at the head of the table.

I lower my gaze in shame.

If he read that article, he must think the worst of me.

Dad takes the seat beside mine. He moves like he wants to take my hands in his but seems to think better of it and reaches for a toothpick instead. He used to smoke cigarettes when I was a kid. Apparently, I begged him to stop when I was in the second grade, so he took up carrying around toothpicks to help with the oral fixation. I've never seen him without a pack. It brings me some weird level of comfort to see him chewing on one now.

"I want to talk about that article," he says gently, "but first I need to get something off my chest. Okay?"

I nod. "Okay."

He blows out a big breath. "I'm sorry, Dais. I am so incredibly sorry that I've made you feel forgotten and alone. And while I had my reasons, it's going to take me a very long time to forgive myself."

With my arms wrapped around my middle, I lift my head to meet Dad's gaze. "I'm sorry, too. I wish that—"

"No." His tone is firm. "No, you aren't going to apologize for anything, kid. How I've been acting isn't your fault, and I should have told you that from the start." When I open my mouth to protest again, he cuts me off with a shake of his head. "I let you believe that you were a problem when, really, Daisy, that is so far from the truth, it's not even funny. Here, I want you to look at this."

Shifting his weight, he reaches into his pocket for his phone. As he fiddles with it, I can't stop my gaze from drifting back over to Weston. He's wearing the same clothes that he left the house in earlier but . . . I tilt my head, staring at the white tag on the neck of his T-shirt. Somehow, he's pulled his shirt on not only inside out but also backwards. Did he get dressed in the dark after the game?

"Note the date, please," Dad says. "And the time."

I force my stare away from West to look down at the phone that Dad has slid toward me. With shaky fingers, I pick it up and read the subject line: **CONCERNING DAISY HALL**. The date is stamped as—*oh*.

It's the same day that Bunny got leaked. And he sent it before I even got to his office.

With his brows lowered, Dad uses his toothpick to gesture at the phone. "Keep going."

The more I read, the harder it is to sit there at Anita's table without breaking down all over again.

"There were a few people on the board that wanted to make Bunny a big problem for you, Dais, but everyone else . . ." Dad inhales sharply through his nose. "Everyone else respected the stance that you'd taken over the years. They understood that you weren't listening in on conversations or breaking NDAs. Yes, there was a few grumbles about how all of this would be easier to handle if you weren't my daughter, but as I pointed out to them—if you weren't my daughter, there'd be no threat of legal repercussions, anyway."

He leans forward on his elbows. "Your posts were inflammatory not because they weren't true but because they were—and you always made sure that your t's were crossed, and your i's were dotted. You came with proof. I'm proud of you, Dais."

My mouth feels like sandpaper. "But if none of the board could find fault with me then why would . . ."

"The commissioner took issue." Wearily, Dad rubs his hand down the side of his face. "He wouldn't let us make a statement offering our support. He threatened to take legal action against the team if we so much as offered you any advice whatsoever. He wanted your presence scrubbed from every trace of the internet, and I—"

"Wanted to walk," I whisper, my gaze dipping back down to the last sentence in his email: **THERE SEEMS TO BE SOMETHING LOST IN TRANSLATION, SIR, SO LET ME REPEAT MYSELF AGAIN: I WILL NOT TAKE A STAND AGAINST MY OWN DAUGHTER, AND IF THAT MEANS I NEED TO RESIGN EFFECTIVE IMME-DIATELY, THEN THAT'S WHAT I'LL DO.**

In all capital letters, too, because Sam Hall knows no other way.

My chest grows tight with guilt. "I never wanted you to quit."

"Resign." His mustache twitches with a there and gone again grin. "You quit your job, kid. I . . . I resigned."

"There's not even a difference!"

"In our hearts, there is." And he places his hand right over his heart, too, when he says it.

I don't want to laugh, but this is *Dad*. I get all of my sarcasm from him. It's a curse.

He clears his throat. "I couldn't support you the way that I wanted to while affiliated with the team, kid. Too much red tape. The Blades have given me a lot over the years but you—" He lightly touches my arm. "You're the reason that I'm alive. I'm sorry if you felt otherwise. I'm even sorrier that it took so long." He pulls back. "Leaving the team abruptly was never part of the plan, and I've been working myself into an early grave to make the transition as smooth as possible—especially because I'm going to be ruffling lots of feathers on my way out the door."

For the first time since coming into Anita's, West speaks up. "You're picking Jackson, aren't you?"

Dad's lips curve in one of his scary hockey grins. "You should see the contract that I have being whipped up right now—it has them all by the balls. But yes, if I have my way, Carter will be the new head coach after I leave."

And I'm sure that he'll get his way, too. Sam Hall always makes lemonade out of lemons.

Gently, I push his phone back toward him. "I wish you had found a way to say all of this before—I would have understood." It hurts to think that maybe he thought that I wouldn't.

His blue eyes turn somber. "I know, kid. I think that when you're trying to protect the people you love, sometimes you get tunnel vision. Plus, well. I thought when you saw me encouraging the wedding with West, you'd realize that I had your back."

I frown. "Why would that make me think you were supporting me?"

At that, Dad gets a funny look on his face. His stare flicks from me to West and back again. "Ah," he starts awkwardly, "because you've been in love with him for years? And I thought—" Red-faced, he shoots Weston another glance. "I thought he felt the same way. Jesus, did I read that wrong? If I did, I'm so—"

"You didn't."

My heart crashes against my rib cage as I look to West. Though he's clearly blushing, he sits with his shoulders back and his wedding band on full display where his left hand rests on the table.

"I was hoping to tell her on her own," he says a little dryly, "but yeah, Coach. I'm in love with your daughter.

Hopelessly. The forever kinda love. If I have my way, we'll be together for the rest of our lives."

Tears burn against the backs of my eyelids. Trust West to march to the beat of his own drum and confess his feelings with an audience.

Wiping my damp cheek with the back of my hand, I confess simply, "I'm in love with you, too."

His smile is soft and only for me. "I know you are, sweetheart."

CHAPTER 34
WESTON

Anita is a gem. She gives us free rein over her apartment for the next hour, in which the three of us get into a heated debate about what to do with Joe Morley.

I draw the line at discussing the details of the article, though.

Coach bristles in that way he does when he's shouting obscenities from the bench in the middle of a game. "Cain, I'm aware that you're now married to my daughter, but let me remind you that I practically arranged this marriage. If I want to discuss with Daisy what exactly happened at Dartmouth, with someone that I fucking *know*—hell, someone that I introduced her to, then I'll—"

"She's seeing a therapist." I don't back down, not even when confronted with of all his red-faced bluster. "And if I'm not wrong, Dartmouth is the reason why."

"Is that true?" He turns the full force of his attention on Daisy, who shrinks into my side. I run a soothing hand up and down her spine, until slowly, the tension bleeds out of her shoulders, and she slumps against me.

"Sam."

With an upward flash of his brows, he turns back to me. If he's shocked that I just used his name for the first time in over ten years, he doesn't tell me to get fucked. Which is good because soon enough, he's just gonna be Sam Hall again and I'll still be married to his daughter. We're about to be stuck with each other for the rest of our lives. In the grand scheme of things, ten years of him coaching me is practically nothing.

His eyes narrow. "West."

Not kid, not Cain.

Guess we're really doing this, then.

I motion to where his phone sits on the table.

"Morley invaded her privacy." If what Daisy said is true about Amber Conners, then good ol' Joe might have some major legal problems coming down the pipeline. Hiding and installing cameras in your ex-wife's home is never gonna slide. Just the thought of him eavesdropping on Daisy's call has my temper rising. "Actually, it's worse than invading Daisy's privacy. He took away her right to process what happened to her on her own timeline—right after she sought someone out, too."

"West, I . . . I need to tell you—I mean, I should say that—"

Immediately, I turn to Daisy, gently cupping her cheek. When her amber eyes finally lift to mine, they're glittering with unshed tears. I lean forward and press a kiss to her forehead. Against her temple, I murmur, "What you need to do in public to right a wrong is one thing, but you don't need to put a brave smile on with me. Go to your sessions. Be not okay. And whenever you're ready, sweetheart— whether it's a month from now or six or even longer—I'll be here to hold your hand and listen."

Her jaw works so tightly that I can feel her teeth grinding against the weight of my palm. Her eyes are shimmering, too, her nostrils flaring with tightly controlled breaths. I know my wife well enough to recognize the signs of when she's doing everything in her power to keep her emotions in check.

Wordlessly, I push my chair back and grab hers by the two front legs. Before she can protest, I'm turning her around so that her back is to her dad and her front is facing the entrance to the kitchen. Then I press my own chair as close to hers as I can get, my legs spread wide on either side of her thighs. I have her wrapped in my arms a heartbeat later, my chin resting on her shoulder. Against her throat, I utter, "Go ahead, Cain. Let it all out."

In the safety of my embrace, she does. Her tears stain my forearms, her fingers press into my thighs. As her quiet sobs push their way free, I give her the space to not be okay, for however long she needs.

WHEN WE'RE BRUSHING our teeth in our bathroom a few hours later, Daisy leans forward to spit her toothpaste into the sink. Her eyes are still bloodshot from crying, and we had to power down both of our phones just to end the onslaught of notifications, but she looks a little lighter than she did at Anita's.

Light enough to say, "I want to move in here. Permanently."

I follow suit and spit out my toothpaste. After toweling off my face, I tell her, "There's a whole house, Cain. You don't need to relegate yourself to only the primary bathroom."

Lips parting with a startled laugh, she grabs the hand towel I just used and thwacks me in the gut with it. "Who made you the way that you are?"

She's being facetious, but I still shrug and give her hell.

"You walked them out the door today like a good little soldier."

Her cheeks pinken. "God, I can't believe that was only today. Also, should I be apologizing for how I handled that or . . ."

"Not a chance."

"Because you feel vindicated that they got to have a taste of their own medicine?"

"No, because that was the moment I realized that I'm in love with you."

Instead of fawning all over me, the way she did earlier, she claps back, "And here I was thinking that you knew that you loved me way sooner than today."

I narrow my eyes. "Are those shots fired?"

"I'm just saying, I found your wedding vows the other day, and I'm *pretty* sure that you were at least ninety-nine percent in love with me before we even got married." Bloodshot eyes and all, her entire face brightens with glee. "Oh, let me read it back to you! We can compare notes."

She's gone.

No, really, she fucking *bounds* out of the bathroom. It's déjà vu all again because here I am, chasing after her. "Daisy," I warn, "you do not need to do this."

"I wouldn't be me if I didn't."

It's true, and I want to laugh so badly, but I would also like to not be the recipient of one of her read-alongs again. It was a horrifying experience. Even if it did lead to the hottest sex of my life—outside of going down on Daisy, that is.

Flinging open her bedside table drawer, she pulls out a sheet of paper with the same flare a treasure hunter might brandish a gold coin. "Here we go. Come sit next to me, West. You are an integral part of this discussion."

She hops up onto the bed and pats the empty space beside her.

Like a total loser, I stand there, grinning, as she begins to recite my wedding vows. As far as days go, today has been one of the worst. If you asked me four hours ago if I'd be listening to my wife try and mimic the sound of my voice—while failing epically—I would have laughed in your face.

I would have laughed because I would have said that there's no way that I can be *this* happy when it's been one thing after another, all of it emotional and traumatic and dark. But the thing is, I am happy.

Because of her.

Because of Daisy.

I pluck my vows out of her grasp and lay them flat on the bedside table. Then I push her down onto the bed and lower my weight on top of hers, not seeking anything more than the kiss that I press onto her lips.

This, right here, is happiness.

She hooks her thigh around my hips to keep me close. Gives me one of those biting little kisses that sends blood rushing straight down to my dick. Groaning, I tear my mouth away and pant harshly into the crook of her neck. "We're not fucking today. Get it out of your head."

Her hand finds my shoulder. "Aw, West, are you being very kind, very respectable again?"

Pushing my erection into her, I nip at her throat. "I'm trying, sweetheart. Failing, yes, but trying."

"Here, I'll help. Let's flip-cuddle."

I pull back to stare at her. "Flip-what?"

She giggles hard enough that a pink blush spreads across her chest. "Like, flip-fucking? But the cuddle version instead."

"I have no idea what you're talking about."

"I know you don't, West. But I'm going to show you, see?" She squirms out from underneath me, turns off the bedside lamps, and pulls back the comforter. In the scant light filtering in from beyond the drawn curtains, I can just make out her pointing to the bed. "It has been a *day*, and physical touch is clearly our love language, so." She motions for me to climb in properly.

Following her lead, I slide under the sheets. "I thought talking was sort of our thing? I mean, you never stop."

A pillow comes down on my face, and her entire body weight follows right after.

Not to be outdone, I wrap my legs around her hips and flip her underneath me. We're both laughing too hard to speak as I pull the pillow away from my face, tossing it aside. I lean down and she leans up, and we meet in the middle for another kiss. It's sweet, almost. It tastes like sunshine, and hope, and strawberries.

It feels like home.

"I love you," I say against her lips.

She smiles against mine. "I've loved you for longer."

All right. Fine. It's another competition that we'll each fight to win, but happiness still stirs in my chest as my wife scoots over and motions for me to roll over onto my side. "C'mon, husband, you can be the little spoon first."

I fall asleep with my wife's arm wrapped around me. And because she's her, she sets an alarm for four in the morning like a total psycho, so I can cuddle her in return.

CHAPTER 35

DAISY

THREE MONTHS LATER

Coach Sam Hall officially retires from the Boston Blades the day after Joe Morley is sent to jail.

I'm not saying that the party we throw for Dad is actually a celly for Morley being locked away, but I *am* saying that there's a general sense of relief as everyone piles into The Box for the festivities.

Even Amber is around here somewhere. It only felt right that she be invited.

West leans his weight into me, his back flush against my front while I wrap my arms around his chest. "You doing okay, sweetheart?"

Since I'm perched on one of the stools at the bar, I'm at the perfect height to press a tiny kiss to the sensitive skin beneath his earlobe. When he shudders at my touch, I give him another kiss in the same spot, then lower my chin to rest on his shoulder. "I don't know. As good as I'm going to be, I think."

After months of conversation with Karen, my therapist, I've come to the conclusion that I'll never be okay with what Morley did to me. Maybe there's some karma in it—you could argue that Joe unearthing my past in such a bloodthirsty fashion isn't so different than what I did to him as Bunny. But after learning just how far he went to keep Amber under his thumb, I don't have any empathy left in my heart for him. He broke into her house multiple times, installed cameras without her knowing, and oh yeah, stalked her for funsies because why not.

Joe Morley can rot in jail for all I care.

I don't feel the same about what happened to me at Dartmouth. It's not that I'm making excuses or anything, it's just that I'm having a hard time coming to grips with the perception that I had as a naïve teenager versus the grim reality of what was truly happening to me.

West is coming in for a session next week, and I'm hoping that I'll have the courage to tell him everything, but he's also assured me more than once that I'm stuck with him until I'm old and gray. Even if it takes another fifty years, he'll be okay with that too. And I think . . . I think all of this has helped me to decide to return to school, to maybe dip my hands into social work. I miss the community. Even more, I miss the happiness I feel in helping someone else.

I won't let Morley take that away from me.

If there's any silver lining, it's that once the top guns at Sports 24/7 discovered one of their junior editors had published a story featuring underage minors, it was yanked down within twenty-four hours and scrubbed from their database.

It's still out there, but I try not to think about it too hard.

I kiss his neck. "Are you okay with your parents coming to the game next week?"

Almost nervously, West fiddles with my wedding ring as he holds my hand. "I don't know. I want to believe what you said to them resonated, but there's a very good chance that they'll play nice for a bit and then go back to same old thing."

"The fact that Tory's decided to move to Boston should shake some sense into them, though, don't you think?"

"Or make them live even deeper in denial."

"I'm sorry," I tell him softly. "I'll hope they'll come around."

West's back shifts upward against me in a shrug. "I've come to terms with it if they don't. And if it doesn't work, then it's a good thing that I have you, and Tory, and all of them." He waves a hand to his teammates, both current and retired. "You said something that hit me—that you chose to leave your mom behind." West squeezes my hand. "I already chose my family years ago, I just never really put it together like that. And even after everything, I still wouldn't choose any differently. I love my life. I mean, I'd probably love it a little more if we were heading to the play-offs this year, but—"

"There's always next year," I say. "You're still young yet."

"Why do I feel like you're poking fun at me?"

"I'd never," I vow, but I do it while snickering into the warmth of his skin. Tilting my head up, I check out the rapidly growing crowd.

Across the way, the Anders brothers are playing darts with Josh, who I'm pretty sure is trying to instigate an argument with the Blades' new left winger, George Hawthorne. Zoe Beaumont is waddling around and way too pregnant to be here tonight; in contrast, I've never seen the big, bad Andre more panicked in his life. Every time Zoe so much as rubs her belly, he's up and out of his chair, running to her side.

Gwen and Hunt are making out in the corner of the bar like shameless teenagers. She's quite literally thrown herself over his lap, and I think they're trying to disguise it as dancing but I'm also pretty sure that no one showed up tonight hoping for a glimpse of Marshall Hunt's dick.

I didn't, anyway.

Henri Bordeaux managed the impossible and snuck in his new beagle puppy. People keep dropping the little guy treats, and Henri must be crossing the line from tipsy to drunk because—

"Did you just see that?" I demand of West. "Look at Henri."

Since people-watching is one of our favorite past times, my husband takes no time to pick out Bordeaux from the crowd. I feel West jerk with surprise. "His ass is going to be out the door so fast."

We watch in mutual horror as Henri holds Crouton the Beagle Puppy in his arms while he proceeds to place an order with the pretty bartender. Crouton alone is enough to see Bordeaux kicked out of The Box, but the fact that the pup is currently snacking on Duke Harrison's retired jersey is tragic. For Crouton and Henri, I mean. Duke is completely unbothered as he and his wife chat with Holly and Jackson.

"What do you think he's going to do when he realizes that this party is for him, too?" I ask.

"Jackson? Cry, probably," West deadpans. "We're going to have to mop him off the floor by the end of the night."

I pause. "But we won't be here that long, will we?"

West goes still in my arms. Then he says, low and rough, "Nah, sweetheart. Me and you are calling it an early night."

It's my turn to shiver. We both know what's going to happen tonight, what we've been leading up to with months of epic foreplay. Wanting to get him started, I turn my head into the crook of his neck again and nip the tendon there.

The hand that was playing with my ring suddenly clamps down on my thigh. He doesn't make any noise— he has too much self-control for that in a public setting—

but he turns himself around to crowd me with his big body. Against my lips, he growls, "Behave yourself, menace."

I bite his lower lip in response.

His green eyes promise retribution.

Just before I can do anything else to drive him wild, there's a loud, tinny sound as someone passes the mic to my dad. Instantly, the room erupts into chants and cheers. I try my best to be one of the loudest. And, okay, if not the loudest then at least the most obnoxious. I know that I've succeeded when even Josh Kammer starts yelling for me to stop.

"Hey, hey, leave Daisy alone," Dad says into the mic with a wink in my direction. "No fucking with the coach's daughter."

From the back of the room, someone shouts, "Tell that to your son-in-law!"

It sets everyone off again. Even from here, I can tell that Dad is blushing. Him and West have formed a new level of respect for each other, but I'm sure he'd rather not think too closely about what it means for one of his star players and his daughter to be married.

"All right, enough, it's my last night. Be nice to the old guy." There's a few jeers about his age, but Dad brushes them all off. Nervously, he grips the microphone and peers out at all the people who have gathered to send him off to the next phase of his life, where he'll be joining a brand-new sports commentary broadcast channel.

The mic picks up the sound of his gulp.

"You know, when I took this gig with the Blades almost ten years ago, I thought they made a mistake. What were they doing hiring some kid out of Connecticut, you know?" Dad gives a little laugh. "And I mean that seriously—here was this brand new franchise trying to get on the up and up, and they looked at me"—he waves a hand at himself—

"and apparently they said to themselves, *that's the guy for us.*"

Everyone laughs, the GM the loudest.

Dad scrubs a hand over his mouth. When he pulls it away, he's not frowning, exactly, but his mood is somber as if it's really hitting him that he's about to walk away from the job that he's had for the better part of a decade.

"I will always be grateful for the Blades." Though his voice cracks, he presses on. "You took a kid out of Connecticut and gave him a reason to fight. In the process, we've lost some, we've won some"—here, the entire team starts yelling about their Cup win last season—"but we've done it all together," Dad goes on. "I've been to your weddings, I've been to your kids' birthdays, and even a few of your house parties." The mic whines shrilly as he leans in to growl, "Why can't all you fuckers be like Harrison, huh?"

The whole room breaks down at the mention of reclusive-Duke Harrison and his habit of staying far away from the media. Even Duke shouts, "There can only be one of me, Coach!"

Dad waves him off with a middle finger.

"You all are my family. Each and every one of you." He wipes at his eyes with the back of his hand. "And I thank you for letting me fight by your side every day for the last eight years."

On cue, navy and silver confetti starts falling from the ceiling. Beaumont and Hunt file forward to snatch up an unsuspecting Jackson from where Holly is already pulling out her camera to capture everything for the press conference tomorrow. Andre gets Jackson's upper half, Marshall gets his lower, and together they carry him to where my dad is waiting like some mafioso don, hands rubbing together gleefully as Carter is deposited right there in front of him.

It's utter chaos as West's teammates start putting together what's about to go down. Josh grabs Bjorn by the hand to swing him into a funky dance. Bordeaux is trying to clap with Crouton stuffed inside the folds of his jacket. Beaumont and Hunt both grab Jackson by the shoulders and plant kisses on the top of his head.

And then there's Dad, who is clearly on the verge of crying. Over the crowd, his gaze looks for mine and he makes a motion at his face as if asking if he still looks okay. We've had some bumps and growing pains since the Fall, but slowly we're getting better. Back to where we used to be. I shoot him a thumbs up and then the heart sign. He visibly lets out a relieved sigh.

Jackson, meanwhile, looks utterly bewildered. Even from here, though, I can see a sheen to his dark eyes as it sinks in that he's officially being promoted.

Dad says simply, "For better or worse, their lives are now in your hands, Coach."

I'm so entranced by the passing of the torch from one generation to the next, so to speak, that I almost miss Weston taking my hand. But then he's tugging me toward the door that leads to the secret passageway, the one you only have access to if you belong to the family of the Boston Blades.

Behind us, the party is still going strong.

I love them all, especially my dad, but I don't look back, not even once.

CHAPTER 36
WESTON

We tumble through the front door at home like teenagers.

Her small fists get a hold of my sweater, and that's all the encouragement that I need to pivot on my heel, ready to yank her into my arms. Hold. Wait. In unison, we kick off our shoes. Shrug out of our heavy coats. When I find her amber eyes in the relative darkness, the anticipation I feel in my soul is reflected back at me in her glittering gaze. It's so tangible, I could fucking choke on it.

"We doing this?" There's no turning back if we do. I'm ready to take that last step but won't if we're not on the same page. We're either in this together or we're nothing at all. "Be honest, Cain."

Somehow, her gaze burns brighter. "I want you."

"That's it?" It's a taunt, a plea, too. This will never be just about getting off for me. "You only want me?"

"I love you. My heart is beating so fast right now, I wish you could—wait, give me your hand." Her chilly fingers latch onto my wrist and then she's tugging me closer so I can press my palm to her heart. "Do you feel it? I'm trying not to freak out, but I am. I want this, West. Not just the sex.

I want to see how I make you lose control. I want that so badly I can *taste* it, and I want it because it's you. Because I've been hopelessly, tragically in love with my best friend for years now, and sometimes it shatters me, you know? Knowing that this is real and that it's not a dream."

"It's real," I manage. "And it's not a dream."

Right there in the foyer, I lift my wife into my arms. With my hands under her ass, and her legs wrapped tightly around my waist, I use her weight to push the front door closed—and then I press her back against it. If I strain my ears, I can hear the sporadic sounds of fireworks as they're set off across the harbor for New Year's Eve. But in this room, there's only the combined sounds of our shallow breathing.

She arches her spine, her fingers clawing at the nape of my neck. "*West.*"

"It's not a dream," I grunt against the parted seam of her lips. "And you and I both know that I've loved you from the second that we met. Now tell me what you want."

"Kiss me."

"No."

My name is a keening cry on her lips. As it shivers over my mouth, I'm so close to giving her what she wants—but I don't, not yet.

I turn my head and kiss her cheek instead. She protests with another cry.

"Does this feel like a dream?" I husk in her ear. "Or does it feel like you're coming out of your skin, you're so desperate to have me?"

She tries to circle her hips, but I pin them, hard, against the door. Lift her higher, too, so she can't rub down on me. Already, she's a wreck. Her blond hair is falling from its messy bun, her eyes are hazy with lust. Daisy gives so much of herself to others but this version of her—this needy, possessive girl who throws herself into the thick of things with no hesitation—belongs only to me. I cherish it. I worship it. I take every opportunity I can to fan the flames and watch her burn even brighter.

Lifting one hand away from her, I plant it against the door beside her head. Lean in close so I'm all she sees. "I can do this all-fucking-night, sweetheart. I'll make you so hard up for me, you'll come without me even putting a finger on you."

A shaky breath slips over her lips. "Please."

"Begging doesn't work on me, Cain. You know that."

With a frustrated noise, she wraps one hand around my wrist, the one that's planted against the door, and tries again to get some friction to no avail. A whine leaves her throat. "I want you."

"I know you do." I press a kiss to her temple. Another to her opposite cheek.

"Then why—"

"Because we both know the minute that I let you get your hands on me, it's over." And it's true. It would be embarrassing except that I know how much she loves having an effect on me. She's merciless, my wife. Only, tonight I want to drive her crazy, too.

We both know that I can.

I do it all the time.

But if mindless lust is her game, then torture and patience is mine.

Daisy's breath audibly catches as her thumb strokes my inner wrist, directly over where my pulse is fluttering fast. "A kiss, then. Give me a real one. You can play with me after that."

Play with her.

Fuuuckk, even the way she says it like that—so nonchalantly as if she isn't fully aware of how quickly it short-circuits my brain—is enough to have my dick going from a semi to hard in less than a second.

I narrow my eyes on her. "You did that on purpose."

She peers up at me through her lashes. "You deserve it."

God, she's a menace.

But it has the desired effect because I tear her away from the door, clasped safely in my embrace, and head for the stairs. With my one free hand, I frame her face and crash my mouth down over hers. Just like that, she turns frantic again in my arms, her own two hands coming up to clutch the back of neck.

She licks at my mouth, demanding entry, but I don't give her more—*patience.* I draw her bottom lip into my mouth, sucking on the flesh until I'm sure that I'll leave a bruise. She fights fire with fire, and suddenly, she's racking up the hem of my shirt, so can she touch her hands to my bare skin.

She tugs on one of my nipples.

Dig her nails into my spine.

By the time I make it to our room, I'm already half out of my mind as I drop her onto the bed and crawl my body over hers. Only, she's fast—faster than I appreciate some-times—and she slithers out of my grasp, rolling away until she's up on her knees and tearing off her shirt, leaving her in nothing else but a thin black bra.

"Shirt," she tells me pointedly. "Now."

I wrap my hand around her ankle and, with her yelping in surprise, drag her back toward me.

"Asshole," she gasps as I straddle her waist. "I can't believe you just did that."

"Better believe it, sweetheart." I drop down so my face is an inch away from hers. "You deserve it."

At her own words from earlier being thrown back in her face, a look of determination comes into her amber eyes. Just like that, I know that I'm fucked. Well and truly *fucked.*

I kiss her again to distract her, to distract myself, even. Our kisses turn heated, filthy, and I realize after a moment that I've completely lost the fight—as in, I've hooked an arm under her leg, spreading it wide, so that I can thrust against the seam of her jeans.

"Take them off," she whispers against my mouth. "Please, West."

Goddammit.

In a rush, I sit back on my heels, my fingers shaking visibly as I undo her button and draw the zipper down. Her belly quivers with each one of her breaths as I sit back even farther so I can wrestle her pants down over her hips. She helps me, the way that she always does, kicking them down her thighs while I drag them the rest of the way off.

She's damn near naked.

Beautiful. So beautiful.

I find her gaze, holding it, and pull off my sweater. Tossing it aside, I awkwardly fumble with my own jeans—until Daisy is sitting up to help me. Her hands tremble as mine do, and it's only then I realize how nervous we both really are.

I shouldn't be.

This is *Daisy*, who I gave my soul to that day we met, whether I realized it or not. Yet, I still can't seem to catch my breath. And when she pushes me backward onto my ass, her hands already reaching for my hard dick, it feels like the world is literally tipping upside down.

She circles me with her hand.

Rubs her thumb over the swollen head.

She meets my gaze briefly, a question in her eyes, and I nod jerkily. Daisy doesn't need any more encouragement than that. She bends over me, her hair falling in front of her face like a curtain. Resting my weight on one elbow, I push her hair back behind her ear, letting my thumb graze the sensitive shell.

The first pass of her lips over my cockhead has my pulse spiraling. I drag one jagged breath after another into my lungs, gasping her name, but she's clearly on a mission to make me lose my mind because she doesn't let herself get distracted for any longer than it takes for her to check in that I still want this.

I do.

Oh, fuck, but I do.

Her lips wrap around me, tongue flicking over my leaking slit. I grasp her hair in one hand and the sheets in the other, trying with everything I am not to push upward into her perfect mouth. She bobs her head, her mouth sinking deeper around me. Sensation explodes in my veins, tremors flooding down my legs.

"Daisy. Fuck, yes. *That.*"

She's touching herself. I can hear her wetness as she sinks a finger deep in her core, and I can feel the moment that her own pleasure skyrockets because her attention on my cock turns almost frantic. Messy. She pulls back to spit on her fingers, then sinks them down between her legs again, out of sight.

With a groan, I release her hair to curve my hand down over the back of her head. "More," I beg roughly. "Use your hand, sweetheart. Stroke me."

Dazed amber eyes flick up to my face. Her cheeks are flushed, her lips shiny and red around my cock. Swear to God, I die right then and there. Whimpering, she wraps her free hand around the base of my length, stroking me up and down. Her lids fall shut again.

"Eyes on me, Cain."

A ragged sound comes from the back of her throat as she obeys. In her heart-shaped face, her eyes are wide and glistening.

"Use two fingers," I tell her gruffly. "Can you do that for me?"

Her head is still bobbing, her mouth still working me over, but I know that she does as I tell her because she squeezes her eyes shut in the same moment that she loses all rhythm. Saliva drips down my length. After a moment, she catches it with her palm, and she pumps me harder. Fuck, that does something to me.

"Look at me, sweetheart. C'mon."

Almost lazily, her lids flutter open. I move my hand from the crown of her head to the base of my dick, taking over for her. On every upstroke of my fist, my knuckles touch those shiny lips of her. Pleasure spirals through me, and I hear myself plead, "Let me have you. Please, let me have you."

She pulls back off of me, gasping. "Yes. *Yes.*"

Because all me and Daisy do is talk, we've already discussed the details. No condom. She's on birth control. We've both been tested. But after I strip her out of her underwear and lower her onto her back, I still check in. As I do, I lower my hand to tease my fingers across her soft skin, her sensitive clit. I press one finger deep inside her, gently thrusting inside and out as I carefully watch her face.

"Are you sure?" I ask.

Her lids flutter closed as sensation sweeps over her, the blush that spreads across her skin telling me everything that I need to know.

"Daisy, yes? Or no?"

"Yes," she begs.

"I love you."

Her eyes shoot open. "I love you, too."

CHAPTER 37
DAISY

I'm a bundle of nerves as West slowly finger fucks me.

I'm hot everywhere, totally restless, ready to burst out of my skin. Going down on him while touching myself nearly pushed me right over the edge. And when he told me to use two fingers . . .

That's the thing about West. He doesn't even try to be sexy—he just says whatever is on his mind as it comes to him, and sure enough, nine times out of ten, its effect on me is catastrophic.

Even now, while he's checking in, his green eyes are dark with desire but he's so casually playing with me that I want to scream. I want to scream, and I want to cry, and I want—I want—

"West," I moan, completely distressed. "You can't just—you're driving me crazy."

His brows lower. "If you need something, tell me."

Tell him.

God, I love him and hate him all in the same breath sometimes.

My hips twitch. "Either fuck me, please, or—or—"

"Or what?"

With a whimper, I shoot up onto one elbow to clasp his wrist in my hand. He doesn't pull his finger out of me, though. Just presses his thumb down on my clit to keep the pleasure cresting toward an inevitable climax.

"Is this what you want?" His voice is pure gravel. He rubs me in tight, little circles. "Use your words, Daisy-belle. We both know that you know how to use them."

It's in that moment that he sinks another finger deep inside of me, and I throw my head back with a cry. "You're an *asshole*."

"So eloquent."

"Fuck. You, West." Gripping the sheets in both hands, I push my hips into his hand. But it's not enough. "Please, I need you."

I feel so empty when he pulls his fingers free, but heat encompasses my entire body the moment that he grabs me by the hips and pulls me toward him. My legs automatically fall open in invitation. His hungry gaze remains fixed on my face as if he can't get enough of seeing me fall apart.

I pull one leg up to my chest to give him room, and with one hand curled around his cock, he runs the swollen head through my wetness before positioning himself at my entrance. His eyes haven't left my face. "Can I, sweetheart?"

"Yes," I whisper. "Yes. Now."

With his eyes on mine, West pushes inside me. A groan escapes him, and—oh—*oh*. He feels big, perfect. When he pulls back to thrust in properly, I release my hold on my leg to hold onto his shoulders instead. He wraps my legs around his waist. Plants his balled fists on either side of my shoulders.

It seems to take every bit of his control, but he never tears his gaze away from mine, not even when he thrusts harder, not even when a flush stains his cheeks. He watches me, he *owns* me, and I'm hit with the stunning realization that he has truly loved me since that first day we met.

He's always watched me the same way he does now—as if he's enthralled by me.

"I love you," I choke out as my nails dig into his skin. "I love you so much."

He leans down, his mouth covering mine in a kiss so sinful, my toes curl. His tongue flirts with mine. It's messy and hot, and I'm crying out against his mouth. He doesn't hold back. When I'm teetering on the verge, I squeeze an arm between our two damp bodies to touch my finger to my clit.

"I'm going to come," I whimper. "West, please."

He sucks my lip into his mouth, growling, "Do it. Let me feel you come on me."

My heart feels like it's going to burst right out of my chest, and yet I'm still touching myself, still rubbing faster, and faster, and faster, until, with a cry, I break apart beneath West, writhing helplessly as I come.

It's the first time that he breaks eye contact.

He sits back on his heels, dragging my ass up onto his thighs, and pistons his hips forward. His jaw is tight, his flat stomach hollowing with every hard breath. He'll leave bruises on my thighs tomorrow, but I can't find it in myself to care. Because West has lost control—and he's so beautiful like this.

"Fuck, Daisy. Fuck, I'm gonna come."

He's even more stunning when he falls apart a few seconds later. His blond hair is damp across his forehead, his wide shoulders trembling with strain. His abs release and contract with every fast, urgent punch of his hips, until his mouth parts on a gruff shout, and he comes deep inside of me.

Slowly, reality filters back in.

The sheets are a mess. Our bodies are slick with sweat.

West stays inside me as he carefully lowers his body on top of mine. He presses his mouth to my throat, to the underside of my chin, to my mouth, feeding me slow, sweet kisses that prick tears at the backs of my eyes.

I wrap my arm around his sticky back, burrowing my face into the crook of his neck. "Do you remember what I said to you that first day? About not falling in love with me?"

I feel him nod, and then I feel his hand cover my hip. "Yeah."

"Thank you for not listening," I whisper. "Thank you for showing me that day and every day since that I'm worthy of something more."

He's quiet for a moment, and then he rolls us over so he can wrap his big body around me from behind. "You deserve the world, Daisy Daisy-belle Cain. And I'm gonna make sure you get it."

Soon, I'll need to get up and clean myself off.

Soon, the rest of the world will definitely come knocking.

But as I find myself drifting off, I hear myself say, "Don't let go yet."

And then Weston's hand curls around mine, holding tight as he threads our fingers together. "Never, sweetheart. Until we're old and gray, and even after then, I'll love you."

WESTON'S WEDDING VOWS

Today, you become my wife.

There should be something shocking about that.

I asked myself last night how we ended up here, with me getting ready to put a ring on your finger, and the only answer I could come up with is that you've been burned into my soul since the day we met.

I've spent most of my life always feeling off-balance.

I'm either too much or too little, too quiet or too loud, and I carried those scars with me until adulthood.

Until you.

The shocking thing about marrying you, Daisy Hall, is that it isn't shocking at all.

You're the one person who sees me.

The one person who never makes me feel like I should try harder to be somebody else.

If someone were to ask me if I had a best friend, I would point to you. And if they then asked if I believed in soulmates, I'd have no choice but to say yes.

Because of you.

I'll hold your hand forever, Daisy-belle. Just as long as you say, "I do."

DEAR FABULOUS READER

Hi there! It's been almost four long years since I last wrote a Dear Fabulous Reader section so please bear with me while I dust off the cobwebs.

This one might be a little different. There aren't any bullet point lists for one. Instead, I just want to say thank you for reading. When I first set out to write West & Daisy's story, I thought, "How fun would a marriage of convenience romance would be? Oh! And what if they were best friends?"

I did not anticipate how emotional this book would be.

I also did not realize how much of myself would end up in these pages either.

If you've followed me at all over the last few years, you may have noticed a lack of books—grief and trauma have a funny way of rearing their ugly heads. It quite literally didn't occur to me until I was more than halfway through the book that Daisy's connection with *Confessions of a Puck Bunny* is a direct parallel to how I feel about my own readers.

When I was sinking under the weight of depression, a message from a reader or a pickle meme (IYKYK) would pop up, and I would smile—sometimes for the first time in days, weeks. It didn't matter if I hadn't released a book, readers would email me or DM me, they would fill my lines at book signings, and I would stand there, awed, that so many people even cared.

In the last seven years, I have built so many friendships with those who have picked up a book of mine. And as the last four years occurred, where I retreated deeper and deeper into myself, it was my readers who always managed to grab me by the hand and yank me back out.

As I wrote Daisy's character, and I thought of the community of support and trust she had built, I wondered how I would feel if my own community was just . . . stripped away. It crushed me. I imagine that Daisy would feel the same, and we see her struggle with her loss.

In the same breath, I would like to touch upon her "experience" at Dartmouth. First and foremost, please no one be knocking down Dartmouth's door to demand vengeance! This particular scenario is very much fiction and a product of my imagination. With that said, it would be remiss of me if I didn't mention that Daisy's own struggles with accepting what happened to her (i.e., grooming, power imbalance, to say nothing of her being underage) is something many people experience in their lives.

Myself included.

I chose to not give the "Dartmouth" man a name. In fairness, it's probably because I choose not to reference the person who SA'ed me by name. It's been over twenty years but some things become habit, and before I knew it, I fed that habit to Daisy.

My intention with Slap Shot was to focus on the healing journey. Joe Morley, of course, got his comeuppance. Off page, I hope that the Dartmouth man would get his as well.

On one last note (a much happier one!), I know you might be thinking, "MARIA, HOW ARE YOU GOING TO

MAKE THE BLADES SUCK SO BADLY?" I know. I *know*. But when I read back through Body Check in lead up to writing Slap Shot, it was the epilogue that stood out to me the most.

We know that Sam Hall retires the following year after the Cup win. And we know that the Blades go on to have three consecutive Cup wins in five years (because it's fiction and fiction is amazing, LOL) with Jackson Carter as the head coach.

Which means that we had to get rid of Hall (sorry, Sam!) and get Jackson into place where he becomes the best coach in the existence of forever. #NotAllSuperHeroesWearCapes

RIP to all the Blades players during this trying season. Better times are ahead but alas, the time for suck-age was now.

Much love,
Maria

ALSO BY MARIA LUIS

NOLA HEART

Say You'll Be Mine

Take A Chance On Me

Dare You To Love Me

Tempt Me With Forever

BLADES HOCKEY

Power Play

Sin Bin

Hat Trick

Body Check

Slap Shot

BLOOD DUET

Sworn

Defied

Grab the Boxset

PUT A RING ON IT

Hold Me Today

Kiss Me Tonight

Love Me Tomorrow

BROKEN CROWN

Road To Fire

Sound of Madness

A New King

Bound To You

ABOUT THE AUTHOR

Maria Luis is an Amazon Top 25 Bestselling Author.

Historian by day and romance novelist by night, Maria abandoned the cold winters of Boston for hot and humid New Orleans (with a pit stop in England, along the way). When Maria isn't frantically typing with hot chocolate in hand, she can be found binging reality TV, going on adventures with her better half and two pups, or plotting her next steamy romance.

Stalk Maria in the Wild at the following!
Join Maria's Newsletter

Join Maria's Facebook Reader Group:
Book Boyfriends Anonymous